The End of the Pier is a striking, compelling debut and a sharply observed evocation of a dying world. The writing is superb, the characters unforgettable and the ending incredibly moving. One of the best debuts I've read. Highly recommended.

Stav Sherez, Author of "A Dark Redemption"

A Tour de Force of observational writing. Convincing characters within compelling prose, laying bare the often seedy side of the variety/entertainment scene. It really got under my skin and I thought the ending was inspired. I found myself rooting for Martin (and Mandy). Loved it!

Sara Elliott, Just Books

The End of the Pier lifts the curtain on the dark reality of summer season shows. The characters are recognisable but stripped of cheap sentiment. A great read.

Tony Peers, veteran comedian, actor and producer

A brutally truthful insight into the veracity of variety, and a great read, beautifully written. So many stunning lines... Laugh out loud stuff! This would make a great independent film!

Sam Kane, Actor

It took me back to our Variety days in the eighties and all that was politically incorrect, captured in an intriguing story. People I knew are so recognisable in the characters, from the stagehand, Martin, who could have been me in the sixties, to Gerry Neon, who could have been many a bill topper from shows of the past. A great read from start to finish.

Ian Tough, The Krankies

Fantastic! Gripping. Nostalgic. Brought back memories. I was there!

Kevin McFarlane, Technical Stage Manager, Lyceum Theatre, Crewe

This is a truly compulsive read that takes you into the minds of the characters. James' observations about the 'back of house' activities demonstrates a unique knowledge and understanding of the world of Light Entertainment in the seventies and eighties. For those of us who were there it is frighteningly accurate!

Alan Cutler, Peel Entertainment

The **END** **of** **the** **PIER**

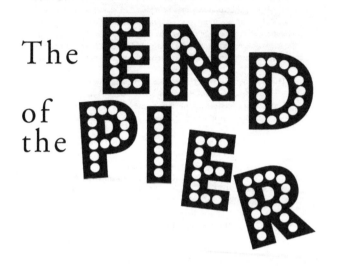

James C. Lee

Matador
9 Priory Business Park,
Wistow Road, Kibworth Beauchamp,
Leicestershire. LE8 0RX
Tel: 0116 279 2299
Email: books@troubador.co.uk
Web: www.troubador.co.uk/matador
Twitter: @matadorbooks

Front Cover Artwork: © Velvet crab drawn (pen and watercolour) by Racheal Bamford

"The Heat Is On" Words and Music by Harold Faltermeyer & Keith Forsey ©1984,
Reproduced by permission of Sony/ATV music Publishing Limited, London W1F 9LD

"I'm So Excited" Words and Music by Trevor Lawrence, Ruth Pointer,
Anita Pointer & June Pointer © 1982, Reproduced by permission of EMI Music
Publishing Limited London W1F 9LD

ISBN 978 1785891 984

British Library Cataloguing in Publication Data.
A catalogue record for this book is available from the British Library.

Printed and bound by CPI Group (UK) Ltd, Croydon, CR0 4YY
Typeset in 11pt Adobe Garamond Pro by Troubador Publishing Ltd, Leicester, UK

Matador is an imprint of Troubador Publishing Ltd

To my Mum and Dad with love
With thanks to Graeme

ACKNOWLEDGEMENTS

In addition to my Double Act Mum and Dad, and my Script Editor Graeme Garvey, to whom The End of the Pier is dedicated, I wish to express my deep gratitude to the rest of my Cast and Crew: my Production Team at Matador, who deserve their stellar reputation; my Set Designer, artist Racheal Bamford who drew the beautiful, slightly menacing velvet crab for my cover; my Ventriloquist, Louise Williams, who expertly proof read my manuscript and corrected my every gottle o'geer to bottle o'beer; my Stage Manager, real life stage manager Kevin McFarlane, who gave invaluable technical advice and feedback; my fellow Follow Spot Operator, Victoria Lister (nee Walker), with whom I shared a childhood watching The 'Weeds, and whose endorsement means so much; my Merchandise Vendor, Sara Elliott, of Just Books (Yorkshire's leading discount bookseller!), whose generous praise gave me a boost when I needed it; my Speciality Act (with comedy), Richard Plummer, who was the first to hear of my plan to write a novel and not only didn't mock my pretentions but positively indulged them; my Musical Director, Simon Berry, who over ten years did mock (affectionately) my slow progress, but in doing so stiffened my resolve; my Costume Designer, Andy Marshall, who shares my love of Lycra and who's enthusiasm for this novel fuelled my own; my merry crew of Stagehands Chas, Liz, Jonathan and Mark, who with their sincere interest in my novel - between quiz questions! – fed my belief; and finally my deepest gratitude is reserved for my Comedian, Singer, Choreographer and Star Of My Show, my wife Nicky, without whose tolerance (and regular absences!) The End of the Pier could not have been written.

1

"Is there anyone in from the Galapagos?"

Martin Collier was forever re-hearing things. Daily his mental Walkman would play him a variety show of echoes. A typical bill might comprise a punchline, a catchphrase, a Scotsman's laugh or, as he could hear now, a juggler's greeting to a half-filled auditorium. On the whole he welcomed each encore as evidence of his perceptive, hi-fi mind; but, if sleepless in bed at two in the morning with the spools still whirring, he wished then that the tape would stop.

Not this afternoon though, and not this audio-clip. In fact the Galapagos opener, which had replayed in his thoughts *all week*, was for him a source of amusement and satisfaction, and for good reason. Hearing it, a smile caused his young eyes to crease.

It was just after four on Friday afternoon and Martin was walking to work. He dipped briefly into Pagoda Park, in the area where the road bridge soared over the glen, before entering Colville Road Cemetery. It was cool and damp beneath the summer canopy and sunlight dappled the gravestones. Again the voice in his head enquired...

"Is there anyone in from the Galapagos?"

He thought of Alfonso Delos Santos, the juggler from the theatre where he worked. He could see him now, resplendent in his mariachi costume and fake moustache, and the lines he delivered between Martin's ears were as good as audible. Just feet from rotting corpses and suited skeletons, he heard gags. The patter came with Alphonso's distinctive pseudo-Latino accent, and the occasional flat stamp of a Cuban heel even augmented the performance. The juggler repeated his greeting for the nth time that week…

"Is there anyone in from the Galapagos?"

Some days Martin would wake up and an insignificant phrase, from a television advert for example, would loop over and over *ad nauseam*: "Yakety Yak, oh my back!" "Yakety Yak, oh my back!"*. However, the Galapagos line that for seven days had possessed his waking thoughts was far from insignificant.

Last Friday, he had been standing backstage on the prompt side, waiting for his cue, when Alfonso came up to him. The "Speciality Act with Comedy" was just about to go on, when he had asked Martin the name of the islands with the giant tortoises; "Y'know, where that monkey bloke with the big beard went?" he had added in clarification, adjusting the chinstrap of his sombrero. It was an unusual question for a spesh act to ask a stagehand, even if he did have a reputation for scholarship. Quizzically, and with some hesitation, he gave the answer.

From the wings, he had then watched as the older man used this knowledge in his act. At the end of a brief

---

*   Radox TV Advertisement, 1985

introductory routine, in which three clubs the size of bowling pins dueled with gravity and the band played La Cucaracha, Alfonso threw the last club high into the air, barely missing the God spot. He spun twice, caught the club, stamped a heavy heeled boot and exclaimed a triumphant "Hey!" Once the eager applause had faded, he greeted the holiday crowd with the unconventional opening line...

"Is there anyone in from the Galapagos?"

Backstage the crew, always primed for irreverence, had sniggered, but quiet-natured Martin had surprised himself by laughing out loud. Even now, here in the graveyard, he still saw great humour in this simple, audacious line – a line moreover he had helped to create. Front of house, however, the gag was met with near silence.

As anticipated there had been not a single holidaymaker in the audience hailing from the Galapagos, an uninhabited archipelago of volcanic islands 600 miles off the coast of Ecuador and a world away from Grumby. What a way *to start* your act, Martin had thought. Never mind the usual north-of-the-border version, with the "Is there anyone in from Scotland?" feed, and the "Who paid for your ticket?" tag; forget *working the room* with audience participation to get them on side, or pandering to their need for a joke that they knew. Alfonso had opened with subtle humour that required intelligence. It had been a lot to ask of the family audience, but it had been piss funny. Indeed...

"Very funny in Ecuador."

...the voice in his head joked further.

Being Friday night, first house, the theatre had been half empty. In this, his second season backstage Martin knew that Friday was changeover day, when one week's herd of holidaymakers went home and the next hundred busloads arrived, most not yet ready to venture into the world of variety. He knew that whenever business was slow, performers might vary their acts – a new line here, an "in" joke there – often more for their own amusement than the audience's. It had never crossed his mind that the Galapagos gag was born of a desire for artistic evolution. Even so, from that moment on Alfonso Delos Santos, Speciality Act with Comedy and third from top of the bill, had earned the admiration of at least one stagehand.

Furthermore, from then on the same stagehand had gloried privately in the gag's existence and had beamed whenever it echoed in his head. He beamed because in supplying a little knowledge to a pretend Mexican, for Alfonso Delos Santos was in fact Alan Sandham from Birmingham, Martin had tasted a kind of fame. It was a deluded belief, he knew, for such a meagre contribution, but all week he had actually felt famous.

On the Saturday following the Galapagos Friday, Alfonso had winked at the stagehand, doffing his sombrero in mock reverence and greeting him in his off-stage Brummie drawl; "O'royt, myte." Even this week knowing smirks had been exchanged in passing, the lad was fairly sure. Either way, each night brought him two shows closer to their next "first house Friday" collaboration; at least that was what he hoped. Now, *Friday afternoon*, walking *to work*, he had only the short hour it would take him to reach Grumby's Victoria Pier Theatre to come up with – to script – fresh material. Passing a particularly grand headstone, he heard another…indeed, he mouthed:

"Is there anyone in from the Galapagos?"

At the boundary with Queensway, he exited the cemetery

and walked into the glare and blare of sunshine and traffic. As he waited for a gap, curbside litter traced swirls and vortices in the wake of each vehicle. The act of crossing this busy road roused him from his daydream and he cantered the last half lane of carriageway. Leaping onto the pavement, he resolved to finalise his suggestion for tonight's location and, with an air of decisiveness, he spoke, he impersonated audibly...

"Is there anyone in from the Galapagos?"

***

After Queensway, Colville Road became more commercialised, many of the houses having been converted into shops. Martin now marched with purpose, searching his mind for Latino sounding locations and his next shot at the Big Time. Mentally he toyed with Acapulco; "Is there anyone in from Acapulco?" he rehearsed. But it seemed to him to lack something; it sounded exotic, but the right name would also need to confuse the audience, at least a little. The problem with Acapulco was that it was too well known, a tourist destination with cliff divers to marvel at; someone may actually have been there. Such a question, he feared, might provoke a response, shouted by a globetrotter in Row J and that would spoil the gag. The humour, the beauty, the essence of the line lay in the moment of silence that followed it. Silence and puzzlement; that was what he was looking for, not holiday recollections.

Nonetheless place names filed through his mind like items to remember in The Generation Game. He weighed up The Alamo, but judged it unsuitable as it lay in Texas, although Mexicans *were* involved. Aconcagua was no good, it being a mountain, and likewise Atacama was a desert. He searched the B's and considered Brazil; but countries were too general, too likely. Bolivia, even? Perhaps the letter C might yield returns... He pondered Chihuahua, but worried that some dog-ignorant punters might not know it as a geographical place at all; the phrase "Is there anyone in from Chihuahua?" would certainly cause confusion, but of a canine strain; he struck it from his mind.

He ditched the alphabetical approach and seized instead upon Ipanema, as in "The Girl from Ipanema". Everyone knew the song and surely the girl of the title wouldn't be in attendance herself; that would be too ironic. He imagined her sat at the back, next to the Boys from Brazil. He snorted at the absurdity. So Ipanema was a possibility.

His mind was now racing; in quick succession up popped Rio de Janeiro, Montevideo and Buenos Aires, but he had little time to reflect on their suitability before Las Malvinas came from nowhere. Thank Christ a subconscious alarm bell sounded, for Britain had only recently gone to war to protect the sovereignty – and the name – of the "Falkland Islands". He didn't want a scarred veteran of the Sir Galahad confronting him at the stage door. So no, not Las Malvinas, he censored himself. What about Tijuana, he went on, or Tierra del Fuego? Where the hell was that?

***

Martin was fast approaching Lorraine's Hairstylist's, which lay on the opposite side of Colville Road to him, but he tried not to acknowledge his location. He was engrossed with his geography of the Americas, which helped, but the fact of his whereabouts kept tapping him on his shoulder. Eventually reality stole him from his script writing.

He just knew that inside Lorraine's his eponymous mother would be combing and snipping quite incidentally while talking the hind legs off some poor regular; an ex-usherette regaling a nobody with tales of glamorous circles formerly inhabited and of stellar shoulders once rubbed against. He knew also that later she'd be hitting the town with a thirst on: how many white wine and lemonades in bars and clubs would she accept tonight? He dreaded to think.

There were times when he had considered taking a different route to work, the slight detour of Sutcliffe Street via Walker Row, the better to avoid his piss-head mother, he thought. But he enjoyed the bustle of Colville Road, The Parade, the architecture... Oh, who was he kidding? The truth was that like a moth to a flame he felt compelled to pass his mother's premises, to spy on her daily, to confirm and then re-confirm that she was still as embarrassing as ever. Not that he could tell much from across the road, that is, but still he would watch her. The irony was that even if he were to bypass Lorraine's it would be an evasion rendered futile by the larger fact of his still living *at home*.

Happily for him though, their paths rarely crossed *inside* the family semi, and so pretty much the only opportunity for mother-son eye-contact was during these Peeping Tom moments; she would glance over and by chance catch her son looking at her, as he was now; she would then beckon him, eagerly, but he would point at his watch and gesture an apology; or else he'd pretend not to see her at all. This state of affairs suited Martin, this estrangement, this surveillance.

It suited him that their working hours and her bedridden Sunday hangovers kept them apart. It suited him that her scrawled reminders to hang out the washing, or afternoon 'phone calls to request that it be brought in ("It looks like it's going to rain, sweetie..."), were practically the only communication they had. These things suited Martin just fine.

Walking slowly, watching her, he could see her holding a mirror behind a freshly permed head of hair. She was presenting its image to the customer with all the drama of a matador holding a cape before the bull; performing as always. She might have been exclaiming "Ta-dah!", or preparing to take a bow to soak up the applause that she seemed to crave, and all the while she beamed with the most dazzling of smiles, a smile that Martin could feel in his guts. He prayed that she didn't look over and see him...and then felt sad that his prayer was answered.

But that was enough confused resentment. Until reaching Lorraine's he had been buoyant and he wasn't about to let his non-relationship with his non-mother scuttle his creativity. In fact, he made a private vow that no one, not her, not anyone, would bring him down *today* – there was comedy to write! His face softened and he continued his commute at pace, mouthing Machu Pichu.

***

As he walked to work, the whole of Grumby seemed to be clocking-off. All around him, home-time routines were evident. In the fishmongers, a man in an apron like a deckchair hosed mackerel blood and slush-ice from a sloping steel counter. Further on, a tan-coated greengrocer was bent over his pavement display consolidating partial trays of soft fruits into a single box, which he then carried inside through the caresses of a fly curtain. "Poets Day", that's how Martin had heard Fridays described; P.O.E.T.S; Piss off early, tomorrow's Saturday! At the T-junction with Morris Lane a white van, bedecked with ladders, cornered at speed, with "Money for Nothing" blaring through the wound-down window and a beefy, weathered forearm slapping the door panel.

After much weighing and gauging he was now decided upon Tierra del Fuego. It met the criteria; exotic sounding, probably unvisited and difficult to place – perhaps even Mexican. "Is there anyone in from Tierra del Fuego?" He could hear the silence and puzzlement even now.

But how and when he should broach the subject with Alfonso was another matter. It had been easy last Friday; all he'd had to do was answer a question, and surely most people knew that Darwin had gone to the Galapagos Islands, didn't they? Tonight he would have to approach the spesh act himself and the prospect of telling a pro their business made the stagehand uneasy. He told himself that at least they had a rapport going, what with the nods and the winks and the "O'royt, myte"s; but even so, he needed a plan.

The key, he figured, was to arrive as early as possible for his 6.27pm cue, in which he carried Alfonso's props onto a blacked-out stage. Early arrival at this point would maximize his exposure to the juggler, who would be waiting in the wings, perhaps making small talk, perhaps racking his brains for just the right place name. Martin could suggest his killer location outright, or else hover expectantly and attempt to catch his eye; surely Alfonso would remember the triumph that was their previous collaboration and would therefore ask for this week's suggestion? So, he had a plan; loiter with intent and supply the line.

Actually, the more he thought about it, the more plausible it seemed. Alfonso was a nice man; why wouldn't he consult other members of the cast and crew? The show was a team effort after all and he'd probably welcome contributions, especially for a Friday first house, just to break the monotony. In fact Alfonso had probably been thinking about it all week himself. The stagehand's confidence was growing.

He began to visualize his imminent success. First there had been "Is there anyone in from the Galapagos?" which had been hilarious, and tonight there would be "Is there anyone in from Tierra del Fuego?" which would be equally hilarious, if not more so. So, two gags on successive Fridays; that would be an achievement!

***

Martin bounded along Eastgate, flew down Cliffside and before long was, quite literally, beside the seaside. The beach was nearly empty now, but in the lengthening shadows there was still an atmosphere of gaiety and timelessness. He watched as a fat and shrieking grandmother flapped at a full-tossed tennis ball. Not many years ago, he himself had played beach cricket with his grandma, his family. He watched also as two boys knelt and scooped wet sand, excavating a channel to their castle moat. Likewise, he too had been a child architect of sandy impermanence, a dyker of tides.

He adored this stretch of the shore, with the Abbey ruins high on the bluff and the towering Victoria Hotel – Grumby's twin sentinels – and with the lifeboat house and the harbour and the cabins selling shellfish. Even the day-old cockles and prawns on a counter to his left, drying and warming in their polystyrene sick beds, seemed appetizing. All summer long these alien beings were forced to sunbathe from dawn until dusk, displaying their cocktail sticks like thermometers. But, even the prospect of food poisoning could seem cozy and benign when Martin was this nostalgic. Besides, optimism trumped botulism; a squeeze of lemon was all that was needed to enliven the little fellows; Granddad had taught him that.

In the space of sixty happy-sad seconds, both departed grandparents had returned to their grandson with the briefest of cameo appearances; beach cricket and crustaceans. And with their homecoming, the past and the present seemed to fuse and his chest flooded with love. Would they enjoy his Tierra del Fuego gag? Probably not; but he knew *they'd* be proud of him, even if his mother wasn't. He continued heading south along the prom towards the pier.

Somewhere along the seafront, between the Victoria Hotel and Victoria Pier, the character of Grumby changed from that of yesteryear's grandeur remembered to that of modern and tawdry commercialism. Martin couldn't with certainty draw a line in the sand to mark this change in character, which he would sense daily as a creeping funk, but the giant illuminated arch that heralded his arrival at Funland, was as good a marker as any. Indeed, whenever he passed by this gaping jaw, it was clear to him that his hometown was at least schizophrenic and probably part-monster.

Once inside the beast anyone could see that Grumby's coastline, proud with cliffs to the north, descended here, like one of Funland's wood-framed roller coasters, to a coarse, eroded shore, where dirt met water. And from this southern extremity, Vicky Pier jutted like a middle finger insult to the sea, and the wind loosened sand from the marram dunes and blew it across the tram tracks.

As usual he was walking on the seaward side of the prom. Here he had only tottering pensioners and seagull raiders to contend with. Over the road, however, one had to run the gauntlet of video game arcades, bucket 'n' spade shops and lock-ups selling greasy burgers and sickly-sweet donuts and waffles of every stripe. On *that* pavement trudged a herd of stupefied punters, corralled and tended to by a posse of hawkers and arcade boys – skinny, feral terriers that stared with mocking fearlessness at anyone who dared to meet their eye. By keeping his distance and by fixing his eyes on the seaward horizon, Martin hid from the vulgarity and the violence that he was sure lurked there.

But those slaggy, shag-me-quick girls! The weekend always brought their wiggle and bounce and he would feel buoyed and then beached by the tides of their favours. They taunted him, he felt, with their choosey availability, their hidden, heaving breasts and their ravening, ejaculating mouths. He couldn't help but glance over, once or twice, just to confirm they were there – consuming, shouting, laughing – even if his desire for them made him nauseous.

His earlier graveyard stroll had accelerated to a bounding descent of Eastgate, but here in Grumby's lowest reaches he felt he was scurrying. There was mounting excitement ahead of any show, of course, and the prospect of another "first house Friday" collaboration with Alfonso only stoked this excitement, but this scurrying was lemming-like and headlong. It was as if he was helpless to the pull of neon and naughtiness, as if spooked by the fun of the fair. And those girls…

He knew he had to shake himself out of this funk. A cocktail of negative emotions – disgust, fear, lust – was threatening to get the better of him; and he had show business to conduct! He'd be at work in less than five minutes and face to face with Alfonso in little more than an hour; he had to get his act together, and quick.

He reined in his legs a little and breathed deeply the seaweed scented air. And then, affecting a carefree disdain, he began to skim and bounce his left hand along the blistered railings, his arm an elegantly flapping wing. Earlier he'd refused to let his mother sidetrack him; well, neither would he now let punters, hawkers and slags derail him. No, he had a plan – Tierra del Fuego, Alfonso, loiter and supply the line – and he *would* see it through. Approaching the pier he knew it would be difficult, however, for this was no place for comedy. His hand soared like a gull over the next dome-topped stanchion.

***

A giant wooden hoarding towered above the entrance to the pier. It could have an almost hypnotic effect on the viewer, like a mobile above a cot, and there was always a number of bystanders staring at it. "Seaside Spectacular '85 – the Gerry Neon Show" it exclaimed in three foot letters. To the right of this verbose headline was painted a bronzed and bouffanted Gerry from mid-torso up. The undoubted star of the show, well known from his many TV appearances, was depicted with warm eyes, a brilliant showbiz smile and with both forefingers pointed at the viewer like pistols, his thumbs cocked. The hyper-real image was the size of a circus elephant. Below Gerry was painted the rest of the bill in the same vivid style and with the same friendly, rounded lettering. Only their heads were shown though, and each became gradually smaller down the board and, to Martin's eye, less recognisable from reality.

Underneath Gerry and to the left, "Ashley Kidd – Top Comedian" appeared cheeky, like he was trying not to laugh

at a blue joke. Back to the right, "Alfonso Delos Santos –
Speciality Act with Comedy" resembled a Mexican bandito,
much to Martin's irritation. And lastly, bottom left, "Amanda
Monroe – Vocalist" looked exactly like...Faye Gold. The
former had replaced the latter, only a week into the season,
after Miss Gold had had a run in of some kind with Gerry
Neon. Now, three weeks in, the replacement's image had yet
to be added to the billboard beside her more easily editable
name. Along the bottom, "The Jilly Conlan Dancers" and
"The Dave Newhurst Orchestra" were advertised in name
only. He half-joked to himself that "Written by Martin
Collier" might one day appear on a similar billboard.

Embarking the pier, his footfalls changed from a concrete
scuff to a wooden bounce. He had heard the permanently
stilettoed Mandy Monroe complain about the pier's
hazardous surface, as there were heel-wide gaps between
the boards, but he rather enjoyed the dizzying glimpses of
the water beneath. By the time he had reached the theatre,
a hundred yards out to sea, he could see slate grey waves
cresting and foaming beneath him and he imagined that the
whole pier was rising and falling like a cruise liner. As he
approached the Stage Door, Martin guessed he was about as
ready for Alfonso as he would ever be. He turned the handle,
pushed and entered the world he was born for, the world of
"Seaside Spectacular '85".

***

"Evening." The doorman greeted him flatly through
the opening of his booth, barely lifting his gaze from a
newspaper. He wasn't rude, merely rationing his effort.

"Hello," Martin replied with scarcely more emotion, closing the noisy stage door behind him. He passed through the small, strip-lit reception area, down a short flight of concrete stairs, painted red, to a door marked "Domestic".

It was last summer, after his A-levels, that Martin had first started at Victoria Pier Theatre. It wasn't the Opera House, as he or his grandparents would have hoped, but it was a foothold. Like every school leaver who worked there, as green and wet as a frond of bladderwrack, he began his employment as a follow spot operator. "Spotlights", he soon learned, were cumbersome contraptions, three feet long, with a gate at the focal point of the lens, into which gobos or "go betweens" were inserted to shape or soften the beam, and it seemed as if his always jammed. The work was hot and uncomfortable. For four tedious hours a night he would pan and tilt his super trouper on its yoke, picking out the performers, anticipating their movements, narrowing the beam, blacking it out. By the end of "Summertime Sensation '84" he could hardly observe a passing tram without his two outstretched arms tracing its path.

That had been his apprenticeship, though; this season he was doing more, learning more – Deputy Electrician, in all but name, he fancied. Since *this* production began he'd replaced fuses and bulbs; he'd ensured the radio mics were properly discharged and then recharged; he'd set up the bomb tank and the flash pots; he'd sat with the Board Operator and had effected several of the lighting and sound cues – not every night, but on two or three occasions at least. This evening he was due to be shown the dry-ice machine, or "pea souper", as it was called; that was bound to be a gas, he had joked, in truth relishing the promise of new knowledge.

First up, however, he had a less glamorous duty to perform. He opened the door marked "Domestic" and grabbed what he needed, before jogging upstairs again.

The thirty minute call was still some moments away and there was little happening either back stage or front of house. The house curtain had yet to be lowered and a cavernous auditorium was dimly visible beyond the footlights. As usual a year-old pop compilation played quietly on the house system, but even Wham!'s "Wake Me Up…" failed to counter the charmlessness of this sixties addition to the Victorian pier. The vast stage itself was brightly lit and empty, save for the single lanky figure that had just entered it holding a broom.

As he swept the boards, Martin reviewed what little he knew of the pea souper. It was "like a giant kettle," Kevin, the Assistant Stage Manager, had told him. Solid CO_2 is placed into a cage that hangs above boiling water inside the "kettle". The cage is then lowered into the water from the outside. The dry ice turns to gas and comes pouring out of a spout. The Scotsman's words came back to Martin verbatim, as far as he could remember. The phrase "…there's a bit of an art to it, though" echoed with real clarity due to the obvious caution with which Kevin had said the words. He didn't yet know the subtleties of this "art", however, or the nature of the pitfalls, and he was intrigued.

***

"Hi, Martin, are you alright? Lovely to see you!" Helen, one of the dancers, had breezed onto the stage. She was all smiles and giggles and her glossy chocolate pony swished above a pink sweatshirt; she had come to warm up, stretch off and turn out. "Am I alright over here? You've finished this bit, yeah?" she asked helpfully, although her questions were pretty much rhetorical and he limited his reply to a grunt.

She sat down, cross-legged, like a schoolgirl in assembly, before shrugging her shoulders loose and twirling her neck. She unfolded her legs and eased them into the widest of box splits. Slowly she leant sideways, rotating her torso and lowering her forehead until it came into nodding contact with her right knee. With her chin, she then touched the floor at a spot mid-way between her legs, before repeating the nodding motion on her left knee, and thus completing a near 180-degree arc.

Still sweeping, Martin listened out for Alfonso's arrival, but his alertness to events off-stage was now distracted somewhat by the contorting dancer upon it. Helen was now standing on one leg while extending the other vertically upwards so that her thigh brushed her ear. He concentrated hard on the pile of detritus he was forming.

Did dancers really need to stretch this extrovertly, he wondered, feeling curiously intruded upon. Ashley Kidd tended to visit the stage around this time, so perhaps she intended to invite his advances – or maybe Gerry's. But Helen didn't really seem the sort to further her career in *that* way, he thought. She wasn't even called Nikki or Vikki or Jakki, or any of the other choreographical names. She was Helen. She even used Martin's given name to address him, not the industry standard "Sweetheart". He decided to give her the benefit of the doubt and accepted her stretching as necessary, indeed professional. However, she was a dancer, nonetheless, and no good could ever come of consorting with her caste. Resigning himself to this fact, he squatted with his dustpan and brushed like the untouchable he was.

After a while, the Wham! track finished and there was a moment of uncomfortable silence before "Let's Hear it for the Boy" lightened the mood. Helen began to adopt more obviously balletic poses; a series of mannered movements with specific foot and arm positions. She even rested her heel on a P.A. speaker, as if exercising at the barre.

Martin, on the other hand, heaped his pan with dust, fluff, and all manner of showbiz litter; errant tassels, sequins and rhinestones, a plectrum and, of course, onion.

"Is that onion, Martin?"

"Er, yes," he answered, reaching for a bin liner.

"What are chunks of onion doing on the stage? The audience don't throw them, do they? ...I didn't think we were *that* bad!" she lowered her voice for this last, self-effacing comment.

"Huh. No, it's the late night hypnotist; he dupes the punters, y'know, fools them into eating them like Granny Smiths." He shook the bin liner open with a flap.

"That's horrible!" She seemed genuinely appalled by the thought of this pungent vegetable.

"And then, when he clicks his fingers, there's this moment...and then they spit it out." Martin shocked himself to add these extra, unsolicited details.

"I'm not surprised! What else is there?" she asked, over-estimating the intrigue of the haul, but nurturing the conversation all the same.

"Oh, mostly decorative stuff that you hoofers lose – sequins and tassles – and some of Gerry's rhinestones – uh-hur-huh." This last, melodic phrase was delivered in sonorous

Elvis-ese, the rhinestones originating from the costume worn by Gerry during his Vegas-era tribute to The King.

Helen giggled. "I'm all shook up!" she also added, singing in the deepest, southern drawl she could muster. They both laughed at her hopeless impression.

This chatter continued for some minutes; Martin tipped and tapped his sweepings into the black bag and spoke with increasing confidence, and Helen swapped legs from time to time, giggling as she stretched. Eventually she headed upstairs to squeeze into her first costume. Martin churned with giddiness, but he also felt relieved at her departure; they had been talking so easily, so naturally, that he didn't want anything – a stammer, a misunderstanding or a clumsy compliment – to spoil what had been a perfect ten minutes.

Other dancers came and went, and pleasantries were exchanged between them as they too contorted themselves. Kevin, the ASM, said "one-two" a lot, and Ashley Kidd did indeed mingle for a time, talking loudly. Drummer Andy took his seat behind the kit and warmed up with the rhythm from a Paul Simon song. Alan Sandham appeared, not as Alfonso but as himself, and then busied himself in the wings with the other man's props.

Martin was more excited than someone sweeping a stage had a right to be; he couldn't wait to have a go himself at the drumbeat Andy had played; the ingenious dry ice machine beckoned and would soon be another string to his bow; *and* he had made Helen laugh so that she had lost her balance. Furthermore, he was no longer fazed by the prospect of sounding out Alfonso; it wasn't as if he was unapproachable, like Gerry.

***

He was decided; there would be no loitering in the wings, no waiting for a chance that might never come; Martin felt confident enough to approach the spesh act directly, and he would do so in the minutes before his entrance. He would simply go up to him and advise him casually to include the place name Tierra del Fuego in his opening line. "Hey Al," he would say, "what do you think about using Tierra del Fuego, blah, blah, blah?"

In fact, dispatching the last dust mound, it occurred to him that he should do it now, this very minute. He rose from his haunches, left temporarily his bin bag booty, and strode with purpose towards his destiny. Tonight's audience would definitely be greeted in a manner of Martin's creation.

He exited the stage to the prompt side, passing between two black curtains that hung parallel to one another. Tierra del Fuego, Tierra del Fuego; mentally he repeated his suggestion. Once in the darkness of the wings, he turned left to see Alfonso ten yards away, his suitcase of props illuminated by a desk lamp. But he halted mid-stride, mid-breath; Alfonso was talking to Gerry Neon.

He felt as if he'd taken a wrong turn in a zoo to find himself *inside* the lion enclosure. He couldn't possibly approach Alfonso now, not with Gerry there. Faking he'd forgotten something, he about turned with an awkward pirouette of endless duration. He could feel his face flush. Why had he been so impulsive, he scolded himself? Hurriedly he ducked back between the leg curtains and escaped into the light of the stage.

He crouched and grabbed his things. The two men could scarcely have noticed him, and even if they had there was no chance that Gerry could interpret his apparent forgetfulness for the aborted meddling that it was. Still, he felt naked to his scorn.

Laden with the bin bag, wood and bristles, he took the long way to the sanctuary of the broom cupboard. He crossed the boards, descended the stairs on the opposite-prompt side and looped back underneath the stage. He re-entered the door marked "Domestic" and pulled the handle behind him with a click. He stood for a moment in the blackness, like a child in a game of hide and seek, his heart galloping. Somewhere above a bass guitar was being tuned, and the low frequencies seemed to be calling him like a whale. Come on Martin, he told himself trying to rein in his thoughts, you're a grown man!

The 6:27pm cue was his best chance, after all; the second house would be too busy, too conventional for his left-field laughs and he didn't want to have to wait *another* week until next Friday. Still, that was what he'd planned in the first place, so nothing was lost – and nothing was going to bring him down today, he reminded himself. In the darkness he resolved to revert to Plan A; loiter and supply. He re-joined the corridor, leapt up the red, concrete steps and landed confidently in the strip-lit reception area.

Kevin, however, intercepted him. "Ah, *there* you are!" said the jovial, no-nonsense and rather bulbous Scot. "Martin, listen lad, there's a problem. Gary just 'phoned, he's not coming in, he's sick. You're on follow spot tonight. We'll do the pea souper another time. Okay? Sorry."

"But…yeah." He had no choice in the matter.

"You remember what to do, don't you? The gate still sticks a bit, apparently, but you'll manage. Okay? See you later." The ASM then disappeared through the swing door that lead to the stage, briefly holding it open for Alfonso and Gerry. The two replaced Kevin in the reception area, laughing and joking with pre-gig exaggeration, and marched straight passed the stagehand and up the stairs to their dressing rooms. Alfonso did not even acknowledge Martin, who stood becalmed, struggling to understand why he felt such a mug.

***

Later, angrily throwing the beam of his spotlight around the stage, he glowered as Alfonso tossed his clubs with what the lad saw as "wanker" hand gestures. He scowled as the band blew raspberries to the tune of "La Cucaracha", it sounding more than ever like an irritating car horn. Indignation burned in him as hot as the super trouper's bulb.

"Hey!" declared the fake Mexican, catching the final club and stamping his boot. Brief, enthusiastic applause ensued. "*Muchas gracias*, many thanks, ladies and gentlemen, boys and girls, *buenas noches*, good evening!" he began in his self-translating, mongrel tongue. "Is there anyone in from Scotland?" he asked, not unpredictably. Martin groaned.

"Aye!" replied a tenth of the audience. Martin groaned again; he knew what was coming.

"Who paid for your tickets?" the funnyman enquired. The pier itself might have groaned, with the ignominy of having to host such humour, its very skeleton creaking as it shifted uncomfortably on its piles.

But the only sound audible was that of laughter. A thousand Mancunians and Scousers, Paddies and Taffies, Geordies and Yorkshiremen, all of them laughing like drains at their conventionally tight neighbours, all of them united in heroic determination to enjoy themselves whatever. And of course the Glaswegians laughed as well; funny is funny, after all.

"Paddy tried to cross the Irish Sea by plank..." Alfonso teed up another. "But he couldn't find one long enough!" More laughter. "What do you call a Scouser in a suit?" Pause. "The accused!" Yet more laughter.

And at the conclusion of this brief review of regional stereotypes, the band struck up with "Cumbanchero", a second representative tune from the Latin canon and sounding a little like "The Flight of the Bumblebee". The juggler swapped his clubs for six flexible canes, a heavy base into which to insert them and some cheap crockery, before impressing with three minutes of plate spinning. Ten-year-old boys watched open-mouthed as the canes wobbled, the plates teetered and as Alfonso attended to them with appropriate brinkmanship.

And all the while Martin groaned and glowered and scowled, and his indignation burned with a thousand Watts, and he thought of The Galapagos and of Tierra del Fuego, and of Gerry, and of Alfonso walking straight passed him in the reception area, and of the unwieldy contraption and the hot light he was trying to steer, and he mumbled to himself: "Fucking Scotland."

"This is your five minute call, ladies and gentlemen, your five minute call. Thank you."

Kevin's melodic Scots tenor came over the theatre's tannoy system and into half-a-dozen dressing rooms. In the biggest of these, Gerry Neon, still damp with sweat from his first house performance, was slumped in a powder blue armchair with his knees at ten to two. He had been sitting that way for the last quarter of an hour and was about as relaxed as it is possible for a man to be, if a little melancholy. He had managed to pull up his briefs, to restore a little middle-aged dignity, but the waistband of his Elvis flares remained snug around his ankles. With the speaker delivering its tinny message, he was oblivious to everything except the cigarette he was smoking.

Mandy Monroe was standing nearby, re-applying cherry red lipstick in a mirror that was framed with ten or more bare, white bulbs. The peppermint cool of mouthwash, recently spat, still burned the singer's mouth, and her knees likewise burned from the carpet, upon which for the previous fifteen minutes she had been kneeling. She clamped her lips onto a Mansize, to blot the excess cosmetic, and was the first to speak...

"Am I seeing you later?" she asked, before checking her huge smile in the brilliant mirror.

"Uh? Erm, yeah. 'Course, darlin'." The star of the show could barely hold a thought in his head, never mind make arrangements.

"I mean, it would be nice to go somewhere after, you know, just the two of us, for my birthday. I'm sure Tricolo's would stay open for us. A bottle of wine? A pizza?"

"Er, yeah, sweetheart, that would be great," came the flat reply.

"You know how well we go together, sweetie, it seems silly keeping us a secret any longer. Don't you think?" The former dancer wrapped her dressing gown more snuggly around still firm curves before perching on the arm of his chair. She embraced his hod carrier's back and kissed his greying hair.

"We'll see," he answered curtly, tapping a worm cast of ash into a tray that brimmed and teetered on the other velour arm. Despite their recent physical intimacy he bristled at this calculated show of affection; he was sick of birds thinking that he owed them something just because they'd slept with him; in his assessment the act itself was reward enough. In any case Mandy hadn't fully slept with him, not properly, not yet, not since she had replaced Faye Gold on the bill, and so *any* expectation on her part showed, to his mind, considerable cheek.

"Okay, baby, okay." She sensed the first stirrings of Gerry's infamous temper, and sought to calm him, keeping her voice soft and stroking his cruel forearm. "I would like to, though, and it is my birthday" she added slowly, pleadingly, pressing her case. He didn't answer.

"I *am* thirty today, you know!" she said, as if it meant something.

"Yeah…" he laughed "…*again!*"

"That's not fair!"

A moment of silence followed until Kevin gave another cue: "Overture and beginners, that's overture and beginners. Thank you."

Mandy looked at the speaker and said: "I've got to go, sweetheart." She stood and moved hesitantly towards the door, retying the toweling cord. "And darling?" there was something else; lately there was always something else.

"*What*, love?"

"You said you'd have a word with Bernie, you know, about the hoarding? I don't want to nag, but it's just that…"

"Yes, I will. Alright?" he interrupted, although he had not the slightest intention of talking to the show's promoter on a matter as trivial as whether or not her mug was on the billboard. He'd got her the gig; what more did the ingrate want?

"It's just that *I'm* the singer on this show now, not that cow Faye Gold, and I hate to see her stupid face every time I walk onto the pier. It's bad enough trying not to get my heels stuck between the planks, without her gawping at me! I know you got my name painted over hers, which I'm glad about, but it's been two weeks now and I want to see *my face* there as well. I'm only thinking of the punters, baby, it must be very confusing for them. I mean she's a brunette, I'm blond…"

"The only confusion, love, is that you're billed as a singer! You're a pair of tits on a pair of legs and that's all. I've said I will, now piss off and leave me alone!" Gerry's building site eloquence would have been amusing, were there neither some truth in his words nor contempt in his eyes.

"Alright sweetie, alright. I'm only saying… I only want what's *right*." This moral claim, though reasonable enough, came as a despairing afterthought, and Mandy knew that she had allowed herself to be bullied. "See me later?" she added pathetically.

"Jesus Christ woman, just go!"

"How can I go on stage *now*?"

"That's your problem! Piss off!"

The woman did as she was told, predictably slamming the door, while Gerry stubbed out his cigarette with unnecessary thoroughness, crushing the filter and soiling his fat, sovereigned fingers. "For fuck's sake!" he hissed to himself. Just his luck, he thought, that practically overnight Mandy should turn into one of those needy birds, the kind that pestered him and got stroppy if he didn't make a fuss of them.

A television rested on the worktop that jutted from a mirrored wall. From his chair he stared at its blank screen, fuming. She didn't used to be like this, he reflected. In the past when they had worked together – at Fagin's, or The Circus Tavern, or any of the clubs on the cabaret circuit – Mandy Shaw, as she was then, had proven herself the most easy-going of hoofers, the most reliable of good-time girls, a Shaw thing. All she had cared about in those days was a spot in the limelight, an after-show bucket load of complimentary champagne and a seeing to from "Big Gee", as she would call him with a wink and a pout. Not now though, he was beginning to understand, not now that she'd climbed to the next rung of the ladder. Of course she'd kneeled and opened her mouth for him, only a quarter of an hour ago in fact, but so what? He could get a blowjob from any ice cream or ticket girl; and besides, it wasn't so enjoyable being on the receiving end – he wanted to get to grips with her, he wanted to show her who was boss, like he used to. But no. Apparently Miss Monroe, diva, was intent on keeping her knickers on and Gerry's balls where she could see them.

"Should have fucking known!" he scolded himself, thinking of the Frontier club, Batley. He remembered how a few months back Mandy had visited him there. In his dressing room she had bared her soul to him, confiding that she'd "outgrown" dancing, and that secretly she'd been having singing lessons, "for years". More to the point she was now *very* ready, she had said, to make the transition to solo artist, to singer, and could he advise. She had then unbuttoned her mac to reveal a boudoir of lace and flesh. Inviting his hands to her body, she had enquired if the star knew of any gigs that were still unfilled for the Summer Season, or of any that might *become* unfilled. The inference could not have been clearer or, as it turned out, more dishonest; Mandy Shaw had been a bundle of fun in cabaret, just imagine what a summer with Mandy Monroe *on tap* would be like! And she had then departed, in a puff of *parfum* and with nothing more than a brief, forceful kiss as a reminder of her passion.

"For fuck's sake!" Gerry repeated, disgusted with himself; so hungry had he been for her, so desirous of her curves, it had never occurred to him that once promoted from the depravity of clubland Miss Empty Promises might then give him the run around on summer season. *And*, to his present and nightly embarrassment, it had also never occurred to him that someone, somewhere should confirm that the bint could actually sing!

Nevertheless, from that moment on, audition or not, the non-singer had joined the cast of Seaside Spectacular '85 as understudy to Faye Gold; the *bona fide* vocalist's name might have been on the contract, but the writing was on the wall. Once the season had begun and Ms Gold had declined Gerry's constitutional and rightful advances, it was only a matter of time. Once Ms Gold had turned down the Top of the Bill, that was all the excuse he needed to pressurise Bernie to release her from her contract and to employ Mandy Monroe, boop-boop-be-do, in her stead; and so it proved.

Now, less than a month into the season, Gerry found himself on a bill with a singer that couldn't sing, and with a bird he couldn't shag. *And* she was starting to make prima donna demands about meals out and faces on hoardings. He actually laughed at the bind he'd allowed himself, like an amateur, to be drawn into. The funny thing, it dawned on him, was that if he wanted this much grief he could get it from his wife. He took the ashtray and banged it against the inside of a metal bin, before tossing it onto a low table. Clapping his hands clean of ash, he knew it was time to get rid.

***

He heaved himself forward to the edge of the seat and reached down to unzip and prise off his stage boots (patent leather, white). It was an effort to breathe, bent and straining in the airless room, and his face bulged, hot with hypertension. He pulled off his Elvis flares (also white) and then straightened up to peel off his cowboy shirt (embroidered with rhinestones, white again). Flushed and breathless, he slumped back into his armchair and sat there seething in just his pants and socks (both maroon). The heavy, gold necklace he wore was not a prop of The King but belonged to his regal self.

He looked at the phone and felt himself sink deeper into the chair. "Right then, you bitch," he said, psyching himself up, "Let's get this out of the way." Dutifully he dialed his home number in Leeds and waited for his wife to answer. "Hello, darling. How are you, sweetheart?" he began with forced optimism. Later... "A *double* oven? What the sodding hell's that?" "What do you want one of those for?" "*How* much?" And finally..."Yes, darling. Promise. On Sunday. Promise. Bye." He hung up. "For fuck's sake!" he spat again.

Outside his door there were intermittent commotions; sturdy dance shoes skipped and clipped along the concrete corridor, accompanied by laughter and exclamations; and between each bout of bonhomie, the band could be heard. The bass and brass of The Dave Newhurst Orchestra hummed through the floor and blared up the stairwell to the dressing rooms, especially whenever the swing door to the stage was opened, which was often. The overture – a rendition of Glen Frey's "The Heat Is On" – was audible inside Gerry's room. It was just after 8:40pm and the curtain would soon rise on the second house performance. The first half would bring a non-singer, a non-Mexican juggler, and then a cheeky comic, all interspersed with further live music and sturdy-shoed hoofing. There was an hour until the interval and plenty of down time for the headliner.

Girlfriend. Wife. Why did he bother? He lit another B&H, took a lungful and tried to coax his agitation out of the red. For several minutes he just sat there in his velour throne, inhaling with a depth and dedication that made the tip of his Benny fizzle orange like blown tinder. This most active of smoking was accompanied by a passive but dawning awareness of events on the stage. He became drawn in by this soundtrack; the riffing, stuttering sax had now been joined by the rest of the horn section for the crescendo of the bridge, and the rising brass seemed to hang like the tobacco plumes above him. In his head he could hear the original version's vocal over this instrumental: "Tell me, can you feel it? Tell me, can you feel it? *Tell-me-can-you-feel-it?*" he imagined. Pause. "The heat is on!" End. Applause. Drum roll. Voice over. He'd heard this routine many times before, but he stayed with the performance; it was soothing.

Kevin's voice boomed over the public address system and up through Gerry's carpet: "Ah-Ladies and Gentlemen, ah-welcome to Seaside Spectacular '85 – the Gerry Neon Show." His almost vaudevillian oration was an octave lower, four hundred miles less Scottish and several decades earlier in time than his normal Perthshire brogue. "We are proud to introduce the ah-Jilly Conlan Dancers and the lovely Miss Amanda Monroe." Applause. Cue Intro.

The band then kicked out a second pop smash from last year, The Pointer Sisters' "I'm So Excited". Gerry visualised the eight dancers jiving onto the pink-lit stage, swinging their arms, clicking their fingers to the insistent pulse of the music; he even tapped his toes a little as he smoked. For a moment someone must have passed through the swing door to the stage because he could make out Mandy enthusing over the intro; "Woo! C'mon! Yeah!" she shrieked. Her over-eagerness made him snigger. And then a little later, in the verse, her reedy voice returned again; "We're going for those pleasures in the night," she piped, not quite in the same key as the band. He spluttered as he dragged. No wonder Bernie was loath to release a proper vocalist like Faye Gold, he thought. In no time this double dose of tobacco and tragic comedy had done Gerry the world of good. And the line – "*We're going for those pleasures in the night*" – the cruel irony of it struck him also. Smirking, he reached over to the table and began to refill the ashtray: "Not now we're not, love," he said to himself as he extinguished his cig.

He jumped to his feet. He caught his image in the mirror and paused to admire the squat triangle of flesh and blood, still muscled in the arms and shoulders, which stood before him. He shot himself a showbiz smile – teeth white, eyes anything but warm – before strutting to the en suite.

The theatre was haunted with strange acoustics – all those concrete stairwells and dry risers carried sound unpredictably – and in the en suite Mandy Monroe was loud and clear and still as flat as a seagull. As he urinated, Gerry joined her in a cruel duet, speaking the lyrics in perfect Elvis-ese; "I'm so excited, baby, and I just can't hide it, no mam, I'm about to lose control…" – he coughed a laugh, amused to see smudges of lipstick on his dick, and then switched to Donald Duck for the last six words – "…and I think I like it!" He shook and flushed and then quacked some more: "Oh boy, oh boy, oh boy! Brrrr!" He was ready for business.

After her second house spot, Mandy took a cursory bow and left the stage to polite applause; her face burned red. She dashed up the stairs to her dressing room and rushed inside, slamming *her* door just as earlier she had slammed Gerry's. As she slid the bolt, she shook with anger. A deep shelf ran along the length of her room and served as a dressing table; it was dusted with face powder and strewn with other cosmetics. On it rested her large, leather handbag. An impatient rummage yielded a half-bottle of vodka, unopened, and a glance at the sink located a tall glass, which she filled and then began to empty in gulps. Unformed questions fought for prominence in her mind; what gave him the right to… how could he be so…what had she done to deserve…? "The bastard!" she hissed with the scolding sibilance of a steam iron. For a while she was too angry to sit down, and so paced as she drank, all the while shaking and fiddling with a tiny silver crab that hung from her neck.

During her maiden season – Blackpool 1973 when she was just eighteen and used her family name of Shaw – Mandy fell in love for the first time. The man she loved was the second-top-of-the-bill: a handsome, young comic with stellar prospects. For most of that summer she spent star-struck nights in the star turn's bed, and the debutant thought herself a woman. But, with a month left for the production to run, he ended the relationship, abruptly one morning, and the experience broke her. For months details would return to haunt her: his yawned explanation about wanting to reach the Big Time and about not being tied down; her hurried dressing in the night-before's clothes; the front door shutting behind her; the brilliance of the morning; her feeling of nakedness in hot pants; the whistles of bin-men. In less than a week she saw him with someone else, another dancer from the next pier along; and he never did make it big.

Early, therefore, Mandy had learned that for a dancer the fabled "world" of show business was little more than a rock pool, in which the men like circling gulls preyed on the soft-bodied, the soft-hearted. But she had endured that debut season, and had prevailed, and by the closing night she felt her own soft heart had hardened. She'd always known her star sign, had always read her horoscope, but from then on Cancer's crab had new meaning for her because she, like it, had grown a shell, to love. And so before she left Blackpool that season she took her final pay-packet to a jewelers in the shadow of the Tower, and as a kind of vow to herself she bought that tiny silver crab, that symbol of her new, calcified self, that constant reminder to keep her heart protected from love.

Eventually she stopped pacing and leant over the dressing table, pressing her palms down on its messy surface and locking her arms straight to support herself. Her head she hung low in troubled contemplation. Tears welled and dripped occasionally, forming dark clumps with the face powder. She stared at the backs of her hands; beneath the right she clenched a tissue, while on the left she had biro-ed three names and a number, but she had neglected to mention Sue and Graham and their son Benjamin's tenth; funny that *she* should overlook a birthday, she noted with a groaning, sinking sigh. She even laughed a little as she blew her nose, but it was heavy levity. Still with her head bowed she watched her crab necklace as it swung back and forth between her elbows, with its shell, and with its claws.

"Bastard!" she repeated to herself, "I'm more than just tits and legs! I'm more than that!"

***

From the office of his armchair, Gerry made a desk of a briefcase. He sprung two clasps with his thumbs and propped open the hinged lid with one hand, while rearranging the contents of the base with the other. Searching, he brushed aside a fat roll of twenties, a screw capped bottle of aftershave, some clean underwear (Paisley), twenty Benson, unopened, and a scrunched up paper bag.

Moving to the lid itself, he pulled a press-stud and three concertinaed compartments dropped forward. Like an office clerk with hanging files, he rifled through roughly opened A4 envelopes, a copy of Fiesta and a tabloid, folded to the crossword. "Where are ya, y'little bastard?" he mumbled. He dug deeper, pulled out a Polaroid of himself wearing an SS uniform and a madcap expression, with the proudest of erections protruding through the flies of the breeches; but that wasn't it.

There was a hurried tapping on the door. "Gerry, its Ray..."

"Yes mate, what can I do for you?" he answered the Company Manager, who half-entered, leaning around the door.

"Everything okay? Need anything? Er listen, would you mind presenting a bouquet in the finale? Duncan from Front-of-House asked me if you would. Apparently there's this old dear in tonight who's a hundred and fifty, or something. Is that okay?"

"Yeah, course I will, no problem."

"Her son will leave them…"

"At the stage door," he interrupted. "Yep. Know the drill. Busy tonight?"

"Sold out."

The door closed and the Top of the Bill continued his search. At last, inside the newspaper, he found his narrow, week-per-page diary. He closed the case and rested the navy book on top of it. Using the red ribbon marker, he splayed the pages to this week, 15th – 21st July. There, entered under Friday, and with an arrow drawn down the remainder of that page and the whole of the next, was the name "Pete", a phone number and the word "Belvedere"; Gerry's oldest pal would be arriving in Grumby tonight. He grabbed the handset, punched the number and waited for the landlady to answer.

"Hiya, Reenie, love, it's Gerry," he greeted. He then remained mostly silent for a good two minutes while Doreen O'Driscoll enthused and reminisced of the old times when he and "the Nobles" played Liverpool, at the Shakespeare Theatre Club or the Wooky Hollow, staying with her in Pro digs. That was a long time ago, the Sixties, before Gerry went first solo and then stratospheric, and likewise before *she* had realized *her* dream of opening a guesthouse with her husband here in Grumby. "So how's The Belvedere going then? Are you still making your wonderful Irish stew?" he interrupted, charmingly. "Mike okay?" he went on, before finally getting to his point; "Has Pete arrived yet?" he asked. "Oh ... right ... I see ...okay then." He accompanied her rambling explanation that Pete, God bless him, had not in fact arrived, but that he had telephoned earlier and had arranged to check in much later, after the show. "Alright, love. I'll expect him *here*, then," he clarified. "Bye, love. Bye. Yes, I'll pop along with him later, don't you worry. Yep. Yep. Goodbye." He hung up with a chuckle; still as barmy as ever, he thought.

Pete Wheeler, he thought. He replaced the diary in the briefcase, and that on the floor, and then got up to make a brew; and so began his nightly routine. With the kettle purring on the fridge, he carefully unfurled his Elvis flares and hung them on a rail to de-crease; a few sequins sprinkled the peach shag pile. The boots he arranged beneath the rail also, and the rhinestone shirt he threw into the corner by the door for wardrobe to launder. Hanging from the door was a white toweling dressing gown, but the heat of the stage lights was still in him, so he remained in just his underwear. The kettle growled. He thumbed the remote and the TV hummed into life with a woman's voice reading the Nine O'Clock News; he watched as the screen slowly revealed Julia Somebody looking...sexy. He bent down and rummaged in his case again, taking the daily, a pen and the paper bag, which he arranged on the arms of the chair. Pacing, he appraised the compact bulk of his reflection; the kettle roared an approval, and he was sure that even Julia would approve. On the balls of his feet now he shaped himself like a boxer and punched at the mirror with two left jabs and a right uppercut. Pete Wheeler, he thought again. "Pete Wheeler!" he exclaimed.

Placing a hot mug on the table, he sparked up *another* cigarette and settled back into his chair. The local news showed a hotel perilously close to an eroding cliff, but he was more interested in "The Roman god of war" nine across, four letters. He barely heard the cursory knock at he door or the gruffly intoned "Wardrobe!" as the damp stage shirt was collected. He did look up briefly, though, as an amiable weatherman with breathy, comedic speech announced that there would be "…an overnight low of twelve degrees with some spits and spots of rain." He took a drag from his cigarette, sipped his sweet, builder's tea and wrote down the solution to his clue – MARS. He gave himself a little smile.

***

Standing over her dressing table, Mandy raised her chin to administer another mouthful of vodka. Her eyes met her reflection. Her pretty face was pink and wet and bore a scowl. She returned the look in kind, scowling at the reflection in that bright, unforgiving mirror, scowling unforgivingly at herself. Why had she pressed Gerry over the meal out and the hoarding, she thought to herself, why had she rocked the boat? "You idiot," she said to herself.

She removed her high-heels and squirmed out of her figure-hugging stage dress. She threw the tiny black number over a hanger and pulled on a white toweling dressing gown with foundation on the collar. At last her legs surrendered to the vodka and allowed her to sit. She folded her body into a two-seater, tucking her feet beneath herself, and sipping constantly now the alcohol like a drip-fed fetus. There was still the rest of the first half and all of the second until her cue for the finale would signal time at the bar, and so she settled down to this most umbilical of drinking.

The anger she felt no longer shook her body or contorted her face, but it remained in her. A crease indented her forehead, betraying another emotion; she sipped and swallowed and closed her eyes in pained embarrassment.

"Oh, God!" she moaned. Her second spot this evening had been a disaster, as bad as ever. She had charged at the Pointer Sisters' number without a thought for her breathing and had sung the whole song from her throat, straining throughout and frequently straying off-key; even her patter in between numbers – so often her saving grace – had been rushed and had lacked her usual warmth. Amanda Monroe had bombed again, and she knew it. She drained her highball.

***

"This is your five minute call, ladies and gentlemen, your five minute call. Thank you," came Radio Kevin over the airwaves.

Gerry swilled the last syrupy mouthful of tea from his mug; the crossword lay completed on top of the briefcase on the floor, and there were now a total of three butts in the ashtray. The call thus ended one trusted routine, private, and prompted another, entirely public. But there was one last thing to be done; he took the paper bag that had rested beside him, untouched but irresistible, and held it in the palm of his hand. This crumpled sweetie bag for him contained the most precious of confections, edible gold dust in fact, and he rustled it open to reveal a million white crystals. His mouth welled with sweet saliva, but the sugary tea would soon be a distant memory – caffeine and nicotine would be distant memories. He wet his middle finger, dabbed at the amphetamine and sucked the bitterest of sherbets from his flesh.

Gerry had been speeding through performances since he first popped Benzedrine on the Reeperbahn. On it, his act would spark and buzz and dazzle like a neon sign, a Neon sign even; one-liners would bolt from his mouth and strike the microphone as if it were a lightning rod; off it, well, he couldn't remember. Even now, after just one, no two, okay three dabs of his finger, the belt of his Van der Graaff was already beginning to turn and a charge was building. He dabbed a fourth time. Current, however, had not yet cracked its whip and he could still function in the real, low voltage world of his dressing room.

He put on his stage suit – not the Elvis get-up; that was a costume change for his closing routine – but rather his standard, dark suit, the kind he had worn for years. As he got dressed, he thought again of Pete, and smiled archly; it was always a right laugh when the two of them got together, and it had been such a long time. Then, sunning himself beneath the bare bulbs, he coiffed and preened and powdered the sheen from his face. Moving closer to the mirror he re-drew a large dot of liner near each tear duct so as to widen the appearance of his eyes. He thought once more of Mandy; she certainly *used to be* a laugh, but then the bint had turned thirty, had hauled herself an inch up that greasy pole and now he would have to deal with her. He dabbed and sucked again.

He bent down for a pair of black Cuban heeled boots and stepped into them, although even in stocking feet he already felt six feet tall. And then, for the last time, he *scooped* at the white powder and shoveled a finger-full into his mouth and made a toothbrush of this same middle digit and brushed his gums, rapidly, gurning. He screwed up and stashed the bag in the briefcase and killed the TV. A surge of current now flowed through *his* circuitry and he bolted for the stage; Showbiz's Monster had risen.

The awkward position he was in caused his foot to hurt, his knee stung from the hardness of the floor and the sustained intensity of the performance burned his thigh. But agony and ecstasy are such intimate bedfellows and, besides, he felt that he was close. Weakness would come soon and then the shakes, but not yet. Experience had taught him to delay the moment, and his class lay in the timing. He felt himself rising with the music, and once he was sure everything was just right, once he was sure The King was ready, Gerry exploded into the chorus.

He sprung from his kneeling, windmilled his arm and punched the air in time to the dramatic orchestrations of An American Trilogy. Dry ice misted the stage, heavenly.

"Glory, glory hallelujah," he sang.

Backlit and in silhouette, he then held *the* classic Vegas-era pose; standing half-turned to the audience and with his face in profile, he raised his arms like a puppeteer's and set his feet as if poised to karate kick. Floodlights dazzled the crowd.

"Glory, glory hallelujah."

From the front again, super troupers spotlit his white suit of flared trousers and high-collared jacket trimmed with gold studs. An eagle, feathered with red and blue jewels, perched emblazoned on his back. The music soared.

"Glory, glory hallelujah."

He punched again, kicked and swung his leg as if mounting a stallion. Red sequined insets in the flares flapped like phoenixes.

"His truth is marching on."

He stood, front on to the crowd, challenging them not to adore him. Breathing heavily in the hot lights, he undid another shirt button and pulled a satin scarf across his brow. The music soared still higher, but Gerry was preparing for a monumental finish. He thrust forward the huge buckle that bulged from his heavyweight champion's belt, and finally he climaxed with an operatic repeat of the final triumphant line.

"His truth is marching on!"

***

Somehow Mandy, angry, embarrassed and becoming drunk, had made it down to the stage door without anyone seeing her. In her dressing gown and slippers, she had sought solace in a phone call. Her head was buried deep inside the hood of a kiosk that was situated next to the doorman's booth. Remarkably she had found the payphone unoccupied by any of the dancers and the reception area was, momentarily at least, empty of ears.

"I mean, it's not like I haven't worked hard at my act…" she was saying.

"I *know* you have, love," she was hearing.

"And I have been going down much better lately…"

"I *know* you have, love."

"Surely it's not a lot to ask for him to sort out the hoarding and to take me for a bite to eat…"

"Of course it isn't."

"And I *can't* go on stage like that…"

"No, you can't."

All that Mandy suspected was now being confirmed; she was a talented professional and a good person, whereas Gerry was a total bastard, entirely in the wrong. Moreover, *he* was largely to blame for *her* performance; her breathless breathing, her strangled singing and the cold warmth of her patter – all had been symptoms of the anger that Gerry had caused. *He* had started the fight, after all, with his indifference to her birthday and his reluctance to speak to Bernie; *he* had been out of order to snap at her the way he had, to say those cruel things about her singing, to tell her to "Piss off" – *just before* her entrance.

"No wonder I bombed after a send off like that!" She snorted. "I mean I was so emotional, so angry, that my throat clenched itself like a fist. How could I sing like that? I should have been in the wings preparing to go on, not rowing with the top of the bill. Even now I can feel a choking sensation…"

"I know, I can hear it in your voice, you poor love. *You* certainly shouldn't feel bad about tonight's performance when it's Gerry that was to blame. It was his fault really, Mandy, if you think about."

"You're right. Perhaps I should stand up to him a bit more…"

"Yes, you should *definitely* do that. You can't let the bastard walk all over you!"

"I mean, I've got my pride, y'know!" she slurred.

"I know you have, Mandy. You *must* stand up to him. You've just got to be brave."

"I will. And then there's always that Cruise Director I have the number of..."

"Yes, you should definitely give *him* a call."

"I will. I mean Gerry..."

"Oh, I know..."

Mandy's victim's logic was thus re-enforced, and the alcohol, which had earlier dampened her anger, now served to fuel that same anger so that indignation burned in her. She hung up the receiver, counseled and cheered to the point of absolute certainty; Gerry had been in the wrong and she would now have it out with him.

In fact, by the time she had returned to her dressing room, she wondered if she might be better off without him. She refilled her glass and drank a toast to her coming independence. That's right, she thought to herself with a grim smile, perhaps *she* should tell *him* to "Piss off". Folding her feet beneath her on the sofa, she sensed revenge – home truths, choice words, his face slapped, her vengeance wreaked – and she searched her thoughts for an opportunity, the more public the better.

Before long she had emptied her second highball of neat vodka and, reaching over to the worktop, she slammed the glass down with the finality of an auctioneer's gavel, as if to declare a closure of some kind. Going once; Going twice; Sold! to the woman with the big hair. Her mind was now set; she would have it out with Gerry *on the stage*, in front of the cast, the instant the curtain had come down on the finale.

***

In the wings stood Pete Wheeler, holding a bouquet of funereal proportions. Although at first distracted by four dancers in bikinis and ostrich feather headdresses, he couldn't help but admire, still, at the thousandth time of witnessing, the resurrection of Elvis Presley that was occurring on stage. What a showman, he thought, and that voice! It helped, of course, that the backing band was top-drawer, and loud moreover – there was serious wattage in the P.A., power more akin to a rock concert than Variety – but all the same… Pete had to admit that, even after twenty years of doing him, no one did Elvis like Gerry Neon did Elvis.

Even so, as Pete watched his old pal, down on one knee, he couldn't help but think how he hated the bloated, Vegas years and this patriotic bullshit about "Dixie", whatever that was. You could keep the jumpsuits and the capes as far as Pete Wheeler was concerned. To him, Elvis was always the Hillbilly Cat, the Pelvis, the white boy that sang like a Negro. It was thirty years since "That's All Right (Mama)" put a power lead up his arse, and he was still electrified.

***

By now Gerry's performance had built to a transcendent degree. The star wrung every last bar out of the closing note and then he and the band signed off with dramatic finality. The audience erupted. For two minutes he stood silent and motionless; the euphoria of the crowd caressing his ears, stroking him, stoking him. The last wisps of dry ice licked at his boots.

"Thank-you-very-much-and-goodnight," he drawled at last. The band reprised the chorus melody as he bowed and exited stage left with a swagger, handing Kevin his radio mic.

"You overran again, Gerry. It's going in the book," stated the ASM matter of factly.

"Sod off, I'm The King," he replied, with barely a rhinestone of irony. In the wings he was greeted with a smile, an outstretched hand and a bouquet. "Stroll on! It's fucking Interflora! I've told you before, I'm not shagging you, y'know! How you doin', Pete man?"

"Better than you, Geronimo. These are for your act!" He gestured with the flowers. "It's dead! I saw you kneeling just then, I thought I was gonna have to help you up! I can't believe you're still doing Elvis! You should bring things up to date, y'know, do some Michael Jackson! A bit of shoe polish, you'd be his spitting image! Can you moonwalk?"

"Sarky bastard! Good to see you, pal."

"Yeah, and you." The two men beamed and wrestled their grips, and would have hugged and slapped like Mafiosi, were it not for Pete's carnations. Even within an aviary of dancers they commanded the attention – Gerry bullish from his ovation, Pete towering and pumped for his entrance to the theatre.

"Can you remember the night he died?" Pete balled, sniggering at a previous irreverence. "...the Lido in the Isle of Man? You asked me to find something black for you to wear during your act, y'know, as an armband, and I said better still you should go on in a coffin and then jump out! You went for me and they had to separate us!"

"I was very emotional! Anyway Elvis lives, haven't you heard? There's been sightings of him, driving a tram! With JFK as the conductor! Trouble is, *he* won't work the open top ones, not after Dallas!"

Both men laughed, and for a moment they were as giddy as the boys on bikes in sunshine they once were. "Anyway Gee, the doorman gave me these." Pete raised the flowers. "They're for…" he looked at the tag. "…Ethel Clemmitt, eighty today."

"Er…just stand here with 'em for now, will yer?"

"Yes boss," Pete replied, doffing an imaginary cap in mock deference. "So…" he said, leaning down to Gerry's ear, speaking more quietly, "which one are you shagging?"

"All of 'em!"

"Yeah, right. You've lost your touch, I can tell. You're not getting any, are you?"

"More than you, mate!"

"Go on, seriously, which one?"

"The singer." Gerry half-lied; perhaps he could extend her run a little longer.

Pete looked around. "Where is she?"

"Dunno."

"Big tits?"

"Like a dead heat in a Zeppelin race, mate."

"Is she wardrobe material?"

"Perhaps."

Gerry smiled slyly, knowingly at his oldest pal and turned his back, ending the banter. The flowers were a nice idea, he thought; an idea he could use himself. Ethel Clemmitt would have to do without.

The band finished the number, a hundred lamps were snuffed and a dark blur of stagehands prepped the finale like bats in a cave. Eight showgirls filed into position.

***

"The finale, ladies and gentlemen; all acts to the stage. Thank you."

Kevin interrupted Mandy's scheming. "Shit!" she exclaimed; the singer was nowhere near ready. She stood up as quickly as her drunkenness would allow, and promptly found herself staggering on what appeared to be a heaving deck of shag pile. There was no choice but to ride out the storm; she kicked off her slippers and threw off her dressing gown, knocking over a can of hairspray, and then lunged for and grabbed her cocktail dress from its hanger. With both hands she held the garment open and tried to step into it, but she kept snagging her foot in its elasticated material, each time losing her balance and swearing and twice almost falling flat on her face. After a hokey-cokey of failed attempts she at last stood with both feet firmly on the floor, lassoed by black, sparkly polyester. Hurriedly she pulled up the dress, wiggling it over her rump like a glitzy sausage skin. She thrust her arms through the padded shoulder straps and managed to pull the back zip almost to the top; as usual this was an exercise in containment that squeezed her breasts into a seaside postcard cleavage, visible above the shelf of her sweetheart neckline. To secure the bodice – and her boobs – she tugged a hook into its eye, and lastly forced her feet back into three-inch heels. Standing there, swaying, she resembled a joint trussed for the oven.

From the stage below came the tune of Mezzoforte's "Garden Party"; the finale had begun. Before Mandy's scheduled entrance there would be brief, warmly applauded solos from each of the three brass men, and then the dancers would take their collective curtsey. She would have, therefore, approximately verse-chorus-verse-chorus to get herself to the wings to make her cue.

"Right then, you bastard!" she slurred; it was time to face Gerry, time to have it out with him. She poured herself one last courageous measure and knocked it back, slamming the glass down a little less accurately than before. Her breath was volatile with vodka.

She unbolted the door and opened it into herself, knocking her left shoulder sharply. It took a moment for her clumsiness to register. She shuffled sideways to re-align herself, but over-compensated and knocked her right shoulder this time on the doorframe. Somehow she made it across the threshold and along the corridor and to the top of the stairs. Lowering her foot on to the top step, she mumbled to herself: "I'll give you 'tits 'n' legs', you bastard!"

She was perilously unsteady on those legs, however, and so paused a while and gripped the handrail. A startling sax solo came up the stairwell. The first note of doubt entered her mind. Had she been too pushy after all, she wondered; should she give him more time to come around? For all her anger and pain, she didn't really know whether to attack or hide in her shell. But, she had a cue to make, and so continued her shaky descent into the foreboding wail of a trombone.

From the reception area she caught a glimpse of Gerry through the swing door; it was a blinding, panoramic glimpse. He was in the wings, laughing and joking with someone holding a huge bouquet, and the sight of him chilled her. The door swung closed as quickly as it had opened and she found herself rooted beneath a strip light, gripped by uncertainty and fingering that tiny Cancer crab, that symbol of something which, like her own feelings, she didn't understand. "Tits 'n' legs, my arse!" she joked, weakly.

She turned to a mirror on the wall opposite the doorman's booth. She made a pretence of preening, but she was stalling for time. She tried to imagine her first post-Gerry gig – a cocktail bar on a cruise ship in the Caribbean, perhaps – but all she could visualize was a dismal holiday camp, a ham-fisted organist, and playing to three rows, with a stage-side message board that read "Baby crying in chalet number 38". A discordant trumpet echoed her fear. She remembered what she had always known, that show business was awash with "girl singers", better and younger than her. She conceded to herself she'd never secure a booking with the prestige of Seaside Spectacular, not without Gerry; and a cruise was just a pipe dream. She was tied to him. He was her meal ticket, her sugar daddy – and she knew it. Drooping, she knocked her forehead on the glass of the mirror, and straightened with a start. There was no way she'd confront him – not now, not ever; it would be professional suicide. And so showbiz instinct, like a cruel lighthouse, directed her away from a rocky but righteous shore and further out into his immoral sea.

Looking in that mirror, staring defeat in the face, she knew that mentally she was already white-flagging an invitation to further abuse – the headliner just didn't know it yet. Even so, she felt too ashamed to look him in the eye, couldn't bring herself to join him in the wings as normal. The best she could do for now was to feign indifference. It was a futile charade – she knew she'd chase any ball or stick that he tossed for her – but she would maintain the act, for as long as she dare, if only to commemorate the pride she had lost long ago. She decided, therefore, to avoid him for tonight and to enter the finale from opposite-prompt.

She made for the corridor that traversed beneath the stage, numbly descending a second stairwell, easing herself down and then up again the hard concrete steps of a bouncy castle, making her cue, just.

***

A hundred tungsten filaments glowed white hot again and the auditorium jumped with the brass and cowbell carnival sound of "Garden Party". The band rendered the fluid syncopation of the number seemingly without effort, and the horn section – three genuine musos, used to playing tented Jazz festivals – dueled their solos with a virtuosity and intensity at odds with the end of the pier setting. Next, eight dancers, seven feet tall in their feathers and with arms outstretched like wings, continued the finale with a brief, pedestrian routine, in which they walked victoriously around the stage to polite applause. Having curtsied, they organized themselves into an inverted V shape, out of which the acts then filed to take their bows in bill order to increasingly rapturous receptions. For Gerry, the star of the show, the star of any show, the fabulous Mr Gerry Neon, the audience lifted the roof. The band signed off with a flourish and then Mr Neon, still in Elvis garb, took a mic from a stand and made his valediction, centre stage.

"Thankyouverymuchladiesandgentlemen," he began his address, his mouth barely keeping up with his brain. "You have been a tremendous audience this evening, really tremendous. Give yourselves a round of applause!" The audience clapped as instructed. "And let's face it, so have I," he observed with playful bravado. The audience laughed, as did the rest of the bill, through clenched teeth.

"Also, please give a big hand for five fabulous musicians: The Dave Newhurst Orchestra. Take a bow, boys." Genuine appreciation poured from the audience and cast alike, towards the sextet. "Yes folks, five really fabulous musicians… and a drummer." The band groaned.

"Now then, ladies 'n' gentlemen. Without further ado, I have some very important news for you this evening; yes, ladesgentmen, I have news of a special anniversary… It's a hundred years exactly, to the day, since the pier collapsed!" The audience laughed again; a few even gripped their armrests. "No, but seriously, ladesgentmen, we do have an anniversary of sorts today; a birthday, in fact."

Ethel Clemmitt's ears pricked up. Mandy, however, wasn't really listening – those last few mouthfuls of vodka, which had left vapour trails on two flights of stairs, had begun to seep through her gut wall like tea from a bag. And as the alcohol flooded her circulation and permeated her brain, she was becoming stupid with it. She stood on the stage, swaying, between a plucked ostrich and a Mexican bandito, and gazed into the spotlights, vaguely aware of her existence and smiling like a vent act's dummy.

Gerry, meanwhile, vacated his position centre stage and briefly disappeared into the wings. Pete handed him the bouquet, saying, "I see what you mean – she's a right hunchfront!" Gerry smiled, tore off the tag and returned to the stage. Proudly, he positioned himself beside the girl-singer, in whom thoughts were forming.

An echo of the word "birthday" finally registered with her and, seeing the bouquet, her plastic smile came alive and a fool's perception flickered in her eyes. Perhaps he was coming around to her after all, she wondered; did he even care for her?

"That's right, we have a birthday amongst the artistes. Yes, Miss Amanda Monroe, the beautiful and talented Miss Amanda Monroe, is celebrating her birthday today... and it's a biggie. Chivalry, ladesgentmen, my chivalry prevents me from saying just how old she is... but it rhymes with 'dirty'."

He then paused and held a wistful expression while puffing his cheeks, all of which prompted a kind of double laugh from the family audience; the first was a universal chuckle at his gall to give away a lady's age; the second, however, came from the bellies of men at his bawdy insinuation – phew, she was hot stuff! And at this nudge-wink confirmation of all they had hoped, the Dads in the crowd roared their approval, while the Mums elbowed their ribs. Discerning adults now knew that Miss Amanda Monroe was *dirty*, and the Star of the Show had inside, first hand knowledge of the fact. Ethel Clemmit's family, however, bore puzzled expressions.

Still holding the flowers, he glanced over to Pete in the wings and gave him a wink; he then turned around completely and aped a female sex pout to the band, who howled knowingly; lastly, facing the audience again, he gave Mandy a proprietary tap on the behind with the microphone, which caused a soft thud to come from the P.A.

The singer's only ignorant concerns in this sneaky boys club, however, were the flowers, the limelight and his tender caress on her behind. At last it dawned on her: their earlier row was no more than a lovers' tiff; it could all now be forgotten. In fact, at that moment, she believed that he might one day love her...as she loved him.

"That's right, ladesgentmen," he began again, "my chivalry prevents me from revealing Miss Monroe's age, and so I'd like to present this beautiful bunch of thirty chrysanthemums..." Someone shouted something from the wings. "What's that, Pete?" Gerry responded, "...I thought that was tinned milk? No? Okay. Er, sorry ladesgentmen, ... and so I'd like to present this beautiful bunch of thirty carnations..." he continued over groans "... to one of the most talented performers I've ever had..." There was another pause and more approving male laughter "...the privilege of working with, that's right, Miss Amanda Monroe. Join me, ladesgentmen, in giving her a big one, a big hand," he corrected himself quickly.

The audience obeyed again. At last, he presented the flowers, with a brief kiss; the smell of alcohol was intense. Placing the mic under his arm, he too applauded, while birthday-girl nosed the bunch and sobered herself enough to shape an extravagant curtsey, like the ex-dancer she was, mouthing several thank yous. "In fact, ladesgentmen," he took the mic again, "*Ha-ppy-Birth-day-to-you, ha-ppy-birth*...altogether now...*to-you.*" He swung his arms like a conductor as a thousand people sang to a complete stranger; the trumpeter even joined in, using a mute to improvise a wah-wah mournfulness to the tune, like a bugler playing the Last Post; and more howls spewed from his colleagues in the band. During the rendition, Gerry spontaneously buttonholed Ashley Kidd, second from top of the bill, and whose ovation had been a little too loud for his liking. Like a Nazi Commandant and only half joking, he screamed in his face with a mock German accent; "You vill zing! You vill zing *now!*" he barked. Kidd, a little afraid, could only laugh with embarrassment.

As the audience finished their tuneless dirge, the headliner managed to calm himself for the close. He retook his position alongside Mandy, who by now believed herself a diva, and with an arm around her waist he finished his address; "Thanks again for being a tremendous audience, ladesgentmen. If you've enjoyed yourselves I'm Gerry Neon, but if you haven't... I'm Cannon and Ball! G'night and God bless!"

The band reprised "Garden Party", and during this celebratory number the cast danced from side to side, waving like children's TV presenters. Two super troupers traced figure eights around the auditorium and the house curtain came down and went up again several times. With each re-appearance of the stage, the performers were shown in ever more outrageous displays of demob happiness. During the first, Gerry was shown kicking an impromptu can-can between two dancers; during the second, he had pinned Ashley Kidd to the floor, and was apparently punching him; and as the curtain was raised a third and last time, he dropped his trousers, but thankfully not his maroon underpants, and mooned the audience. And with that final visual gag, a thousand cheerful mums and dads and boys and girls stood and left the world of Variety for another year.

By now Mandy's drunkenness had returned like a deep breath of dentist's gas and she beamed inanely, oblivious to the mayhem around her. Not a single thought of her planned confrontation remained in her head and, as far as she was concerned, they were lovers again; in fact they were an item.

As described in the BECTU handbook, an employee is free to leave his place of work as soon as his last call has been completed; stagehands, therefore, tend to bolt like rabbits the moment a theatre's house lights come on.

For sure Martin felt no inclination to hang around. Normally at the close of the second house his final tasks would be to strike the stage in preparation for the late-night show and to dock all the radio-mics into the discharging / charging unit. Kevin, however, had given him no such call via his headset and so he figured that tonight someone else would be taking care of the broom and the mics, probably. To be frank, having been banished to the super troupers for four hot hours, he wasn't about to break any more sweat worrying about it. He shut down his spotlight and was relieved to depart with the punters.

A thousand holidaymakers stood up and filed into the aisles. Quickly he found himself trapped within a tight column of people, each shuffling softly up one of three carpeted slopes that led to the single exit at the back of the auditorium. Many had been amused to the brink of incontinence, and there was a cheerful, excited hum.

The bottleneck out of the auditorium led into the foyer, which offered its own obstacles. There were queues for Gerry Neon merchandise and for the ladies' toilet, and plumb in the middle of the foyer a small island of OAPs stood waiting for something, oblivious to the choked flow of people trying to leave. At last Martin made it out of the theatre and into a fresh sea breeze. A chill touched his neck and wherever perspiration had caused his shirt to cling. He zigzagged free of the crowd and began to stride down the pier. He saw clouds scudding above, and to his left waves caught the moonlight as they broke and foamed creamy white. In an instant he felt starving hungry.

His desire to eat was irresistible. No longer did he care about Alfonso or The Galapagos or his temporary demotion to follow spot operator, the only thing on his mind now was a cheeseburger. He passed under the hoarding at the end of the pier, crossed the road and the tram tracks and placed his order at "Bryan's", a lock-up that backed onto Funland. Almost eleven o'clock, the rides had stopped spinning and dipping an hour ago and presently the promenade's slot arcades were being silenced and darkened. All along this stretch of Grumby, kiosks and booths were closing for business; panels were being hung, flaps lowered and shutters pulled to and fastened with hasps and padlocks, but Bryan kept his burger bar open later than the other lock-ups and Martin was a nightly customer. He paid and leant an elbow over the lip of the serving hatch. As he waited, the sweet tang of fried onions and beef fat caused his mouth to well with saliva. In the day he hungered after shellfish by the harbour and tended to look down his nose at the vulgarity of his current fat-spitting location; but he always found it easy to swallow his culinary pride when he was this famished. Besides, the feral fairground youths and the kiss-me-quick crowd had all but disappeared back to their caravans and guesthouses or else on to nightclubs.

"Busy night?" enquired Bryan.

"Er, not bad – two-thirds full in the first house and the second house was packed. There were a lot of Scots in."

A squirt of ketchup under the lid, and no first mouthful was ever more delicious – starving, ice age cavemen, feasting on roasted bison, could not have enjoyed a meal more.

"See you tomorrow, Bryan." He sucked his fingers, wiped his mouth with a napkin and set off for The Galleon as happy as a carnivorous sand boy.

**

The Galleon was an underground bar in the centre of town that operated after hours as a jazz club for members only. For all the world, though, it seemed the only criteria for membership were thirst and insomnia, and anyone connected with any show in any way was allowed in free. "A gallon at The Galleon", therefore, was a phrase familiar among stagehands at the Victoria Pier Theatre – a nocturnal, thirsty bunch to say the least. Likewise the crews from Grumby's other theatres and cabaret venues also regarded the bar with similar affection because each night it crawled with flymen, electricians, soundboard operators, follow spot operators, ASMs, and whoever else was at a loose end. The Opera House, being just around the corner, was always well represented. On any night of the week, therefore, Martin could be fairly sure to turn up and find himself among his kind.

At the entrance desk he signed himself in, and the lean doorman, all tattoos and tendons, waved him down the stairs impatiently. At the bar he surveyed the clientele, furtively, so as not to catch an eye; there was no one here yet that he recognised. He bought himself *two* pints of bitter and went and stood against a wall, as far from anyone else as was possible. The place was still only a quarter full and this afforded Martin relative privacy and space, while he was still absolutely sober.

There were two dim, low-ceilinged rooms in The Galleon. The main room housed the bar and a tiny stage in the corner, just big enough for a small drum kit and electric piano. There were tables and stools around the edge and standing room in the middle. The adjoining room behind the bar was smaller and contained proportionately more tables; a snug to the taproom. Martin was standing in the larger room near the duo, who played cocktail lounge Jazz and did not play loudly.

Well salted by his earlier burger, the first pint barely touched the sides; the second he drank more slowly and he could feel himself relaxing into the funny-odd, funny-ha-ha ambience of this nautically themed bar. He allowed his gaze to drift over walls decked with old maps, ships' wheels, lengths of thick rope tied into knots, anchors and lobster pots containing plastic lobsters. As usual he smiled at the life-sized torso of a Pirate Captain – a dark faced dummy, adorned with large hooped earrings, eye patch, sash and cutlass – that looked out from a shelf behind the drum kit. The house drummer himself was a sight, well into his seventies, bow-tied and severely cross-eyed.

By now some familiar faces were standing at the bar. There was Gary and Alan, flymen from the pier, and two other men Martin believed worked the Opera House. All of them, like Martin himself, were dressed in regulation black. He didn't think his workmates had noticed him, however. He considered going over to join them, but decided *they* would probably come over to *him* in due course. Besides, he had a good spot, over here, by the band. He took a mouthful and continued his visual voyage of discovery. Screwed to the wall behind him he found a map of the Caribbean Sea entitled "Haunts of the 'Brethren of the Coast'" and he lost himself in its strange cartography – the ragged coastlines and the exotic inscriptions – and the duo played Take Five.

He felt a tap on his arm and a voice said: "Hello Martin!" He turned to see a kind, round face looking up at him.

"Oh, hello Dennis."

"Long time no see! Planning your holidays?"

"What? No, I was just, erm…" Dennis was right, the two of them hadn't spoken properly in ages, perhaps years. Martin felt self-conscious.

"You alright then? I thought I might bump into you down here – the young lads from the Opera House are always going on about the place, telling me about the lock-ins, trying to get me to join them for a pint after work – and I figured your lot would be regulars here as well. Seems I was right. Mind you, you're all the same you stagehands. I bet they have to pour you out of here at sunrise!" Dennis paused and looked around for a moment, and Martin watched his mum's friend take in the chaotic decor of this grotto of kitsch. "It hasn't changed much…"

"Did *you* used to come here then?"

"What, you mean when I was your age? Oh, I've been coming to The Galleon since the early sixties, just not lately.

I remember when old Albert over there had two good eyes – that's a glass eye, you know, it's hard to tell down here in the dark – and there used to be a fake ship's figurehead next to the bar, a big paper mache mermaid. Her tits got worn away though, from blokes touching them, right back to the wire mesh, and they had to take they her down. They could have put a bra on her, I suppose."

"Huh, yeah. I like the pirate, myself."

"Oh, yeah? Captain Blood."

"Is *that* who he's meant to be?" Martin was intrigued…

"I don't know, er, I suppose he might be."

"Oh," …and then disappointed.

"Funnily enough, there's a story behind the pirate. Albert – huh, he's a character, been playing here since the fifties, you know, on and off – anyway once he performed *dressed* like a pirate. It was years ago, just after his accident. You wouldn't think it to look at him now, but he used to play these really wild solos, and once, one of his sticks – it was all whittled down from overuse – it split and then it snapped, and the free end, a giant splinter really, it flew back and stabbed him in the eye."

"Ouch! No way!"

"Seriously. He had to go to hospital, but he got an infection and lost it. Really sad. So, for a time he had to wear a patch, and Albert being Albert he got an idea. Peter Pan was on at the Opera House – it was around Christmas, mid-sixties – so he asked me to wangle for him the costume for Captain Hook, you know sneak it out of the theatre as I was locking up and bring it down here for him to wear. I shouldn't have done it, but I did. So he put it on in the toilets and it was massive, far too big for him. He looked ridiculous walking out and getting behind the kit, with his eye patch, dressed like a pirate, but everybody laughed and applauded."

"I bet they did!" Martin remembered what a nice feller Dennis was.

"Some of the cast were in, and they loved it. The trouble was, though, he got completely pissed, walked home in it – *in the snow* – and slipped on his backside. He got grit and slush all over the trousers, and he *tore* the elbow, and there were these leather shoes with big shiny buckles and they got soaking wet, ruined. There was a show the next night, and when he brought the costume all filthy and torn round to mine, his elbow was the size of a cannonball! Mind you, it was his fault, the daft bugger. Wardrobe went spare, and I got into a bit of bother with the Theatre Manager, almost lost my job... but still, it was funny! And so that pirate dummy behind the kit, Captain Blood or whoever he is, was mocked up soon afterwards, you know, as a nod to Albert. Can I get you a pint?"

"Er, yeah, alright. Bitter. Thanks."

By now The Galleon was heaving, and the cheerful stage doorman soon disappeared into the dark of the crowd. At the edges, amber spilled from shaded wall lights but could only lap at the central darkness. A single spot cast a wide cone of grey light on the duo, and in its diffuse beam hung smoke. Elsewhere steam mushroomed from a glass washer, just opened, and Martin watched it billow and cling to the low ceiling. The bar glowed golden.

He had always liked Dennis, ever since he was little, and ever since he had first understood that he didn't have a dad. The boy grew up knowing the man as a neighbour and a friend of his mum's, but she would never refer to him as *Uncle* Dennis like the other "Uncles". Those flash gits would breeze into Martin's life bearing Lightsabers and Scalextric sets, only to vanish a month later, their Capris and their Stags never to be seen again. Dennis had never vanished, though, and he had never given Martin anything except time and patience and attention. Sometimes he would take the youngster to the Opera House during the day and let him stand on the stage, awestruck by the towering silence of the empty theatre; and he would lead him down beneath the stage and into the band pit, and let him sit behind the drum kit and bang around until he had found a rhythm. As a kid Martin had wondered why this kind, caring man – this avuncular man – could not be called Uncle, and sometimes, grazed and crying after a fall, he had wanted to call him Dad.

Tonight, though, he simply found Dennis good company, and the combined effect of beer and bonhomie had really brought him out of himself. Before he knew it, he had even returned the smile of a pretty blond girl. Fleetingly her face had glowed like limelight in the murk, and he had beamed his own helpless, desirous smile. He followed her bare shoulders with his eyes as she took the passageway to the smaller room, and then she turned and smiled at him again before disappearing.

"There you go, son." Dennis handed Martin a pint.

"Cheers, Dennis."

"Before I forget, how's Kevin? Is he alright?"

"Er, very well, I think. Yeah, he's a nice bloke. Helpful. Taught me loads."

"I knew he would. Give him my regards, will you?" Martin replied that he would and Dennis went on: "As I said, I haven't seen much of you lately. I've *heard* you though – every time I walk Freddie past your house you're either in your bedroom knocking seven bells out of your drum kit or else you're huffing and puffing and clunking your weights in the garage. You seem to be filling out a bit…"

"D'ya think so? I still feel a bit lanky, myself. I eat for England, but I can't seem to put any weight on. I suppose the walk to and from work every day must burn it off – I'm always starving!"

"Well, whatever you're doing, you look good on it – 'athletic' I'd say, not 'lanky'." The balding, beer-keg of a man couldn't believe that such a strapping lad, handsome with his strong nose and cleft-chin, could be so unsure of himself.

"Thanks, Dennis, but, er…" And then Martin volunteered something: "It's my drumming that I'm most pleased about…" He paused and took a sip.

Dennis nearly dropped his pint at this new-found eagerness to speak, but said calmly: "Well, I'm no expert, but you certainly sound to be getting better." He was right, he wasn't an expert, he didn't have the ear to discern a drummer's improvement, but he was enough of an expert in human nature to know he should stroke the lad, and give him an audience. He made a guess and told another white lie: "What's that rhythm you've been practising lately, over and over? It seems to be coming together."

"Oh, that half-time shuffle beat? That's Jeff Porcaro's, from the track "Rosanna" by Toto. Do you know it?"

"Er, I think so." Dennis had no idea. "Is he good?"

Instantly Martin seemed to leap out of himself, enthused by this chance to reveal his own specialist knowledge. "Good? He's amazing! Overall the beat sounds easy enough, quite slow. It's in triplets with the first and the last on the hi-hat, like this: one, three-one, three-one, three-one." As he counted the rhythm, he whisked his hand as if tapping an imaginary stick on a make-believe hi-hat. He went on: "But it's deceptive because he plays all these little ghost notes on the snare in between. Then over the top of that you've got the bass drum, mostly on the *off*beat, and the *accented* snare on the back beat, like this…" With both arms he now played a whole invisible kit, voicing the rhythm. "Duh – d'ga – duh – – duh – – ga – duh – d'ga – duh – – duh – – ga."

Dennis had been quite concerned about Martin. Lorraine Collier, fully worried, had told him of how she "no longer knew" her son, "not since puberty", and of how he was "permanently down about everything", possibly even "depressed", and of how he would "fly off the handle at the drop of a hat". Dennis himself, on the few recent occasions they had crossed paths, had found the teenager increasingly surly and evasive. But now, as he watched the lad banging away on his air drums, he was reminded of the little boy he had known – the excited, little drummer boy in the band pit – and he was reassured to see the same rapt enthusiasm in Martin the near grown man. Possibly puberty *had* left him confused or shy, perhaps even darkened, but he was not "depressed", he was probably just angry at his foolish, boozy mother and his absent dad. Dennis guessed he probably just needed the love of a good woman! He smiled and said: "Impressive! I *think* I know what you mean – it sounds really difficult! And you can play that?"

The Jeff Porcaro-wannabe happily continued: "Well, I can do the overall beat, and separately I can do the triplet hand parts, but no way can I do the two together. I've bored myself to tears with it, but it's too hard! And *then* there's the arrangement of the song itself *and* he puts in these *monster* fills – he really builds a shed! I've seen it transcribed in one of those drumming magazines, but it just looks like hieroglyphics to me. I'm self-taught, you see, and that's well beyond Grade Eight – *I* don't even have the rudiments." He paused a moment, and then said: "But you know what my Mum's like, she wouldn't pay for lessons ..."

"Wouldn't she?" Dennis had wondered if the lad might get to his mother.

"No, she wouldn't," he said coldly.

The conversation halted abruptly. Dennis watched Martin's eyes fall to floor and his shoulders drop. He took a long drink from his pint, trying to think of something to say, to restore the mood, to pull Martin back from whichever abyss he was staring into. The duo ended one jazz standard, with little applause, and began another. And then the young lad's demeanour changed; his jaw muscles began to bulge, he raised himself to his full height, puffing out his chest, and he fixed Dennis with combative eyes. The older man could see that their conversation had only just begun.

7

"But let's wind it back a little," Martin said with a swagger.

For him, most if not all thoughts lead to home, and so it was only a matter of time before he remembered one childhood grievance with his mother or another. She, in particular, was the terminus for his mind's less attractive bus-routes. And so, with this inadvertent remembering of her denial of drum lessons, practiced details of the whole festering saga came pouring out.

"I only got my drums in the first place because my grandparents bought them for me," he continued. "I'd been pestering *their daughter* for months – I was thirteen at the time – and I even found a second hand kit advertised in the newsagents – Premier it was, cherry red, with Zildjian cymbals and an absolute bargain at thirty quid. But she just refused point blank, saying I should forget about being a musician. It wasn't even the expense, because she bought me that stupid bike instead. The only reason she gave was that I should concentrate on my schoolwork, so that when I left Field Grove I could get a job "*in a bank*, or something" – I was only in the third year!"

"Right," Dennis said, thinking he might have to pacify Martin somehow. He began to consider what explanation he could give that would sweeten the lad's bitterness without hinting at the truth of the matter, which he had always known.

"Anyway, around my fourteenth birthday, I went to my grandparents' for tea, but only my grandma was there. She said that Granddad had had to go out somewhere – it was all very strange. But when I got home he was in my bedroom, on his hands and knees, arthritic and completely failing to set up this *brand new* drum kit, which was in a hundred pieces on the carpet. I could not believe it. I was so happy! And so I figured that my mum could at least pay for some lessons, surely she couldn't refuse me that! But when she got home – probably stinking of booze or something – she went apeshit, absolutely mental. She started screaming at my granddad, about how *she* knew what was best for her son. She even screamed at *me*, as if it was my fault. There and then I promised myself I'd become a pit drummer, or do something else – anything – in showbiz. I think it pisses her off that I work at the pier – she never asks me about it..." His face contorted in the dim of The Galleon.

"That doesn't mean she's not interested, Martin, or proud of you. She loves you dearly, you know." He tried to reassure the lad.

"But why was she so against me learning the drums?"

"She was probably just trying to protect you."

"Protect me?" Martin said, not comprehending. "From what?"

"From disappointment."

"Well it didn't work, did it!" he mocked.

"No, Martin, protection from disappointment *later* in life, when it's more serious. It's almost impossible to make it in music, to become famous – a chance in a million – and she didn't want you to suffer the disappointment of failure." Dennis was fairly pleased with this line of reasoning, it seemed believable; but Martin didn't buy it.

"I never wanted to be a *famous* drummer, just a good one, a pit drummer, and what's wrong with having a dream anyway? If you don't dream you end up a lush, working in a crappy hairdresser's."

"That's not very nice."

"Well, I'm not the one who can't get out of bed on Sundays because I'm too hung over."

"Your mum likes a drink on a weekend, I'm not denying that, but she's no 'lush', as in *alcoholic*." Dennis realized he had underestimated the depth of Martin's resentment. He gave a measured response, trying hard to sound both magnanimous and wise. "Look, you're right, it's important to have dreams, and I suppose it was *me* who introduced you to drumming, with our secret visits to the theatre, backstage, but your mum's right also; you've got to keep your feet on the ground and get some qualifications."

"I did! Why do you think I stayed on in the Sixth Form? I could go to university with the A-levels I've got!"

"Yes, I know you did really well in your exams, but your mum couldn't have known that when you were thirteen, could she? She only wanted you to, er, maximize your chances of getting a job later, and I suppose she saw drumming or joining a band as a distraction." Dennis was beginning to see through his own arguments.

"You've changed tack. First you said it was to do with protection from disappointment, and now its distraction from schoolwork? Which is it?" Martin was sure there was something else.

"Both." The older man knew he'd been found out; Martin was too sharp for him by half, and moreover he was bent on answers.

"Yeah, right… Look, my mum has always been totally unsupportive about my drumming, about me going to the Opera House with you or my grandparents, about me working at the pier, especially on *this* show, with Gerry. Last year she just about tolerated me working there, but *this year!* If I even mention Gerry Neon she gets really off with me, or leaves the room. I'm beginning to realize that she's got a slate loose. Seriously! There's clearly something bugging her, and it's got something to do with me and show business, or Gerry Neon in particular, or I don't know what… But *then* she's always talking about when she was an usherette and about all the famous people she met. I don't know what to think…it's like it's all this huge contradiction."

"Alright, Martin, alright." He spoke as softly as the jazz duo would allow. "Listen, like I said, your mum loves you dearly and I *know* she's very proud of you. But perhaps you should go easy on her – life's been cruel to her, you know? She's a beautiful lady, but she's suffered because of her beauty, because of a few bad choices. You see, the very worst kind of man was always attracted to her – real Flash Harrys and Fancy Dans, only interested in her because of her looks – but she's got a soft heart, you see, and she's been hurt many times. You know, walk a mile in my shoes, and all that…"

"But why won't she ever talk to me about *my* life?" There were tears in Martin's voice.

Dennis knew there was no way – ever – he could tell Martin the *whole* truth, the truth that he by accident had witnessed; but it seemed now unavoidable that he would have to tell him *part* of it. He chose his words carefully; he knew the lad was ultra-sensitive and would jump on any inconsistency or any word or phrase that came across as contrived. "I suppose it's because deep down she's still upset about her time at the Opera House." He started his sanitised version of events.

"Go on…" Martin folded his arms.

"Because of what happened."

"What *happened*?" He did not understand; Dennis seemed to be hinting at a single event or episode as having taken place – this was news to him.

"You know, how it went for her, at the Opera House," he checked himself.

"But she was only an usherette – how traumatic can it be tearing tickets? Huh. So how *did* it 'go for her' – did she get the sack, or something?"

"Is that what she told you? That she was only ever an usherette?" It was clear that Martin knew little of the truth; there might yet be a way out of this for Dennis, and ironically for Martin. "Listen Martin, you know how your mum can sing?"

"What, you mean when she's pissed up at Christmas? You call that singing?"

"Perhaps you *don't* know. Well, *your* mum, *Lorraine Collier*, has got a really good voice." Now Dennis was swaggering, confident of *his* specialist knowledge. "I mean it. And back in the sixties when she was a girl of fifteen-, sixteen-years-old, showing punters to their seats, she was forever singing to herself. She knew all the hits, but her absolute idol was Dusty Springfield. And she had lots of nerve as well – she'd arrive to work early and find some reason to go on the stage during the sound-check. Once there, she'd charm the pianist and ask him if he knew any of her favourites, like er, oh I can't remember, doesn't matter anyway. Before long, she was singing *with* the band *on stage*, at the sound-check! People were surprised, of course, but really quite impressed too – she was very talented. And she always looked the part as well – tall and blond and with such a pretty face. Already you could see she was destined for stardom."

"So what happened?" Poker-faced, Martin felt a stirring of affection for his mum, but it was mixed with anger that she had kept this from him.

"Well, I don't know precisely how it came about, but with a week to go of the Summer Season – Doddy was headlining, and The Nobles closed the first half, you know, Gerry's old band – but with a week to go, the real girl singer on the bill, I can't remember her name, she just left under a cloud and didn't come back. I was in my booth at the time, when she stormed out of the theatre, slamming the stage door behind her. So, with only a week left to run and no girl singer, you can guess who filled in…"

"Miss Lorraine Collier?" Martin managed a smile.

"Actually she called herself "Dusty" – she sounded a bit like a coalminer, "Dusty Collier", but in her mind she was Dusty Springfield. It was the happiest week of her life – can you imagine! – and to say she was only sixteen she did really well, she went down a storm. She planned to get an agent and to go pro."

"So why didn't she?" Her son was intrigued.

"Well, it all ended a bit sad, really. At first she didn't tell anyone about her "promotion" – I suppose she was bit embarrassed, or perhaps didn't want to jinx it – but news spreads and quickly she became the talk of the town. People she knew starting buying tickets *just to see her*. On the closing night she had her own fan club in – aunties, uncles, neighbours, friends from school. Your grandparents were given free tickets – like guests of honour they were – and even the press was in. The trouble was though, apparently that last performance, on that closing night, wasn't her best. I think she'd had a falling out with someone backstage, or perhaps it was delayed stage fright – I don't know, but whatever it was she seemed distracted and didn't smile all night, and she sang awful, and she flopped. I was in my booth, but that's what I heard."

"Shit," Martin empathised.

"It was a terrible disappointment to take for a young girl. She acted brave, mind, but I don't think she was ready for it – you know, one night she's this wonder kid, living her dream, and the next she's a flop – and it all happened in front of her friends and family. And with the season ended, she had no chance to redeem herself. Your mum thought that opportunity had knocked and she'd blown it, she thought she'd missed her chance; that's what she told me. Other shows came and went and she continued for a few months as an usherette, but it was galling for her, you know, after her success *on the stage*. Anyway, she soon started showing with you and eventually she had to leave."

"I had no idea." More shocked empathy.

"She came back for a while, once you were old enough, and worked the bar – your dad was long gone by then. There was a sadness to her, though, like she'd lost something. It seemed like she was just hanging around, waiting, and I think it was then that she started sneaking shots of vodka. And after the shows, when the stalls' bar became the artistes' bar, every randy comic or crooner would be sniffing around her, promising her auditions and gigs, which never materialised. And she was weak for them. Working there was no good for her, I tell you, and anyway you can't really work with a little 'un at home with its grandparents – it's not conducive – so she left the Opera House for good. It's fair to say she had a sour taste in her mouth *then*, and I don't think she's *ever* got rid of it. It's a cruel business, you know, this show business, and like I said, life's been cruel to your mum. I don't think she'd have got through it if she hadn't had you to love."

Although it gave him no satisfaction, Dennis was sure he had potted convincingly the Collier history, and from the shocked and saddened look on Martin's face he knew he hadn't needed to reveal the whole truth. It seemed the *apparent* truth – the *public* version of events that countless people had witnessed those twenty years ago, but which Martin had never been told – it seemed that *that* truth was sad enough for him to understand his mother's repulsion from and her attraction to showbiz

"Did you know my dad?" Martin was calm now, but flat. If he knew nothing of his mother while at the Opera House, he knew even less about his father.

"Er, not really. He didn't hang around long – like I said, a right Flash Harry. You're better off without him, son."

"Right." He felt hollow. He thought of Gerry Neon. He was about to ask if Gerry, or someone like him, was, or could be, perhaps...

"Listen, this is all a bit heavy for a Friday night..." The older man wound up the conversation and returned to his colleagues, but Martin had stopped listening anyway. He slumped against the wall, his eyes cast downwards at the floorboards on which Dennis had been standing. A cigarette butt lay extinguished and crushed. And yet behind his defeated demeanour, Martin's brain staged a frenetic drum solo. Thoughts rolled unstoppably around his mind like blurred sticks on taut skins; his dad's anonymity thundered like a floor tom; his mum's tragic stardom grooved briefly, a cowbell carnival, only to bomb with a crash of cymbals and a dull, kick drum thud. There was no rhythm to this silent cacophony and he couldn't isolate his thoughts one from the other, never mind understand them. He didn't stay much longer. He didn't talk to his workmates, he didn't rejoin Dennis, if only to say goodbye, and he didn't notice the pretty blond girl walk closely past him *twice* more. The next thing he did notice was a cold, wet sea fret on his face.

***

Jacketless, he strode for home. The flesh and blood humidity of The Galleon condensed quickly beneath his shirt, and the fine drizzle that hung in the air collected about his features. Before long it spilled in rivulets down his cheeks, and dripped from his nose and chin. In the absence of heavy rain, he soon became soaked. Hunched and shrugged in futile defense from the wet, he squeezed both hands into tight jean pockets, until the seams burned his flesh with each stride. The physical discomfort he felt, and the exertion he put in to this route march, were at least distractions to the chaos of his thoughts.

He steamed through the town centre; amongst the banks, bookies and bakers, there were hoardings chained to roadside railings and fly-posters layered over bus shelters; only these communicated anything like glamour. They assaulted the reader with promises of "Family Funtime", "Midnite Mystique" and, of course, "Seaside Spectacular". Nothing, however, could glamourize the aqueous drabness of urban Grumby at one in the morning.

Martin stared at the pavement, each slab appearing and then disappearing like frames of celluloid in a miserable film. This silver screen, however, glistened sodium orange and was strewn with pizza boxes, chip trays and beer cans; and it was lain with dog shit, like so many wet slugs; and the film was underscored with silent drizzle, the wet woosh of passing taxis, and then more silent drizzle.

A pair of white stilettos hove into view, from the top of the screen as it were, and he looked up to find a plump young woman in his path. Dressed in a turquoise top and white ski pants, she meandered slowly in a slalom of drunkenness. Around her neck hung a pale green chemi-luminescent necklace – the kind tourists buy for a pound – and it glowed weakly from beneath her wet-mop hair like a vulgar neon sign that someone forgot to turn off.

To give her as wide a berth a possible, he checked to his right. But as he overtook her, she stumbled a little and he was forced to sidestep further, into the road. His foot landed in a puddle. Remounting the kerb, he scowled at her over his shoulder as his sock squelched. He could see that her bra was visible beneath her sodden top. She looked lost and pathetic. The thought of walking into something broke his stare, which had at least softened from contempt to disgusted pity. "How could she allow herself to get into such a state?" he could hear his mother saying.

The surroundings became semi-residential, and the earlier high street feel gave way to B'n'Bs and takeaways. He could have sworn he passed Gerry Neon loitering sheepishly in one of the gardens – he was imagining him everywhere! – but it was only a glimpse and he dismissed the thought out of absurdity. Fifty yards later he heard a commotion coming from outside the same guesthouse, and so looked over his shoulder to see a woman screaming obscenities, screaming "Animal!" and attacking the man, who was laughing his head off. "These people!" he heard himself say.

Over the road and a little further down, he saw three white-shirted lads stabbing forks into trays of steam. The first to finish balanced his container gingerly on the summit an over-filled bin. He took a cigarette from his breast pocket, before padding himself down for a lighter or a match. "Oi, mate! Have you got a light?" he shouted over to Martin, who answered flatly in the negative. The frustrated smoker then mumbled something to his mates, who sniggered.

Before long he had passed the trio and was striding away, ten yards, twenty, but then the clink and scrape of a thrown bottled caused him to stiffen. The projectile skidded across the tarmac and hit the kerb by his feet with a crack, before spinning back into the road. A contemptuous "Puff!" was shouted, followed by raucous laughter. Time slowed. Martin slowed, readying himself. Like a bushman in the veldt his senses sharpened. At three against one he would be outnumbered, but he felt no fear. Indeed, as he strained his ears, he was almost eager for the scuff of pursuing footfalls.

Perversely the phrase "Nice tits, love!" rang out, however, followed by a chorus of jeering approval. The drunken woman with the luminous necklace had reached the three lads. "Get yer tits out!" yelled a second voice. Martin felt almost disappointed that he had been upstaged, robbed of the possibility of combat. But then a chivalrous instinct caused him to stop altogether and to turn around.

The woman had folded her arms across her chest, and was now walking soberly, linearly, exactly. The man with fags but no flame, the top dog, began to cross the road towards her, a study in mock meekness. "Come 'ere, love," he said confidingly, beckoning with an arm. "Have you got a light? I'm gasping!"

"He's gasping *for it!*" Clarified one of his mates, with a snigger.

"Go on, Jas'!" encouraged the other, and then both jeered excitedly. Martin bristled. The one called Jason held his arms out, palms up in supplication, his eyes as wide as a puppy's. He had not yet made it beyond the white lines and so retreated to let a vehicle pass, but before he could reacquaint himself with the woman, she had disappeared into the "Marinara" B'n'B. Sexual insults then filled the wet air and another bottle was thrown, this time smashing into the guesthouse. Martin turned and resumed his walk home.

He marched quickly. In no time at all he had crossed Queensway and was climbing Colville Road, which felt to him more than ever like a dark tunnel. To his left was the low wall of the unlit cemetery and a row of mature trees that bordered it, and to his right was a dead jam of tightly parked cars. Dense foliage above clouded the streetlights, and beneath the vaulting of the branches the pavement was slippery with sap. Martin remembered how when he was young, Dennis would quip that Colville Road Cemetery was the dead centre of Grumby; but he was in no mood for humour now. Over and over he imagined his teenage mother dying on the Opera House stage, fleeing from it to the sound of sparse applause, fleeing from it her whole haunted life in fact. And he tried to visualize his faceless father, in the wings watching his mother perhaps, but all he could see was that bastard Gerry Neon.

Suddenly and unconsciously he broke off a car's wing mirror; in a spontaneous outburst of blind violence he just kick-stamped it with the sole of his right trainer. It snapped back, and off, clattering onto the pavement. Only afterwards did he understand what had happened; he noticed the detached mirror and the spider's web that decorated the glass, and he felt a throbbing in the ball of his foot. Only then did he understand his vandalism, his raw physicality. A feeling of power surged through his limbs and he set off at a sprint, not because he was in a rush to get home or because he was now on the run from his crime, but because he couldn't contain his anger any more. For ten, twenty seconds he sprinted, his thighs straining against his wet jeans. For thirty, forty seconds he pumped his arms with angry uppercuts, droplets of water rained from him. Even after a minute he was charging, his heart beating like a boxer's speedball. Some other time questions would come to Martin; long ignored dark voids in his life's narrative would open up again, and even the blackness of its earliest chapters might demand his brave enquiry. But for now he sought only the distracting pain, the pleasure of physical exhaustion; and he ran until he had found it.

Earlier that evening, twenty minutes after the finale, Mandy was walking up the pier, towards the shore. There was a stiff breeze at her back and it caused strands of hair to whip at her face and to catch in fresh lipstick. No longer did she feel anaesthetised to a depth conducive with dentistry, as she had done on stage, but she was still drunk. Barefoot, she imagined herself skipping along the boards and flitting over the gaps between them as if she were on a shell-strewn beach; and she finger-twirled her high-heels by their straps as a paddler might a pair of sandals. From the crook of her elbow swung her bucket and spade handbag, and in her other arm she hugged her beach ball bouquet. Escorting her was her date, her man, Gerry Neon. He was close enough that they might even have held hands, she fancied, were she not so laden and were he not a yard in front of her, leading the way.

Beside him though there strode a towering, black-haired man, whom Mandy thought she recognized, perhaps from the cabaret circuit. Who *was* he, she wondered, and why was he here with them? Earlier she had glimpsed him in the wings holding a bunch of flowers, the same flowers that Gerry later presented to her on stage, and which she now cradled. But he was no florist's van man, no harbinger of romance. He had the swagger and build of a doorman and keen eyes that sort out ears to thicken. He looked like violence. It didn't matter, though, she told herself; it was *her* birthday, *her* night, and he was bound to be leaving them soon, whatever his dark identity and whatever his relationship with Gerry.

As they approached a small crowd Mandy accelerated and managed to catch up, bumping into her man's arm and meaning to, inviting him to encircle her with it so that the punters would see his affection for her. A youngster ventured from the gathering, egged on by his proud parents, and he offered Gerry a brochure and a pen with which to sign it; the star refused curtly, however, and then added something inaudible that made the taller man laugh. That's right, thought Mandy, no autographs! Not here, not now! The boy's parents should have known better; they should have waited by the stage door with the rest of the fans, not pester the star when out on a date. Mister Neon was off-duty now, busy dedicating himself to his *lady friend*, on *her birthday*. As they exited the pier, she paused to replace her shoes, which might have been glass slippers. "Hang on!" she called winningly.

On the prom, Gerry conceded to himself that they had better wait for Mandy. The two men stopped a moment and turned around to see the singer hurrying hen-like to catch them up, tip tapping with quick heels on the concrete apron. Already the headliner had begun to doubt the wisdom of giving her the flowers in the first place, never mind of allowing her on their boys' night out; but seeing her in her skimpy, stretchy dress, as voluptuous as any man could desire, he knew that she at least made him look good. A quick glance at Pete's wide eyes and slack mouth confirmed this as fact. Nah, there was no problem; he could give her the elbow some other time. "Eh up!" he said affectionately, "'Ere's me tits, me arse is following!"

He led the way to the nearby Sands Hotel, in whose grounds artistes from the pier were provided parking. At his car Mandy stood presumptuously, a passenger for the front seat, Pete's seat. But Gerry was having none of it. He opened the rear on-side door for her with a Parker-esque "M'Lady," before adding: "There's more room for your flowers on the back seat, love." Mandy accepted this dishonest thoughtfulness, and the star slapped her arse as she got in the back. Three heavy doors thudded closed and the Jaguar smelled of leather and cigarette butts and motorways.

Pete saw dials dance in the mahogany and felt the jag's four-litre power; the tape deck winked with orange points of light and The Eagles filled the car.

"Nice motor," he shouted over the music, before adding royally "I wonder what the poor are doing?" He looked over his shoulder at the back seat passenger. Mandy was adjusting her wiggle dress, smoothing it down over her thighs. She then attended to a large diamante brooch, that was pinned to her stressed-denim lapel but which did not distract from her top-shelf cleavage. Only when she raised her eyes to his, and he saw them hardened from his voyeurism, did he turn around. As fit as fuck, he thought; he would certainly have to okay it with Gerry so that he could have a crack at her.

***

"Dead, totally dead. First house they're playing to four rows, that's what I've heard. One night they shot a stag on the balcony!" Gerry said.

The three had arrived at the Belvedere guesthouse, and were at the bar. The two men stood arrogantly, an item, smoking and drinking cold lager; Gerry in beige Farah slacks and a burgundy Lacoste polo shirt; Pete in black trousers, white shirt and black leather bomber jacket. Mandy, however, was perched on a high stool, adjacent but mostly ignored; she had hooked her heels over the stool's foot rail and was holding onto the bar, swaying, half-smiling, not really listening. Before her rested a white wine and soda, barely touched.

On the other side of the draught taps and the drip trays stood Mike O'Driscoll, the proprietor of the guesthouse. His rolled-up shirtsleeves strained at the hams they contained and from a belt-loop hung a bunch of keys the size of a prison guard's. Notoriously he possessed an entrepreneurial disregard for the terms of his licence, much at odds with his wife's curfews and crucifixes approach to boarding houses, and he would often invite artistes from the shows to his place for "refreshments" after hours. In fact whenever the whispered word got around the various productions that Mike was having a lock-in, it was only a question of *which* of Grumby's acts would turn up. Tonight, with Gerry Neon in attendance, he'd hit the jackpot.

"It's a shame they're not doing the business, though." Gerry continued charitably. "It's a lovely old theatre, the Opera House, but I'm not sure about this kid they've got headlining, the young comic. Queer as a hairy egg, apparently. I forget his name. I've heard big things about him, though, to be fair, but his act…it sounds gimmicky, y'know? Fire-eating and too many props..."

"*You're* packing them in though, aren't you?" Mike flattered his V.I.P., placing on the bar a huge tray of sandwiches, adorned with a cucumber twist garnish. "Compliments of the Belvedere," he said proudly.

"Er, thanks…Yeah. Sold out. Every night. It's a big production, you see – eight dancers, and the best band you've ever heard. They cost a packet, mind, *and* the PA's not cheap either. I told Bernie to hire *the best*. So he did." He took a grated cheese and pickle. "At last, the backing I deserve, eh Pete?"

"Get stuffed!" laughed the former Nobles' bass player, already on his second ham, a smear of margarine on his moustache.

"I get some real pond-life in, though. Honestly. Thick as pig shit. Er, laugh now. Clap now. *Piss off now!*" Pete laughed again. "Tonight, first house, there was this coach load of head-bangers in. I could see them thrashing around in their wheelchairs in the aisles, and they were shouting out all these animal noises in between the numbers. I thought I was at Flamingo Land!" Mike howled. "I got loads of laughs thanks to 'em, though, poor bastards." He ate as he talked. "And the pensioners! Fuckin' 'ell. Some nights there's this sea of grey. You can smell the piss!" Pete and Mike howled together. "And they're all there adjusting their deaf-aids – "What's he saying, Cyril?" or moaning – "It's too loud!" They've no idea who I am. Honestly, my act's wasted on 'em. Still… bums on seats!" he concluded sagely, to nodding approval. He finished his sandwich, downed his pint and pulled a wad of notes from his seat pocket.

"You sold a few brochures tonight then, I take it?" observed Pete.

"Yes, I'll be notifying the taxman tomorrow," he joked, thumbing a twenty from his undeclared earnings. "Er, a large rum and coke, please Mike. Pete?"

The barman set Pete's lager pouring and turned to the optics for a double pump of the nautically themed spirit. Beside the bottles hung a cardboard display of bags of peanuts that revealed more and more of a topless model with each purchase. He bent down to a fridge for the mixer, decapitated it on the bar-mounted bottle opener and poured half into the rum. He flipped the lager tap with a splash and placed the drinks on a beer towel, next to a collecting tin for The Spastic Society. Mandy raised a hand to her mouth and yawned.

"Here you go, gentlemen. So, aren't you gonna introduce me?" said Mike, looking at the woman that sat beside Gerry, all curves and cleavage, mane and manicure. He extended a huge hand.

As the star did the honours, Mandy dazzled. She thanked Mike for his hospitality and said what a nice place the Belvedere was, but Gerry soon spoke over her. And as the fat barman squeezed her hand, she looked through him, through his iron filings stubble and the sheen of sweat on his forehead, through his vascular nose. Her gaze instead fell on the postcards and the foreign banknotes pinned to the wall behind him, on a crucifix, and on signed publicity photos wedged into the optics, which she read: "Best wishes to Mike and Reenie. Tommy and Bobby"; "Thanks to Mike and everyone at the Belvedere. Sid and Eddie"; "Mine's a large one! Gerry Neon". Her smile faded. She reached for her spritzer and drank. Someone was speaking to her. "What? Sorry, I was, er..." she said, blinking, dazzling once more.

"I said, you don't look like your picture on the pier..." repeated Mike. "I thought you had dark hair?"

"Don't *you* start!" interrupted Gerry, laughing and coughing up smoke, before facing Mandy. "Yes, it's not a very good likeness, is it dear?" he said, placing his hand on her thigh, gripping firmly, his eyes fierce.

"So how's Reenie then, Mike?" interrupted Pete, sensing Gerry's irritation. "Past her bedtime, is it?"

***

For his tenth birthday Gerard Noble received a huge pair of crimson boxing gloves. He and Peter Wheeler took turns with the right hand glove, the other boy with the left, and with skinny, windmill arms they went timeless rounds together. In back yards and front rooms they threw blind, benign punches until exhaustion and laughter brought their collapse. But as boyhood thickened to manhood, and as Pete got his own pair of Lonsdales, it became clear that Gerry was no match for his stronger, longer reaching pal. Gerry was hard all right, especially after tough summers labouring for his uncle – digging foundations, carrying bricks in a hod – but Pete was the scrapper; no one messed with Pete Wheeler. So when they and three other Leeds lads first performed as "Gerry Neon and the Nobles", it was always Pete that sorted out the front man's messes. During that early-sixties pre-history their beat combo played violent pubs throughout the West Riding, where cavemen fought with heavy dimpled pint glasses; and the stocky front man was forever chatting up someone's bird or else shagging them in the back of the van; and his giant bass-playing lieutenant was always at the bar, buying the unwitting cuckold a drink; and if crumbs fell from Gerry's table, Pete didn't complain. But if it came to a fight, like it often did in Hamburg, Pete was a madman. So, when the front man went solo and swapped The Yorkshire Hussars for The London Palladium, it was no surprise that Pete was retained as "Road Manager", a catch-all euphemism that throughout the seventies and up until the early eighties described his best mate's various roles of runner, driver, negotiator, enforcer...

***

Fifteen minutes later, Pete had polished off most of the sandwiches, a resident had approached Gerry and struck up an "I saw you in nineteen-sixty-something" conversation, quickly terminated, and the saucy peanut girl had revealed yet more of herself. Mike was collecting glasses and Mandy was in the Ladies'.

"Mandy seems, er, nice," said Pete, grabbing the last ham.

"Fit as a butcher's dog, you mean?" corrected Gerry. Both men were now seated at the bar.

"Well, yeah, I suppose... You're not kidding, actually!"

"Thought so. I saw you, licking your lips!"

"It's the sea air, I can't help it. One sniff of seaweed and I'm like a tripod! Anyway, what's she like? Bet she bangs like the Duracell bunny!"

"She *used* to. A bit of a handful. Well, more of a screamer, really – used to deafen me! But lately… I think she's become a born again feminist or something, like that Faye Gold dyke – now *she was* uptight! But Mandy won't let me shag her either, not any more, not until I've wined and dined her, or some other romantic bollocks. She'll give me a gobble… but I want to knock the back out of her, you know, show her who's boss."

"You've lost your touch, Gee! I told you, you've lost your touch!"

"No, seriously, it's Mandy… She's changed. She was a right goer on the circuit, when she was a dancer – bags of fun; used to scream her head off, like I said – but now that she's a singer… Well *that's* a joke for a kick off. Have you heard her sing? Can't hold a note; as flat as Blue Bass fart! It's embarrassing. Like a fucking seagull! Anyway, she *thinks* she's Barbara Streisand, or some other diva. Started giving me a right runaround. Honestly. And *I* got her the gig! I can't believe it. She's forever hassling me about meals out, and about this, and about that. And as for her picture not being on the hoarding – I mean, where's her sense of humour!"

"Yeah," Pete laughed. "She sounds like your missus."

"Oh God, do you know what *that* bitch wants now?"

"Go on…"

"A new kitchen! She can't fucking cook! *Everybody* wants *something* from me."

"So what are you gonna do, then?"

"Buy her a kitchen."

"No. About Mandy."

"Oh. Give her the elbow, I suppose."

"I could take her off your hands."

"I knew you were gonna say that! Be my guest, but, er, not just yet. Wait until I've kissed her goodbye."

Mike returned from his glass collecting.

"A straight vodka, mate. No ice," ordered Gerry. He took the glass the barman handed him and poured its contents into Mandy's wine and soda, Pete watching. "And she thinks I'm unromantic!" The two men laughed.

***

The door to the entrance hall opened and in walked Darren Daniel, the bill-topper from the Opera House. "Dazzler" Darren, as the local press had dubbed him, was accompanied by two statuesque women and a soberly dressed older man carrying a Filofax. Pete saw him and whispered the fact to Gerry, who remained looking at his pint and tapping ash from his Benny.

"Good evening Darren, Roy, ladies," said Mike. "Good of you to come, nice to see you again. What can I get you? On the house."

"No, you're okay thanks, I'll get them. A bottle of champagne, two glasses, please, and er…" the comic surveyed a shelf below the optics. "Two Remy."

"Take a seat, I'll bring them over." His entourage moved to a table in one of the two large bay windows as suggested, but the young star remained at the bar looking at Gerry Neon's back, waiting. "You know Gerry, of course…" said the barman, privately excited that Grumby's two biggest acts were both here as his guests.

"No, we've never met, actually," said Darren.

"Who's this then?" said Gerry, turning slowly to see a tanned, slender man with a shock of bleached hair, wavy at the back, and wearing a pair of white trousers and a white V-neck beneath a baggy, apricot suit jacket. "Oh, hello. It's Darryl, isn't it?" Pete laughed.

"Funny cunt. Hi Gerry, how you doing? It's a privilege to meet you at last." He held out his hand.

"Of course it is." The two stars shook; Gerry squeezed hardest. "And you."

"No, seriously. I remember seeing you on the Royal Command Performance on television when I was kid. You were brilliant, I remember laughing my head off. You're one of the reasons I went into the business."

Gerry pointedly looked at the two lovelies the young pretender had entered with, saying: "The other reason being women, I suppose." Again Pete gave a knowing laugh.

"Er, not my type really."

"No, I didn't think so. Thanks for the compliment, though; I always wanted to be Elvis."

"You don't say. Of course, I'm not up at your level yet."

This was said as praise, but Gerry sensed a barb of emphasis on the last, competitive word. "Perhaps not. So, how's business?" he retorted, giving one last squeeze before letting go.

Darren's hand hurt, but he didn't show it. "Well, we were a touch quiet the opening week, as I'm sure you've heard, but then as the word got around about the show – it's a great show, a bit different though, very modern – er, and as the word got around business really started picking up. Now we're packing them in."

Papered, thought Gerry; a few hundred complimentary tickets could make anywhere look full. "Really," he said blandly. "A few comps, perhaps, to get the ball rolling?"

"Oh come on, everyone gives free tickets. I do, you do, we all do. What's Landladies' Night, if it's not papered? In any case we're sold out tomorrow, advanced sales, both houses. Anyway, like I said it's good to meet you. Come and join us later, if you like." He turned with a flap of linen and strutted towards his companions.

"Yeah, see ya later," said Gerry, before facing Pete, whispering: "He can stick 'modern' up his arse!"

Mandy returned from the toilet, but didn't sit down. "Gerry, I want to go home. Ask Mike for a taxi for me," she instructed.

"Oh, darling… I've been ignoring you, haven't I, sweetheart?" Gerry had no need in his world to crawl or to worm and so this unpracticed and inexpert attempt at diplomacy, this sham sympathy, sounded patronising to Mandy, and her stone face developed a contemptuous fault. "Oh don't be like that. Come 'ere, love, come 'ere…" He extended an arm, but she stood her ground. "Look, I know I haven't given you enough attention this evening… I meant to… And I drove all over to find a florist's for your flowers, y'know for your birthday… It's just that me and Pete, we go back a long way, right back to when we were kids…" Her face softened a fraction. "And I haven't seen him in over a year. Listen. We've been talking about the hoarding, haven't we, Pete?"

"We certainly have," lied the man in leather.

"You're right. It's diabolical that Bernie hasn't sorted it yet, er, totally disrespectful to you as an artiste. I'm gonna phone him tomorrow morning, first thing, I promise. If your face isn't plastered all over the pier by tomorrow night, then I don't go on." At last he'd hit the right note. "Come on, love. Sit down." She did so. "Here, drink your drink," he said, passing her the spritzer doctored with vodka.

***

"Champagne, Mike. A bottle."

"No Gerry, really. I'm okay. I'm struggling with this as it is."

"Nonsense. It's your birthday."

"We have Moet and Chandon or white Lambrusco..?" said the sommelier.

"Er, whatever Miami Vice had."

Mandy looked over. "Is that Darren Daniel?" she said, with a little too much excitement for Gerry's liking.

"Er, yeah. Fucking shirt-lifter."

Pete laughed.

"Really? I didn't know. He's very handsome in person."

"You sound disappointed, like it's a waste or something. Why don't you try and convert him? You'd better ask him to wash his dick first, though."

Pete laughed again.

"Don't be disgusting! Anyway, honey, you're the only man for me." She squeezed his upper arm.

Gerry tensed his muscles. "Is that a fact?" he said, and looked at Pete and winked.

***

Two pints, two rum and cokes, and half a bottle of bubbly later, Pete was reminiscing. "Do you remember, Gee, that old Thames van we had?

"Yeah, mate. I don't know how you kept it going for so long."

The ex-mechanic faced Mandy and spoke kindly. "I did all the servicing, you see love, and it used to bleed oil constantly. There was this metal seat next to the driver that you could lift up to access the engine, and we used to add motor oil *while* we were moving. We went through gallons of the stuff."

"So, did you have a roadie to drive the van?" Mandy replied; Pete seemed nice enough.

"No, this is before we got Colin. In the early days there'd be just the five of us crammed into it, with all the gear as well – amps, drums, suit bags – and we were forever driving over the Pennines, doubling Fagin's with the Poco in Stockport, or playing the Northern Sporting, or the Talk of the North, Eccles... Once at the Settlement Club in Altrincham we shared a dressing room with thirteen strippers! And then there was Liverpool. And remember, this is all before the M62 was built, so we had to go via Halifax. And we left oil slicks the whole way."

"I like to hear about Gerry's past. He never tells me anything, do you sweetie?" said Mandy, playfully. She reached to squeeze the back of his neck but slid half-off her stool and so had to hold on to him. "Oops-a-daisy!" she joked. Gerry supported her.

"Steady girl! You okay?" She righted herself. "Good. As soon as Colin drove the van with the gear, we got a second-hand Bentley S1..." continued Pete.

"We did some miles in that!" said Gerry.

"Round the clock twice, nearly. It was a huge old thing, and it meant we could travel in comfort for a change. Anyway, Gerry crashed it – nearly killed us all!"

"Aw, here we go again! How many times...?" Gerry played along with Pete's story, feigning embarrassment.

"Oh, no!" cried Mandy, horrified. Fascination held her drunkenness in abeyance.

"He was legless as usual – we all were – and he lost control coming out of a dry underpass into the wet, er, near Preston it was, 'bout three in the morning. We bounced off a concrete wall, mounted the embankment and ploughed right through a road sign, knocking it over. Any other car and we'd all have been brown bread, but the Bentley was like a tank. No one was injured, surprisingly, just shaken. But we'd caused a lot of damage and we were all pissed so we had to get out of there sharpish. And the S1... it was still ticking over! Driveable, if not exactly road-worthy – the doors were all stoved in, paint scraped off, lights smashed, and we had to prise a wheel-arch off a tyre so it would run smooth..."

"He's exaggerating, it was just a scratch."

"...But, and this is the thing, the boot had sprung open during the crash and all these publicity photos, *with contact details*, were blowing around all over the wreckage of the road sign! And there we were, scrabbling around the road, slipping on the steep wet grass, pissed and pissing ourselves trying to recover the evidence. And all because Stirling Moss, here, can't hold his ale!"

The two men laughed. "Oh, God!" said Mandy, also laughing but frowning too. "You were *so* lucky, sweetie. You could have died!" Again she squeezed Gerry's neck, leaning into him.

"Nah. Praps..." he said. "We got *you* though, didn't we Peter?"

"How d'ya mean? When?"

"With the low-loader."

"Bastards! I'd forgotten about that. I shat myself."

"What happened?" asked Mandy, still intrigued.

"We broke down on the M1, love," began Gerry, turning to Mandy, "driving back from Bailey's, Watford. Pete was completely unconscious in the back seat of this Ford Zodiac we had…er, modified, it was, with an extended wheelbase like a stretched limo. Anyway, it broke down, and since our resident mechanic was totally out of it, we had to get a tow. And did we wake Pete? Did we heck! We left him in the back seat, drunk and asleep, and the recovery bloke allowed the car onto a low-loader, with Pete still in it! It was a right laugh!"

"Right…" she said, puzzling over the significance, stifling a yawn.

"Yeah, and when I woke up," Pete took over, "I was alone on the back seat, still on the M1, still moving – road-signs and lamp-posts whizzing by – and I thought where the hell *is* everyone. And so I sat up and looked in the front, and was gonna ask Gerry where everyone was, but there was no one there either, and no one behind the wheel! But the car was moving at seventy-fucking-miles-an-hour! And I thought: Who the fuck's driving? I shat myself!"

Mandy laughed. All three laughed. "Great days, mate!" said Gerry, shaking his head, smiling. "We had some right times together, didn't we?" He placed his hand on Mandy's knee, looked at Pete, and winked.

"Sure did, Geronimo," said Pete, placing *his* hand on Mandy's other knee, refilling her glass, and thrusting the bottle back into the ice bucket. "And we will…," he added quietly.

There was a break in the banter. But, as Mandy watched the bubbles stream in her glass and as she yawned contentedly, her two companions exchanged glances and grins and gestures. They mouthed words and pointed secretly at their watches and held up furtive fingers and mouthed more words, and Pete coughed a disguised laugh and Gerry lit a cover-up cigarette. In a previous decade, a board rubber may have struck one of them. And Mandy was still yawning, and she felt now those bubbles on her tongue and she heard the fridge give a click and she listened to it whine and a hum in the classroom quiet.

The owner appeared with a tea towel over his shoulder. "Right then, Mike. I suppose I'd better check in," said Pete.

"I'll get your key." He disappeared again, but only for the time it took Pete to stand up and to grab his sports bag. "You're in number three, at the front. Nice big room. Up the stairs, turn left. If you need anything…it's late, so don't bother asking!"

"Huh, no problem," agreed the new resident, taking the key. He kissed Mandy on the cheek and patted Gerry on the shoulder. "Right then. I'm off to bed," he said.

"Goodnight. Nice to have met you," said Mandy; finally she would have Gerry to herself, she thought.

"Yeah, see you later," replied Pete, looking to Gerry.

"Don't forget to check the wardrobe for monsters," said the star, grinning.

"I won't," he replied, resisting his own grin.

The promise of mischief flashed between them.

***

By 2:00am the residents' bar was empty, save for Gerry and Mandy. The two had moved from their backless high stools to the more comfortable seating that curved around the bay windows. The middle-aged man sat so that he could see the door to the entrance hall, his younger woman with her back to the door.

"It's like I'm swinging a tiger by its tail," Gerry was saying, staring into the stale air. "Business is going great, don't get me wrong, but sometimes, I don't know…"

"Go on…"

"Well, sometimes I feel like I can't handle it, like it's too much for me. There's a lot of responsibility on my shoulders, you see… it's *my* name at the top of the bill, it's *me* the punters come to see… and so there's a lot of pressure to keep on coming up with the goods. But I'm fully booked, this year and next. There's no end in sight. My agent, Frank Gillespie…"

"I know, love, I know," sympathized Mandy, taking his hand clumsily, willing him to look at her, to let her in. Her head swilled and sloshed with alcohol like bilge in a boat, however, and so as she listened to his monologue she caught only fragments and phrases. "I know exactly what you mean, sweetie," she said.

"My agent, Frank Gillespie… it's like he's this slave driver, and I've got no control. He keeps ringing me… 'I've got you Purfleet, seven nights,' he says. 'I've got you The Lakeside, seven nights.' 'Batley, *fourteen* nights…' It's hard to say "No". I'm at The Opera House, Blackpool next summer, and with the illuminations it's *twenty* weeks for the season. I'll be there 'til fucking Christmas! There's no end in sight." He shook his head slowly, sighing, still staring into the distance. "I'm just a passenger in my own career. But, at ten grand a week, it's hard… It's like I'm swinging this tiger… Like I'm riding a bull, and I can't get off or it'll gore me."

He felt Mandy's grip tighten, her two thumbs now massaging the back of his hand. He turned to look at her and saw immediately that her cobalt eyes had moistened. She looked concerned, caring. The sob story had clearly worked, and he knew now that she was finally his to do with as he pleased, as Pete pleased. He poured her the last of the champagne and thrust the empty bottle neck-first into the melted ice so that the domed bottom presented itself from the bucket.

"I know, love. I know exactly what you mean," she repeated, kneading his neck. "It must be really hard for you, you poor love." "Why didn't you tell me this before?"

But something did not sit right with Gerry. Despite the certainty that he would now possess Mandy, as he had done before her recent teasing denial of him, despite all of this he felt no mounting excitement, no pending triumph. In fact, looking at her lovely, loving face, he felt empty and sad. "I'm telling you now," he said angrily, wishing that he could keep talking, keep telling her all his doubts and fears. There was so much to say. He even wondered if perhaps he should invite her back to his empty apartment, with its empty drawers and empty units, where they could carry on this grown up conversation, and to hell with the prank that he and Pete had hatched; Pete would understand; Pete could piss off!

"Go on, sweetie. I'm listening." She felt him soften and yield into her. "We can talk all night, if you like…"

But then that same Pete poked his head around the door, as planned. Gerry tried not to notice his pal's re-appearance in the room, over Mandy's shoulder, and the huge thumbs-up he was giving and the schoolboy's grin that was fixed on his face like a laugh frozen; he tried to hold down the bubble of excitement that was swelling inside him and to resist the smirk he felt creeping onto his own face. For all of five seconds he tried to ignore these things, but a comic's instinct is irresistible; if there's a feed line, there must be a punch line; if there's a gag to crack, it will be cracked.

"Listen, love. I know it's a bit, er, presumptuous, but I spoke to Mike earlier, while you were in the loo, and I've sorted a room for us, here, tonight."

Mandy was both pleased and, looking at the drab surroundings, disappointed. "But I saw "No vacancies" on the way in…?"

"Er, yeah. There was a cancellation," he lied.

"Well, yes, it *is* a bit forward. But, I don't mind, really," slurred Mandy after a moment's thought. "What about your apartment, though?"

"Oh, er, Jilly's staying at the moment." He lied again.

"I thought you said it was all over between you and her," she replied quickly, possessively.

"She wants to patch things up between us, give it another go."

"What do you want?" Jealousy pulled at her. His answer took forever to come.

"I want you," he said at last.

She kissed him.

10

Inevitably Gerry led the way upstairs to number three. The unlocked door gave to his push and he entered the room. In the corner stood a standard lamp, already switched on, and its tasseled shade spilled an amber light, showing a space crowded with dark wooden furniture. He noted the king-size bed, the towering wardrobe.

Mandy followed, closing the door behind her. She made straight for Gerry, embracing and kissing him with challenging, overpowering passion. But her passion was also clumsy with drink, and the pair of them fell about the room, pushing and pulling each other in a fight for balance as well as dominance. Trampoline floorboards creaked under heavy feet, and the fringe of tassels now swung beneath the lampshade.

Surprise brought a muffled laugh from Gerry's mouth, but he managed to throw off his amorous assailant, pushing her down onto the bed. The headboard knocked against the wall. He stood over her and began to unbuckle his belt. But she jumped to her feet and came back at him, kissing him even more forcefully, pushing him with her mouth. Again he stumbled backwards, this time falling onto a dressing table that occupied the bay window, disheveling the doily that covered it and upending a basket of *potpourri*.

And still Mandy kissed him, so that her teeth indented her own lips. And she clung to him too, so that her arms ached. And she leant into him heavily, knocking a chair over, pushing him backwards with dancer's legs. The desire she felt to have him, to take him, was total.

"Bloody hell!" thought Gerry. He'd had women throw themselves at him before, but never quite so literally. He threw a hand back to grab something, anything to steady himself. His hand found the top edge of the dressing table's mirror, which tilted backwards and then rotated freely away from him. He fell back further, losing his arm over the top of the mirror and between the bay's curtains, and banging his ribs on the lower edge of the mirror that had spun up to meet him. The whole dressing table rocked backwards and seemed to hang, teetering in the sodium orange of the parted curtains, until it came down with a thump and a rattle of four metal drawer pulls.

All was motion and noise; the trampoline floorboards, the metronome lamp, the boomerang dressing table; even the wardrobe, apparently untouched, seamed to shift and creak in the loud struggle. Finally, Gerry muscled Mandy away, holding her off with his left hand and raising his flat-palmed right as if to slap her. Fear flashed across the woman's face, but then a delicious smile broke out and she relented. She sat down on the bed like a good girl, reaching down to unbuckle her high heels. Calmly Gerry walked over to the lamp, felt for the switch, and then stood before her in the street-lit semi-darkness, unbuttoning, unzipping.

***

And then the commotion began again. The bed bumped heavily on dead springs and groaned as it swayed around loose joints; the headboard hammered the wall. Quickly it became a cacophonous vehicle of love, protesting noisily, rhythmically at its cargo of two. Mandy began to gasp and moan in nearing ecstasy, and Gerry grunted his approval.

From inside the wardrobe, Pete had been spying with great amusement as the couple made their violent, comic love, over the dressing table and now on the bed. He supposed he might as well enter the fray now. The star had the woman's face pressed into a pillow – there was little danger of her seeing him – and so he made to catch his pal's eye.

Unheard, the wardrobe door creaked open a couple of inches. From the edge of his vision, Gerry noticed the dark profile change slightly, turned and saw Pete peering out of darkness. No way was he ready to hang up, however. "Not yet," he mouthed with exaggerated lips and an irritated shake of the head. The door closed again.

He began to soften. He'd already produced the goods this evening, reclining in the arm chair of his dressing room, and that earlier emission together with all the speed he'd taken – the shriveling, shrinking speed – made him feel he was in danger of flopping, and Gerry Neon never flopped, certainly not with Pete Wheeler looking on. He changed his angle slightly and began to squeeze the back of Mandy's neck, re-establishing his control. He felt a thin-chained necklace impress his hand. "Who's the boss?" he asked, only half-joking, playing to Pete, not really thinking of the pain he was causing. "Who's the boss now, eh?" he demanded rhetorically, squeezing harder. The woman's cries were muffled by polyester and foam; the spider-silk chain gave under his force. At last he released her, winked at the crack in the wardrobe door and slapped her backside; spoils of the war that tonight he'd won. There was a thumping on the wall and angry words coming from the room next door. "Sod off, y'puff," called Gerry, "can't a gentleman make love to his lady any more?" A snigger came from inside the wardrobe, and the star brayed, tumescent as a teenager.

Mandy hoped the strange interrogation had been just banter, the painful squeezing merely horseplay... but analytical thought on the matter was beyond her addled mind. "Oi, you, be gentle! I bruise easily," she slurred playfully, struggling to get the words out.

"Sorry, love. Thought you'd like a little massage, to relax you," he mocked, before leaving another stinging handprint on her rear. He laughed again, and Pete added a faint echo.

She couldn't be sure with all the noise – the bed, the swirling hum in her ears – but Mandy could have sworn she'd heard a sound inside the room, a human sound that was not of their making. It must have been someone from next door, she told herself

The hammering of the headboard petered to a halt and the bed went silent. But then there were more creaks from the floorboards, more heavy feet as Gerry lead Mandy across the room to the dressing table. He bent her over it, so that she lay face down beneath the underside of the mirror, and so that her arse was displayed. For the final time he took her, looked over his shoulder to the gap in the wardrobe door and, with grim inevitability, gave a nod; after all, if there's a feed-line, there must be a punchline.

**

Whatever Gerry's reasons for being rough, Mandy was now doubly confused by the use of the dressing table. She could feel the cool, hard wood on her stomach and the rough *potpourri* on her breasts. Surely he didn't think this would be a turn on for her, or even comfortable? Never mind. She would grant him his kinky desires for now, and within reason. But then she felt him again, felt him thrust into her with very definite force, and she understood that in reality her body was not her's to grant, but his to take. She could only hope he wouldn't be too rough, and tried to unstiffen herself.

She felt as if she'd been dragged to Funland and was being forced to ride the Wild Mouse, an old wooden mini-coaster that threw its helpless passengers against the sides of the cars on the hairpins and which made them nauseous on the drops and on the rises; certainly she felt sick. And slung there over the dressing table her whole body began to hurt – her pelvis banged against the edge of the table, her elbows and knees found other places of hard wood. She fought back; but this only brought more pain from the furniture, and from Gerry's strong hands. She couldn't help but call out. Her mind again turned to holiday camps, and ham-fisted organists, and playing to three rows, and her calling bingo numbers, and she knew she would just have to grimace and bear it.

In private desperation she felt for her crab necklace, that symbol of her inner strength, but it wasn't there. Her heart sank; she was defenseless now in every way. Blankly her inanimate face returned a lurid orange from the streetlights as she was driven again and again between the curtains, against the wood. Her dead eyes refused to cry. And as blood hummed in her ears, there was still the clatter and groan of old furniture, the rattle of drawer pulls and the squeak of floorboards beneath the carpet. Gerry lowed like a bull.

***

The wardrobe door opened with a creak, but unnoticed, and Pete clambered out. He went and stood behind Gerry, dropped his trousers and shuffled closer and closer to the action.

Gerry was gladdened by Mandy's dumb appreciation: her "Oohs" and "Ahs"; her "Ows". And he took as encouragement her every utterance: her every "Yes"; her every "No"; all her "Nos". He knew she loved it really, and it was good of her, the old pro, to put on an act like this, to pretend it hurt, to help him along.

He found he had really hit his stride now; sweat seeped from his brow and trickled from his armpits, and his thighs burned, his hod-carrier's thighs burned and his rough hands gripped Mandy tightly like when he used to climb ladder after ladder. He felt again the woman struggling and heard her calling out – she always was a screamer. But this was different somehow. No matter. She was a big girl now, she could handle a bit of rough and tumble, a bit of slapstick sex. And then he heard his own grunts and snorts, and he felt powerful, vital, and then he screwed his eyes shut and Mandy ceased to exist at all. And then he went quiet and became lost and jolted violently, slowed and it was over.

But it wasn't over, not for Mandy, and not for Pete. It took Gerry a moment to sense the hand on his shoulder, and then a further moment of dazed shock to comprehend its meaning. When he turned around he saw a brief grin on Pete's face and then a look of serious concentration, and he was queuing with such eager proximity that his erection actually bobbed against Gerry's side. Briefly, four hands mauled ignorant, stupid Mandy. The star slapped her arse a final time and stepped aside, and then Pete was at it. Like a relief driver taking the wheel from his colleague in the dead of night on some French autoroute with the coach still moving at a hundred kilometres per hour and the passengers oblivious, he took over.

Rarely in the past had it worked so smoothly, thought Gerry; it must have been the sneaky vodkas, the spikes with which he had laced Mandy's spritzers and champagne. It was a wonder she hadn't vomited from all the alcohol and all the rocking back and forth and he felt relieved to have got off when he had. For a while he just stood there like a naked dog-walker waiting for Pete to finish his business.

***

Unusually he began to feel awkward. He located his clothes and got dressed quickly, quietly. But still he felt awkward, squirming inside, and he looked at the door and thought of the staircase, the building's exit, his car.

Normally he would have waited for the punch line, that piss-funny moment just before the penny dropped and the shouting and swearing began when the girl would turn around and see the unexpected and her face would be a picture. For sure Mandy's face would be a picture, and Pete would doubtless howl with laughter as he fought rodeo-style to stay on, but tonight for some reason the star didn't fancy it. He simply couldn't watch the graphic zoology that was occurring, and he couldn't face a knowledgeable Mandy.

He patted Pete on the back and made for the door. His pal glanced around with a puzzled, slightly worried look on his face, and then shrugged and carried on, and Gerry turned the handle. Light leaked in from the landing and he sidled through as quickly as possible, closing the door softly. And then he was down the stairs, through the exit and onto the gravel pathway.

A young lad was walking past the Belvedere. Gerry recognised him as one of the crew at the pier, but shied from his eye. He halted short of the gate and turned around, scratching an ear that didn't itch, trying to hide himself in the open garden. He looked up to the first floor bay window and saw movement behind the curtain. And then he saw a palm press against the glass, Mandy's palm.

His thoughts lead him back upstairs and into the bedroom again. He felt a pull to be there, to be with his pal for the funny aftermath. And he thought of Mandy and of what Pete was doing to her. But the main entrance had closed with a click, locked, and he wasn't about to knock up Mike. He felt stranded. He raised his eyes to the window again. Between the ruffling curtains he glimpsed the crown of a blonde head. "She's a big girl," he told himself, but in his mind he saw her pretty face and he heard her kind voice; "You poor love" she was saying to him. He felt sick. In his confusion he felt like screaming. He bent down and clawed a handful of gravel. He wanted to join in with Pete again; he needed to be with Mandy. He walked through the gate and out onto the pavement, stopping beneath the lamppost. He sighted the window, gauged the distance and reached out in the only way he could; he threw the gravel.

***

Mandy was still slumped in a fireman's lift position over the dressing table, little more than a corpse, dead to the act that was occurring. She had stopped protesting; indeed she had stopped making any sound at all, other than a regular low groan. A dull ache had spread throughout her battered body, a dull ache now given sharp relief by a drying soreness between her legs. All she could do was try to relax, try not to vomit, and wait for Gerry to finish. A few moments ago she'd mistakenly thought he had finished, but then he'd started up again, continuing as before, only more so, as if he'd got his second wind, or something. Now, she didn't know how much more of him she could take, but still the tears wouldn't come.

This was more than a shame. In the bar earlier she had felt so close to Gerry – he had laid himself bare, confessing his insecurities, and she had heard his confession. He had disclosed to her for the first time that he actually cared; "I want you," he had said to her, and it had seemed to be more than just his lust talking. She believed him. She trusted him. And then here in this room she had at last given herself to him, totally. They had kissed, and they had made love with passion and with heart. But then… But now…

She tried to catch hold of her thoughts, but a shoal of notions swam like mackerel through her mind, each slippery idea following the former and leading the next, each blurred question darting this way and then that, everything going nowhere. All bore the mark of truth: Gerry was drunk and powerful and didn't realise the pain he was causing; she was no better than a minx and deserved to be put in her place; he was a cruel woman-hater, bent on her pain and humiliation; she was a blameless victim, whose only crime was to love him. God help me, she thought; she *loved* him. She loved him, and it wouldn't matter how much he hurt her. At last tears pooled in her eyes and spilled down her cheeks, and she tasted their bitter sweetness.

Suddenly a splatter of multiple impacts came loudly from the windowpane. Like a wind-gust of hail or a volley of something hard hitting the glass, it was startling. Mandy's mouth and eyes made wide circles and shock snatched the air from her lungs. It took a moment to understand the din. She visualised a handful of gravel leaving a hand and striking the window. But whose hand? "Who the hell…," she said, surprised and relieved by the interruption, which she hoped would be final. "We'd better see who it is," she said urgently to Gerry, straining to look over her shoulder at Gerry, hoping she would find agreement in his face. But the mirror blocked her view of him, and Gerry didn't stop his thrusting, or even reply. He must be close, she thought. Only another burst of gravel on glass took Mandy's attention away from the man that was screwing her.

At this second clattering communication she faced the window again. She reached forward with her right arm, threw open a curtain, which ran a few inches on its rail, and then craned her neck to look. There was a man beneath the lamppost. But her view was fogged by a layer of condensation, and she couldn't tell if she recognised the man or not. She tried to wipe away the million tiny droplets of breath, but Gerry was becoming especially vigorous behind her and was now pulling her backwards onto him as he thrust, so that she couldn't quite reach. For a few moments she rode the waves of this pushing and pulling until she was once more within reach of the wet glass. She flattened her fingers onto the surface and wiped until water ran down her wrist. With Gerry nearing his climax, and making sounds that were most unlike him, she made a window in the window, as it were, and through it she couldn't understand what she saw. Through the clearing in the condensation, she saw Gerry.

***

"You animal! You bastard animal! How could you? You bastard! Bastard!"

Outside the Belvedere, Mandy was attacking Gerry. The knowledge of her deception, her rape, which she had learned indirectly from the remote actions of this coward, had roused her to desperate bravery. On hearing the gravel and seeing her supposed lover through the window she had fought with every nerve and fibre of her body to void herself of the alien that was inside her. She had heaved and twisted until somehow she'd freed herself from under the mirror; and she had then elbowed and scratched at the man behind her with such ferocity that he'd backed off. Free, she had then vomited utterly, on the carpet. She had then pulled on her dress, grabbed her bag and shoes and had hurried barefoot from the guesthouse.

Now, down on the pavement, Mandy was bent on hurting Gerry. As inaccurate as she was determined, she slashed at him with one of her high heels, making giant X-shapes, missing him, missing him, and then catching him, on the forearm and again on the neck. And she clawed at his face with her other taloned hand, drawing blood from the side of his nose, and all the while obscenities and gastric spit sputtered from her mouth. "You bastard animal!" she kept screaming, over and over, "You bastard animal!"

But enough was enough, as far as Gerry was concerned. He grabbed hold of this mad woman's arms, and with all his strength pushed her away from him. He then watched as she stumbled backwards, falling and landing chaotically on the paving slabs, spread-eagled. "Fucking calm down, love! It was just a bit of fun, alright?" He stood over her, braced for a second wave, but it didn't come. "Look, it was just a laugh, and anyway I thought you liked Pete."

In shock, Mandy withdrew herself into a ball, hugging her knees, and she stared palely at her dirty feet. She felt her heart pound, and her battered, numb body trembled from the fight. She sensed that Gerry was standing over her, but she didn't look up, and her only words were "Bastard. Bastard," which she whispered to herself like a mantra.

"Fucking hell, Gerry, I see what you mean about her being a screamer! I could hear her from upstairs," called Pete. He had appeared at the main entrance wearing only his unbuttoned shirt, but with Mandy's knickers hanging from his unspent erection, and with her bra on his head like a flying helmet. Gerry gushed with laughter at the sight of his pal modeling lingerie in such a fashion.

Seeing Mandy through the open gate, sat on the pavement, Pete continued: "Here love, you forgot these," he said, swaying his hips so that her panties swung from side to side. There was another toilet flush of laughter from Gerry, but Mandy refused to acknowledge her tormentor. "Why did you have to leave in such a hurry, anyway? I hadn't finished. I'm not like Gerry, y'know…I don't chuck my muck early doors! I like to take my time when I'm making love." There was more laughter from Gerry. "You can finish me off now though, can't you? Come on love, I'm all backed up. Tell her, Gee, tell her to come over here and finish me off!"

There was a pause in the banter. Gerry noticed a light come on in the guesthouse. He pocketed his hands and then removed them again; he looked over his shoulder at nothing in particular. Not really knowing what to do, he offered to help Mandy to her feet, but she slapped away his hand. "Right then," he said to Pete with an unconvincing air of purpose, "I think… I'm off home. See you tomorrow."

"Yeah, and I'm off for a wank," came the reply. Both men laughed, weakly.

Still refusing to look, Mandy heard the guesthouse door close, and then the Jag's. The engine rumbled and then roared, pulling the car away. But still she sat on the pavement. The cold, wet stone began to feel cold and wet. A bang on her elbow began to throb. With the taste of exhaust fumes in her mouth, she waited until she could hear the Jag no more. When she was sure both men would not return, when she felt able to face an empty street she got up off the slab. Still shaking, she fumbled on her shoes, and rotated and straightened her dress into some semblance of decency. Clutching her handbag, she limped away from the Belvedere. Out of habit she reached again for her cancer crab, but felt only bare neck.

11

Martin endured a fitful night, at times unsure if he was awake or if he was asleep but dreaming he was awake. Whatever the depth of his consciousness, he was certainly *aware*; the rabble of birds that squawked at him through the ajar casement, the hourly clunks from the lounge clock that forced him to count – but did he hear three or four? And with each dawning he could tell that more and more light was coming through the blind-less velux, and he felt increasing discomfort from his bladder, until he could no longer ignore the fingers of pain that reached through him like a glove puppeteer's. By the time he heard his mother flush the toilet, as if to mock *his* need to go, he was fully awake. Only once she had left for work with a door thud that carried through the semi and into her son's head, however, did he feel able to leave his room and venture to the bathroom.

Stood there swaying, he watched as Friday night's beer streamed into the lurid, evergreen water, and he felt that he too might fall into the disinfected bowl. Somewhere behind his eyes a splinter caught on something tender and he screwed his lids tight. He didn't immediately notice the warm splashes that wet his shin and foot, but once he heard the dull pouring of urine onto the toilet mat, he opened his eyes and righted himself to the vertical.

Back in the horizontal haven of his duvet, he stared upwards through the velux. Sometimes on brilliant winters' nights he would polish both sides of the glass and lose himself in the beauty of the moon. This morning, however, Martin saw nothing beautiful in the pristine clouds that floated through the blue and gold; instead he saw ominous zeppelins of heavy water, and he imagined them falling and crushing him. The doorbell buzzed angrily, taking Adam, his half-brother, out to play with another tectonic door slam; and somewhere nearby a lawn was being mowed, rusty blades hacking bluntly at the grass.

He rotated onto his front and stared at the floor. Last night's wet clothes lay there in a pile and he saw his trainers beside them, kicked off and upended. He thought of the wing mirror, but felt no guilt, or satisfaction. He remembered the three lads and the beer bottle and the chemi-luminescent girl, feeling no emotion he could name. What was wrong with him, besides a hangover? Why did he feel so raw, so under siege? He beat his pillow into shape and rifled his body inside the barrel of the duvet.

In the kitchen he medicated himself with fresh orange, administered orally direct from the carton, and he ate cornflakes dosed with copious milligrams of sugar. Whisking three eggs he remembered Dennis' words: "Walk a mile in her shoes." He forgot whether he'd added salt or not, added it anyway and allowed the first two rounds of toast to burn. Scraping the blackened squares over the pedal bin, more of Dennis' words came back to him: "He didn't hang around long."

When he finally came to eat his scrambled eggs, which may or may not have been double-salted, he barely tasted them. Why *should* he care about his piss-head mother and his deserter father anyway, he asked himself. The only answer he could think of – because they were his parents – didn't seem good enough. He finished his breakfast with toast and marmalade and sucked his fingers clean, out of habit and without relish.

Instinctively he knew he had to keep busy. He washed the dishes, hung the clothes out to dry, screwed up the note asking him to do so and threw it triumphantly into the bin. He then multi-tasked a cup of coffee with his drumming magazine while on the toilet. He started an article on traditional versus matched grip, but couldn't finish it. He resorted to flicking through the pages, looking at the photos, reading the captions. It seemed the best drummers – the jazzers, the fusion guys, the guys who endorsed products and had session credits – it seemed they all had exotic, tough-sounding names like Terry Bozzio or Vinnie Colaiuta. Even Porcaro sounded like a sportscar; The Porsche Porcaro. But "Collier?" He had the wrong surname to be a drummer! And *who was* Collier, anyway? Not *his* father, he observed. Collier was his mother's family name. Even Adam had inherited Berry. No, Martin had the wrong surname, full stop. He threw down the magazine and flushed.

In his bedroom he dressed in jogging bottoms and a Level 42 tee-shirt, and he hung his work clothes from the curtain pole to dry. The day stretched before him like a prison sentence. He jostled himself behind the drum kit that was assembled tight in the corner of his cramped bedroom. Clangs and chimes accompanied his passage there. He slumped on the stool and picked up his sticks, without enthusiasm.

The doorbell buzzed. He had little appetite for drum practice, but even less for talking to anyone. Huffing he stood and re-negotiated the gauntlet of cymbals and floor tom, wondering who was taking him away from his own distraction. Not next door complaining again, surely? He hadn't hit a skin in anger yet, and besides it was after eleven – *their* curfew. There was another long buzz. "Alright, alright," he said. Turning the Yale, he heard stifled laughter and fleeing footfalls. "Ha, ha!" he called, stepping through the open door, "Very funny! I know it's you, Adam, *and you*, Stinker. Go play on the main road!"

Behind his kit again, Martin snatched up his sticks and began to drum loudly. Irritation gave him an artificial sense of purpose. He tore into the beat from Herbie Hancock's "Chameleon" – on record a slow, loose groove with an off-beat on the snare drum – but in his irritated, distracted hands it sounded jerky and brittle and he played much too quickly. And the sticks in those hands, so often obedient extensions of his flesh, began to feel less like hickory and more like dead eels, and they began to slip from his grip. He tried a fill on the mounted toms, but hit more rim than skin, and later, when moving from the hi-hat to the bell of the ride, the right eel seemed to wriggle free, and his empty hand struck the cymbal with a pathetic low chime.

He threw the remaining stick at the wall opposite. But in the ringing quiet a second rhythm was taken up by a second drummer; paradiddle, paradiddle, paradiddle went the doorbell and knocker. He knew straightaway it was Adam, a paradiddle being the one thing his brother had allowed Martin to teach him, and the youngster now used the rudiment to torment and to mock his sibling. Martin leapt from behind the kit, jumped up onto the bed, pulled open the velux and shouted "Adam, just pack it in!" Stinker must then have joined in as a battery of raps to the door's glass and of tap-taps with the letterbox duetted with the knocks and the buzzes. Martin flew downstairs and out onto the driveway. "You little wankers! Just sod off!" he shouted as they sped away on BMXs, pissing themselves like the ten-year-olds they were. He didn't see the elderly neighbour look up from her pruning, as he marched back inside and pulled the door to violently.

***

Later he swapped his joggers for shorts, laced his Silver Shadows and went for a run: his hour in the exercise yard. He descended through the wooded glen, following the stream out into Pagoda Park. The path curved with and carried him over petalled water that poured down shallow cascades and into an artificial lake. On an island at one end of the lake rose a tiered Japanese temple that gave the park its name, and families in pedalos pedaled around it. He saw fuzzy, mustard goslings peck the mown bank, as pensioners on benches scattered their packets of seed. He leapt flowerbeds to avoid rolling roadblock families, with hand-held children and dogs on leads. He crossed the road by the outdoor pool and the cable car, almost low enough to touch with a jump, and he passed through the open-air theatre, beside the moat that separated the stage from the steep seating. At the beach, he inhaled the sea air and ran free along the prom, north towards the cliffs.

"Hiya Martin!" He was entering the footbridge that lead to the cliff path when a melodic greeting broke his runner's trance. Helen stood square in front of him on the narrow bridge. He had no choice but to stop running and to jog on the spot, as if waiting for a break in the traffic. He wiped sweat from his eyebrows. "Wow, you run fast! I'm glad you saw me, I thought you were going to knock me over!" said the dancer. She was with a smartly dressed elderly couple – a man in a brown sports coat and leather shoes and a woman under a cumulus of grey hair – and the two of them looked at Martin with a mixture of surprise and disapproval. "Er, sorry, these are my grandparents," she said gesturing, "and this is Martin, from the pier."

Still shifting from foot to foot, he dried his sweaty fingers on his shorts and took two outstretched palms. "Hello. Nice to meet you," he panted, feeling like a Weimaraner in the Obedience Ring at Cruft's. Heel. Roll over. Shake hands. Once the mention of the pier had registered, however, the couple seemed to warm to him, and the grandma even uttered a sound of recognition, as if she had heard her granddaughter talk of him by name. At last he stopped shifting about and stood still. "Please excuse me, I'm a little out of breath," he said with a smile, wondering why Helen would have talked to anyone about him.

"So, where are you running, then?" she asked.

She seemed younger and more petite than the dancer he knew from the pier. "Oh, not far. Down through Pagoda Park, avoiding all the goose guano, y'know, poo. Along the prom, dodging the old codgers. Er, sorry, I mean the *really* old codgers. Up onto the cliffs – I hope they don't collapse *today*. And then along the main road, back home." As he spoke he described the route with his finger, and judging by the chorus of chuckles he was relieved to have caused no offence with his playfully ageist remark.

"Well, I'm out of breath just thinking about it," said Helen modestly. "Where is 'home', anyway? Where do you live?"

"Glenside, at the top of the, er, glen. You?"

"Oh, four of us live together in South Shore, behind Funland…Sandhills Avenue?"

Martin thought of four girl dancers sharing a house in a holiday town. "Sounds like fun…"

"Well, it's been an eye-opener. I must have lived a sheltered life, I'm not really used to…"

"Is this the young gentleman you told us about? The one with the onion?" interrupted the grandma, moving closer, getting a good look at the lad, the nice young man…

The show dog now sensed he was being judged further, for temperament and coat perhaps, but he felt strangely un-self-conscious and he even puffed out his forequarters. As he made polite conversation with the old couple, who he soon learned had once been frequent visitors to Grumby and its tea dances at the Empress Ballroom, he increasingly became aware of Helen. She had moved so that she was now standing by his side, and he felt an urge to turn and to look at her. But he looked straight ahead, almost unblinkingly at the faces of the old timers – the moist, grey eyes and wrinkled mouth, the corned beef cheeks – but still he could sense Helen's softness in the periphery of his vision. And it seemed also that he was being pulled towards her, as if within her slight frame she possessed the gravity of a mountain or a moon.

They bid their farewells – the old couple, the nice young man, the pretty slip of a girl – but Martin sensed a pushing, pulling contradiction in Helen's "See you later" that was beyond his male comprehension. With strange relief, he tore himself away. He crossed the bridge and then scrambled up the unclear path between the gorse bushes, leaping the eroded steps three at a time. He was giddy and confused and reached the top in no time. She had spoken coolly, indifferently words that meant goodbye, he knew that much, but her eyes had for eternal milliseconds gazed into his with such intimacy that her "See you later" felt like a promise; and she had touched his elbow to seal that promise. Darting now along the cliff top, this virile virgin, a hundred feet above the rocks and the grounded sea, without a care for his foolish mother or his absent father, he felt as if he had caught the wind and was flying with the birds.

***

Early for work, he bounced the length of the pier and pulled the stage door towards him as if throwing open curtains on a sunny morning. Like yesterday, like every day, he began by sweeping the stage, but on this early Saturday evening he had a reason to do so beyond housekeeping, and he thought of those slender fingers touching his elbow, and he bubbled with the possibilities of life. Before long the stage was spotless, but he continued sweeping nonetheless, waiting for Helen. "See you later", she had said, and he knew just where and when to meet her.

Andy arrived behind his kit and a crisp, rich sound filled the stage. Jack plugs crackled and amplifiers hummed as other musicians took up their instruments. Sheet music was sorted, guitar strings tuned, lips and fingers limbered up, but there was no sign of Helen as yet. Not a speck of dust remained on that stage, but the stagehand kept sweeping, waiting.

"Evening Martin, bad news I'm afraid. Gary's off again, should be back Monday, so you're on follow spot for another night." Again the assistant stage manager re-deployed his man.

"Right."

"And there's a problem. Mandy's got a dickey tummy so she won't be working tonight. Al and Ash will do a few extra minutes each, and I'm sure Gerry will milk it a bit more than usual."

"Right."

"But listen," Kevin continued, "I'll show you the pea-souper just now – it'll only take a wee moment, and then you can do it yourself on Monday. Come with me."

Martin, thinking only of his imminent "date" with Helen, followed the ASM into the wings. They reconvened by the Le Maitre dry-ice machine and straight away Kevin squatted and began his instructions.

"So, twice a week we get a delivery of solid carbon dioxide, Ellis and Everard supply it, and it's kept in the freezer, down the way," he pointed. Martin grunted his understanding, bent forward, his arms locked against his kneecaps. "It comes in a big block, about a foot cube, and you have to break off a chunk with this hammer and put it in the bucket – you *must wear* the rubber gauntlets! It burns. The hammer and the gloves are kept *in* the bucket, which is stored here," he pointed again. He listened as attentively as he could, but felt quite flat and disinterested after having been stood up, as he saw it, by Helen: "See you later" she had said. He continued to hear Kevin's words, but struggled to follow them.

When his attention returned, the ASM was saying: "…and then you lower the cage into the hot water using this lever and the dry ice sublimes and comes pouring out of the spout here." Martin nodded and expressed his total understanding, as if he'd followed every word of the in-service training. "But the important thing – and you must be canny about this – er, actually the *two* most important things are the water level in the kettle and…"

At that moment Martin became terminally distracted by the presence, at last, of Helen, who had entered the wings from the reception area, followed closely by Gerry Neon, his hand on her waist. As Kevin gave instructions with voice and finger, as he passed on essential technical wisdom, Martin followed not one word. Instead he twisted and craned his attention towards Helen, towards the star and his dancer, and he tuned his hearing to catch their conversation.

"So, there you have it," said Kevin, unheard. "Any questions?"

"What? Yeah, I mean No," said Martin, glimpsing that Gerry had his arm around Helen's shoulders and his mouth to her ear.

"You'll be fine, Martin. It looks more complicated than it is…it's a cinch, really, once you have the hang of it, so don't worry."

The stagehand heard an echo of Kevin's words and thanked him with a smile. He witnessed that Helen was laughing now, throwing her head backwards, revealing her neck. He then watched as Gerry kissed that neck. He looked down, saw the hammer in the bucket and imagined the hard, heavy feel of its wooden handle.

***

Martin tried not to look at Helen but, having to point his super trouper at her, it was difficult. God, she looked pretty. Even from the back of the auditorium her smile reflected his spotlight tenfold. But her sweetness towards him, her apparent innocence within a corrupt cattery of dancers, now seemed an act. Flirting with Gerry earlier, standing *him* up for a better offer, she was no better than the Vikkis and the Jakkis. He tried not to think about it, but there was no escaping the realisation that before long Helen – like every woman; like his teenage mother, probably – would sleep with Gerry, and his famous dick.

12

Helen's change of heart, only hours after her promise to him, sent Martin into a spin. He could now only imagine what might have been between them, and this made her fickleness, her betrayal, somehow more difficult to bear. Throughout Sunday he struggled with opposing thoughts. He still craved Helen and several times caught himself lost in a fantasy of touching her, as she had touched his elbow, and of kissing her... And during these masochistic imaginings he would soar as he had on his cliff top run. But then reality, like gravity, would pull him back to earth, and a gnawing jealousy would take over. After all it was *Gerry*, not he, who had kissed her soft neck, an image which the cruel projectionist in his head played and replayed and which his mind's eye, lidless and staring, could not evade. Forced to watch this betrayal again and again he tortured himself with thoughts that later, in private, she had kissed him back, had lain down and had opened her legs for him. He could feel Gerry inside her. Sunday dragged. Monday dragged. He felt each second. Leaving for work as late as he dare, he knew his only options were to concentrate on his job and wait for these feelings to pass, or else he could fight Gerry for Helen, as if his life depended on it.

At the pier, something was different about the hoarding. It took Martin a moment to realise that the image of Faye Gold, which still smiled beside the words "Amanda Monroe – vocalist", had been altered. Ms Gold's hair, previously black, had been painted over with egg yolk yellow, as thick as custard. Her face, however, remained there unchanged and still appeared nothing like Mandy Monroe beneath this graffitied clown's wig. He boarded the pier, shaking his head at this sloppy retouch.

He swept the boards quickly – he didn't hang around – and went to familiarise himself with the dry ice machine. Crouching in the wings, he operated the handle and watched through the open lid as the basket descended into the water and then rose again. He took the gauntlets from the bucket next to the pea-souper, and went to the freezer to sneak a look at the dry ice itself. He weighed the berg of carbon dioxide in his hands, watching with something like awe as the solid sublimed into wisps of white gas that fell away and vanished. He returned to the corner, and inspected the radio mics, lifting and then re-docking them into the chargers, their LEDs glowing orange, or green, depending…

Cast and crew arrived: Helen sickeningly cheerful as usual; Mandy Monroe apparently well again; stagehand Gary likewise recovered from his illness, and back on spot. Martin would have preferred another night front of house behind a super trouper. At least there he'd be hidden from Helen, from Gerry. But now with Gary back…never mind. He'd just have to tough it out here in the shadowy conspicuousness of backstage. He waited for the show to begin.

***

"Oh, I wasn't expecting him. Er, send him up. I'm just off for a crap, but, er…tell him to make himself at home. Ask him if he knows a decent painter and decorator."

Gerry hung up with a snigger and locked himself in the en suite. Pete thanked the doorman with a laugh, before climbing the stairwell to the star's dressing room. The first house was well on the way, Mandy Monroe just finishing her spot, Alfonso Delos Santos, three clubs in hand, about to commence his.

"Oi, what you doing in there?" The visitor hammered on the toilet door.

"I'm unpacking my arse! Piss off and put the kettle on."

Pete made two teas and began drinking his, sitting on a powder blue sofa, smoothing his moustache. Trumpet rasps filtered up from the stage; Gerry added his own echoing accompaniment. After several minutes the star emerged from the en suite, satisfied that he was now down to comedy weight. "Well that's the best part of me gone! Bloody hell, it was like Dunkirk in there!" he said.

"I know, I could hear you! Jesus, Gerry, you smelly bastard…did something crawl up your arse and die? Shut the door, will you. Your brew's over there…and summat else as well…"

Gerry immediately saw the crumpled paper bag next to his mug. "Oh. Ta. Thanks, I was running a bit low." He collected the mug and lowered himself into his armchair. "So, Michaelangelo…I take it it *was* you who touched up Mandy?"

"I think we both did a bit more than that, mate! Er, yeah…Well, I knew *you* wouldn't sort it with Bernie…and I thought we owed it to her…"

"Owed it to her? Don't include *me* in your charity work! It was *you* that took advantage of her." Gerry sparked his lighter and lit a Benny. Perhaps he should have spoken to Bernie, but in his experience these things had a habit of sorting themselves out. "You always were the guilty type!" he said.

"Huh...*Anyway*, Saturday morning I went to find a newsagent's. Just round the corner from the Belvedere there's this parade, with a hardware shop on it, and I thought: "I bet they do paint!" Funnily enough Dulux don't do "Blond" so I bought "Buttercup" instead. And then this morning...Jesus, the old dear at the ticket office took some persuading... what a battleaxe! Where did they find her? The Gestapo? Anyway, there's this gantry at the foot of the hoarding, and I had to climb up through a trap door in the ticket office to get access. Luckily, Mandy's bottom of the bill, so I could reach her no problem. Trouble is, I was laughing so much I couldn't keep my hand steady!"

"Well it looks very professional, mate." Gerry laughed loudly. "Bloody hilarious! She looks like Ronald MacDonald! I pissed myself when I saw it on the way in. She'll be livid..." Both men roared.

For some moments they sat, the comic in his armchair smoking, his erstwhile road manager uncharacteristically on edge, as if he was waiting for something. Eventually Gerry said: "So, to what do I owe this unexpected pleasure? Bowling's not until tomorrow night, y'know."

"Yeah, I know. I have a business proposition for you."

"Oh, yeah?"

"Manage me."

"You what?"

"Manage me. I'm sick of doing this and that, driving for whoever. I want to perform again."

"What? Re-form The Nobles! Are you joking?"

"No, not that. I'm gonna be a comic."

Gerry spat his tea. "I can see it now…" He wiped his mouth and then motioned his arm through the air, slowly tracing an imaginary sign with his finger, gazing into the distance beyond. "Pete Wheeler, Comedian, written in coloured chalk."

"Get stuffed, coloured chalk…Anyway, I was thinking of Pete *Noble*."

"You can fuck right off! You're not using my name."

"Why not? I was a Noble when I backed you for almost fifteen years."

"That's different."

"Gerry Neon *and the Nobles*." He said, stabbing his own finger through the air. "So why not Pete Noble?"

"It's *my* sodding surname!"

"Use it then, instead of that Neon bollocks."

"Yeah, I'll ring deed poll tomorrow." Gerard George Noble took a mouthful of tea. "I knew there'd be a reason you contacted me again, out of the blue."

"Why not manage me? You have the contacts. You'd get your cut. *You fucking owe me!*"

"Owe you, my arse! Besides, you couldn't time an egg."

"Funnier than you, y'cunt."

"Yeah, right."

"I mean it, Gerry. I'm serious. Manage me."

***

Martin ghosted through the first house. He performed his cues without ceremony. He prepped the stage between acts, he attended to Alfonso's props, and all the while he managed to avoid Helen and / or Gerry. He collected the dry ice from the freezer, breaking off a chunk with the hammer, and was now on the corner loading it into the Le Maitre.

On the stage, the evening's first resurrection of Elvis was in full effect. Raised from the grave he postured and strutted once more, and the drummer caressed his snare – the intro to An American Trilogy. Martin monitored the performance, crouching in the wings, his hand resting on the handle of the dry ice machine, waiting for the middle passage and the lyrical cue. Gerry's voice came deep and warm and full of power in reserve.

The stagehand worried for a moment that he hadn't filled the cage with enough solid CO_2, or that he hadn't topped up the reservoir sufficiently, or that he'd misunderstood the timing of the cue and that it was in fact earlier. He turned briefly to Kevin, who was sat behind him on a high stool, and sought his eye and in it found reassurance. Everything was fine. He tightened his grip on the handle.

On the very first phoneme of the first word of the cue, Martin lowered the cage into the water.

But nothing happened. A few wisps and streaks emerged from the spout and then were gone; there was nothing like the billowing torrent that engulfed the stage twice nightly. Martin froze. Kevin jumped down from the stool, nudging the youngster aside, and forcefully raised and lowered the cage. A little more dry ice came out, a puff and a spill, but still no blast, no deluge. For a split second, Gerry glanced over, but then Elvis looked away again. Thankfully the audience knew nothing of the missed cue, and sat rapt and in awe of the King. But Gerry knew.

Martin got up and moved out of the way of Kevin's paramedic urgency. He stood looking down at the pea-souper, his forehead fluted with incomprehension. What had he done wrong? Finally something like a cloud came out of the spout, some even reached the stage. But the number was almost over; it was too late. As the band crescendoed and as Gerry climaxed with operatic loudness, a fart of white gas seeped across the stage and began to gather at the star's Cuban heels.

Kevin prevented further too-little-too-late flatulence with a large cork, which he plugged into the spout. Open-mouthed, Martin stared at the machine, at the handle, and at the power lead that snaked along the floor and into the wall socket. And he watched as Kevin turned to him, and he heard him, with a hint of an edge to his Perthshire brogue, say what he now knew: "You didn't plug it in, did you? The water's clap cold."

***

For all his hoped-for invisibility, Martin felt as conspicuous as a streaker doing cartwheels. He stowed the pea-souper out of the way, and returned to the corner where Gerry was talking to Kevin, the band playing the outro.

"Where was the fucking smoke?"

"Yeah, sorry about that Gerry, my fault."

"Another cock-up!"

"Yeah, I know. Won't happen again," said the ASM, unaware of any other missed or fouled cues.

Gerry heard this apology but didn't believe it. "I'm not fucking joking! It's a disgrace," he said, moving closer.

"Alright, I heard you. It's no big deal. Listen to the crowd…" Cheering could be heard over the band.

"If I say I want dry ice, I want fucking dry ice. Elvis played Las Vegas you know? Not fucking Cowdenbeath, or wherever it is you're from!"

Now Kevin moved forward. Eye-to-eye with the star he said: "I've said I'm sorry. If that's not good enough for you, you can go through the official channels." He turned his back and spoke into the microphone, telling all acts via the intercom to be in place for the finale. Gerry squared up to this disrespectful back for a moment, before walking off, shouldering Martin painfully in the bicep as he did.

Instantly the youngster's heart began to beat hard, and he felt himself coil. As soon as the curtain came down he sped onto the stage and removed to the wings the heavy mic stand, as if it were made of cane or balsa. Waiting for his next cue he shifted on the balls of his feet, his fingers curled tightly into fists. Kevin reached an arm around him and, cupping his words, spoke into the lad's ear. "Don't worry about Gerry," he said, "but next time I won't cover for you."

"What about the second house? Am I doing the dry ice again?" said Martin, his knuckles still blanched white. "I want to."

"Yes, same again. Well, huh, not the *same* again…" Kevin laughed a little, some of the tension appearing to leave him. "Look…Remember I said it was like a kettle? Yeah? Well, you've got to turn it on! And give it plenty of time to heat up. You'll be fine. Just don't cock it up again!"

***

In the second house Elvis again punched and windmilled his way through An American Trilogy, and Martin this time produced sufficient dry ice, exactly on schedule.

In the finale, however, it was Gerry who missed his cue, or rather he delayed it. He took his bow and the ovation crested as normal – cheers drowning the score, people standing to clap. When the Musical Director silenced the band, the applause continued, roaring like radio static. Eventually those standing retook their seats, the roar became a riffle and then a patter of handclaps, and an expectant hush descended – all this proceeding as normal.

But Gerry, standing centre stage, did not address the audience right away. Instead he left his position beneath the God spot and began walking around, inspecting his cast. From the wings Martin watched as slowly the headliner moved from singer to spesh act to comic. He straightened Alfonso's Mariachi bow tie and, coming around behind, flicked an imaginary speck of dust from Ashley Kidd's shoulder. He even looked over to confirm Kevin was watching him, before pointedly checking his Rolex. That's right…he was over-running again and there was nothing the ASM could do about it. The performers smiled like mannequins; the audience went along with the improv, or whatever it was.

Strolling yet more leisurely Gerry now appraised the line of feathered dancers in bikinis that held elaborate poses, stage right. The band's was now the most prominent laughter. He inspected first Vikki, then Becky who giggled, good girl, then Suzi, and finally Helen. He stopped behind Helen. Folding his arms, cocking his head to one side, he looked her up and down, plumage to calf. Sniggers, but also coughs and shuffling could be heard in the audience. Ten feet away, Martin looked on, inching forward.

The top of the bill now circled the dancer, curb crawling, until he faced her front on, his back to the audience. Privately he once more took her in, cleavage to thigh. Helen held her pose, her smile, but looking straight ahead. Gerry pored over her young body, imagining his hands on her, the feel of her waist. Even the boys in the band had fallen silent by now, and Kevin had to half-restrain Martin, again putting an arm around the lad, easing him back into the wings. When Gerry had finished assessing, scheming, he returned to centre stage, slowly nodding his head, satisfied that she was the one. He cleared his throat and spoke into the microphone:

"Well, ladesgentmen, boys and girls, you've been a fabulous audience, you really have. Give yourselves a big hand." The crowd applauded, as they always did, but this time there was a palpable sense of relief, as if collectively they were glad to be back on script. "I've just heard the weather forecast for tomorrow, ladesgentmen…" he continued, "Yes, there's good news…It's gonna be eighty degrees. That's right, forty degrees in the morning and forty degrees in the afternoon!" Laughter once more filled the auditorium, enthusiastic and out of all proportion to the joke's merit. He went on with this conventional, comforting humour. "So, ladesgentmen, like I said you've been a fabulous audience this evening and if you've enjoyed yourselves half as much as we have then we've enjoyed ourselves, er, twice, no, half, er, wait a minute…" He touched his temples and screwed his eyes shut, and mumbling quickly said: "…one times two is two, two times two is four, there's twelve pence in a shilling, two hundred and forty pence in a pound, five two eight zero feet to the mile, so that's…" He opened his eyes wide and, with a look of surprise and delight said: "…we've enjoyed ourselves *twice* as much as you have!" More laughter. More forgiveness. "So, if you've enjoyed the show, make sure you tell all your friends…and if you haven't, keep your gobs shut! Thank you and good night!" The band played out. Rows of seats sprung upright as the audience filed into the foyer. Excited, happy chatter floated through the glass doors and into the night air. Gerry's dirty-old-man power trip was now a distant memory. In fact by the time the crowd had reached the promenade, it had never happened.

13

Martin wanted answers. He cocked his right fist and pounded hard on the stage door of the Opera House. While he waited he felt no pangs of nostalgia and did not, with wistful reckoning, estimate the number of years that had elapsed since he had last entered through this same door, the guest of caretaker Dennis. Neither did he remember that doing so always gave him a feeling of excitement and privilege, this being the artistes' entrance, untraversed by the general public. And certainly he did not reflect with pride that this place was where it had all begun for him all those years ago, with boyhood visits here which had ultimately inspired his career on the periphery show business. What he did do, however, was knock again, even louder, and after an interval so brief as to advertise his impatience to anyone within earshot. He wanted an answer; courageously, he wanted *the* answer.

"Alright! Alright!" Dennis turned the Yale and was only half surprised to see Martin, who without invitation stepped straight across the threshold, filling the door's frame with his own. "Come in, why don't you?"

The sarcasm was lost on Martin. He continued his

ingress and would have walked right into the fifty-year-old, had he not backed out of the way. "'kyou," he mumbled, unheard.

"You're welcome!" More sarcasm.

"I said 'Thank you'!"

"Alright, calm down. I didn't hear you."

The teenager stared at the floor, convinced and doubtful in equal measure of the legitimacy in his being here.

"Anyway, why didn't you use the buzzer?"

"I needed to hit something."

"What's wrong? Your Mum?"

"My Mum, my Dad, Gerry-fucking-Neon... Take your pick!" He looked up and sought the older man's eyes. "Dennis, I need to ask you something, and I need you to tell me..."

"Right," said the caretaker, in the manner of a quiz show contestant saying "Pass". He closed the old door with a rattle, thinking. He tried to imagine how he might respond. "Look," he continued, turning around slowly, "you wait here while I finish off my rounds. I won't be long." He held reassuring eye contact while he spoke and then disappeared to complete his duties, whistling cheerfully, but dreading his return. Since their chance meeting at The Galleon and the partial revelation he had been forced to disclose, he had come to realize two things. Firstly, he had answered Martin's questions – about his mother, his father, his provenance – the only way he could: with honest lies. Secondly, he knew his incomplete answers could only spawn a nagging dissatisfaction and that the lad would eventually seek out his lying confidant, which he now had; he was bound to have more questions. Dennis hoped that by the time he'd pulled windows to, thumbed light switches off and turned keys in their locks, he would have an inkling of how further to lie.

Martin palmed a belch and tasted burger. Thirsty as hell, he poked his head inside Dennis' booth, but divined no bottles of pop or cartons of squash. There was a thermos flask, though, and he grabbed it through the stable door and gave it a swirl... No good; empty. He replaced it on the counter next to a closed-circuit TV set, still on. In silent black and white, the monitor showed Dennis walking down a corridor, towards the camera, his bald head sinking below the bottom of the screen. Martin reached into the booth and pushed a button. The monitor now displayed a grey stairwell and only for a moment before a second push brought another monochrome corridor. A third... and a mostly black screen scintillated like a snowstorm in the dark. A final, inevitable push returned Martin to the first corridor, now empty. His impatient, pointless surveillance complete, he began to pace. He tensed and squeezed his bicep, which felt tender, and he wondered if he had a bruise where Gerry had shouldered him. "Bloody hell, Dennis!" he said to himself, "Where are you?"

Eventually he found distraction in a collection of old posters that hung on the wall opposite the booth. Phil Ray, "The Abbreviator", had played the Opera House on Whit-Monday 1910, with That Brute Simmons below him on the bill, and so too had Vesta Victoria, and Vulcana. All unknown to Martin. On another poster, another occasion, Else & Max Arbra had performed "In a Novel Equilibriatic Act," but they and George H. Chirgwin had worked *not* the Opera House but Zalva's Hippodrome. Cissie Lupino, however, had worked the *New* Hippodrome, she being billed as a "Clever Dancer", whatever that meant. Martin imagined her reciting pi, or twisting a Rubik's cube, but he did so purely out of comedic habit and without pleasure. Fucking dancers, he thought. Fucking Helen.

With simmering anger, he read on. Percy Hannan was "The American Baritone" and G. H. Elliott was, astonishingly, the "Chocolate coloured Coon". He found the Thomas Street, Grumby address – the same as the current Opera House – and he heard in his head his Granddad's voice saying the word "Hippodrome". The old man had sometimes referred to the theatre by its earlier name, for the simple reason that *his* grandfather had called it that. Martin felt a bubble of intrigue in this personal connection to the past. There was no softening of his face, however, not even as he pictured his great-great-grandfather, with waxed moustache and starched collar, paying sixpence to witness Little Tich "and his Big Boot dance".

All these exotic names, and the appearance of the bills – the pastel backgrounds, the capital lettering, tall and narrow – seemed to belong, not only to another age, but also to a different kind of entertainment. Vaudeville, was it called? Or Music Hall, perhaps? Certainly he saw nothing of its kind displayed at the Pier. There, pinned to the notice board by the payphone, he'd seen publicity *photographs* for "Mr. Graham Binmore...almost sophisticated" and "Clive Webb...is definitely barmy!" These bills, here at the Opera House, were no more than framed gravestones. They named only the dead, all long gone and with no living witnesses. He read the names again: Zalva's Hippodrome, Vulcana, Little Tich, That Brute Simmons, Vesta Victoria, That Brute... Vesta Victoria...

Still no Dennis. Still thirsty. He explored a passageway that lead to... Matcham's Bar, yes Matcham's *bar*, with glasses and running water, orange cordial even, and beer of course. He tried the handle... No good; locked. He almost punched the door. On the walls of the passageway a collage of framed photographs caught his eye, however. Each informal snapshot documented that someone famous had once drunk here. In black and white he recognized immediately Eric Morecambe and Tommy Cooper. A fresh-faced Jimmy Tarbuck smiled for the camera, mop-topped and gap-toothed. In seventies colour Les Dawson mugged a world-weary expression framed by huge sideburns, and a dental Ken Dodd gurned with wild eyes and electric hair – informal but still performing. This was more like it, he thought; acts he could relate to.

In none of the photographs was the star alone – a young lady was often in the shot, or else the star was snapped beside a suited dignitary or within a coterie of drinkers. It was interesting to play spot the celebrity, to see Tarby so young, and Tommy Cooper so huge, but Martin also found a measure of interest in the faces of the peripheral characters in the photographs, the onlookers, the hangers-on, the wanna-bes, the witnesses... He observed how they sometimes looked at the celeb and not the camera. He tried to read their emotions. In one face he made an I-was-there-smugness, while beneath a Ted's quiff he detected an I-could-be-him contempt. He saw handholding possessiveness, he saw boredom. He even spotted Dennis *with hair*, making himself useful in the background, collecting glasses. And then he ID-ed Gerry Neon.

The star of the future sat beside a man with bad teeth and of a similar age, early twenties perhaps, and both men wore the same white shirts. He imagined a narrative: they were band mates, post-show, too thirsty to change. Gerry's stage shirt was unbuttoned to the chest and he wore an expression of arrogant indifference, in contrast to the other, obediently smiling Noble. And Gerry's hair looked to be darker in those days and his face, Martin had to admit, was a defined and handsome face; indeed, upon his thigh rested a female hand, slender-fingered and wearing a large dark stone, it's owner out of shot. But the most striking thing about Gerry's appearance, then as now, was his eyes, which glared from the photo, as cold as a goat's.

And then Martin remembered what Dennis had said, that his mother used to work the artistes' bar and he wondered if her teenage image could be found here on this wall, within this rogues gallery of graveyard teeth and quiffs and mop tops. He searched deeper within the photos, scrutinizing every pretty face in the background, every half-turned head and hair-do. Was that his mother's shoulder, her bare arm, her hand on Gerry's thigh? His eyes darted. He had to find her… And then he froze, shocked by the realization that perhaps an image of *his dad* was on this wall as well. Was *that* him, in the corner with the dark hair? Was *that* him, with the prominent jawline smoking a cigarette? Perversely star-struck, Martin imagined his dad might in fact have been a performer, famous even…"Every randy comic and crooner" would chat up his mother, that's what Dennis had said; "Every randy comic…" Was Gerry Neon his dad? He felt sick at the thought. He almost laughed at himself for having such a ridiculous idea – their difference in heights; the absence of *any* facial similarities between them. But still… He didn't know what to think.

Dennis knew, he was sure. He'd replayed over and over the mental tape of their conversation at The Galleon. There was something perceptibly jarring about the way Dennis had ended the exchange, as if he'd revealed more than he should have and had bailed before blabbing more details. He said his Dad "didn't hang around long…" Well, long enough, bet Martin, for Dennis to know who he was. And now Martin wanted to know – he wanted a name, a description – and, with all these photographs to choose from, these mug shots, this parade of suspects, Dennis wouldn't even need to speak. All he had to do was point.

"Martin? Ah, there you are. Admiring the photographs? There's a good one of…"

"Who is it? Where is he?"

"What are you… what are you talking about?"

"My father. Which of these bastards is my father? Show me!"

Talk about getting to the point, thought Dennis. "They're just random photographs, Martin, that's all."

"I know what they are, and he's on one somewhere. I know it. Is that him, there? Is Gerry Neon my father?"

Dennis knew that Martin was, chronologically at least, an adult. But the angry adolescent, the hurt little boy was still very much present in this pre-man. He clearly still had a lot of growing up to do. "Martin. You've got to try to calm yourself down. You…"

"I've had enough of staying calm. I'm pissed off. I have a right to know. Show me who it is! Point at him!" Martin modelled the action violently.

"Martin. Please. Stop shouting at me." Dennis lowered his voice. "There's no photograph of your father there. That would be…"

"So you *do* know who he was, *is*, then?" The lad moved closer, almost squaring up to the caretaker.

Dennis, beginning to feel threatened, backed into the wall. "No, I didn't say that, I…"

"Well, what are you saying? The other night you said 'he didn't hang around long.' Well? That sounds to me like you knew him." His eyes filled and his face began to contort. With a strangled voice, he said: "*I want* to know him."

"Martin, lad, try to calm down." He reached up, placing a hand on his shoulder. "Look, you need to talk to you mother. She's the only person that can help you."

Martin began to weep. "I can't. I can't talk to her. I hate her."

"No you don't. No son hates their mother. You've just got to be strong, Martin, and talk to her, like a man. You're carrying a lot of baggage, a lot of pain. I can see that, but I think it's time for you to grow up, son. You must talk to her. Tell her how you feel."

He threw off Dennis' hand, shouting: "Grow up? Is that the problem? *I* need to grow up?" Anger rose in him like magma and, with an inhuman scream, he punched his fist squared in the face of Russ Abbott, smashing the picture glass two inches from Dennis' ear. He rushed for the exit but spotted a fire extinguisher on the wall by the stairwell. He lifted it from its bracket, raised it above his head and, with Dennis shouting now words of caution, hurled it with all his strength through the open door of the booth and into the TV monitor.

14

There was a grind and a flutter as two plastic flaps toppled forwards and 08:19 slowly became 08:20. Martin stared at his ancient clock radio, waiting. He had spent all night waiting: waiting in the black and the blue light for sleep that never came; waiting in the bruised jaundice of a Tuesday sunrise for the moment, yet to arrive, when he could get out of his bed and begin his investigation – for he had an idea. Now, clock-watching these last few viscous minutes until his mother finally left for work, it was as if time itself had thickened and slowed. With mechanical effort, 08:20 became 08:21.

After an entire night awake, his knuckles cut and throbbing, he felt light headed and incapable of clear thought on all subjects bar one: his mother's jewellery box, or more specifically an item within it. Upon this subject he was possessed of a monomania that was crystal and without end. The box was wooden. It had a hinged lid. Under the hinged lid it was divided into several compartments, in two layers. In one of these compartments he was sure he'd find something; a specific something. The box was wooden. It had a hinged lid…

The door slam that signified his mother's egress from the family home came like a starting pistol. In no time he found himself standing beside her dressing table, naked. He thumbed the clasp on the lid of the jewellery box and lifted it. He began a fingertip search with breathless, clumsy rapidity. A dozen silver chains ensnared his fingers. At least two unfastened brooches pricked his flesh. Stud earrings spilled from one compartment into the next. He scraped at the velvet lining, but still the object of his monomania escaped discovery. He lifted the tray and searched the bottom layer. A heart shaped locket contained his image. A charmless charm bracelet entangled several other items; what was it with women and cheap tat, he asked himself? Why a hundred pieces of jewellery and none of them of any worth? And then he found it. Priceless. For some reason it had been threaded onto a necklace, but there was no mistaking its identity. He unchained the ring – his mother's Whitby jet ring, passed down to her from her mother – and he squeezed it tight in his fist.

"What you doing, you homo?"

Martin nearly jumped out of his naked skin; he'd forgotten about his younger brother. "Oh, it's you," he said with as much composure as he could muster, poking around in a jewellery box, in the nude. "Er, nothing. Just looking for something. It's not important."

***

Left and then bandaged right, Martin's fists slammed into a heavy bag. Like the belly of a fat man belted with gaffer tape, the punch bag swung from a rusting joist beneath the roof of the garage. Each determined body blow caused it to jump, and the stiff joist bowed under the weight. Flakes of rust fell onto his bare arms and, as each bloody knuckle thud filled the concrete shell, a hollow formed in the bag.

Exhausted, Martin lowered his arms. He bent over as if to vomit, and coughed and spat on the floor. His belly too felt hollow, and yet also filled with a sick excitement. He walked over to the muscle mirror. Around his neck, held now on a string necklace, the jet ring rose and fell with each aerobic breath. He wiped his brow and the back of his neck and then took the ring between his wet fingers. The gemstone glistened in the sweat and, like an infant, he placed it in his mouth, tasting salt. Still staring in the mirror, he saw only Gerry in black and white looking back at him from the photo on the wall at the Opera House. And as the punch bag swung gently to and fro, it's rope creaking, he heard Dennis' voice again: "He didn't hang around long."

"But he's still here, Dennis," said Martin.

He made for the DIY shelves at the back of the garage. He picked his way around the weights' bench with its barbell, and between the dumbbells and the old paint tins that littered the floor. Reaching over a rickety once-used barbeque, he searched through his granddad's hammers and chisels and bradawls, all oiled and previously cared for, all since bequeathed to an impractical daughter and thrown into a biscuit tin like the haul of a knife amnesty. Rummaging loudly, blindly, the grandson selected his weapon.

***

It was only mid-afternoon when Martin reached the centre of Grumby, at least two hours before the pier theatre even opened. Sunny, the streets were thronged with shoppers and there was a cheery, carefree mood in the air, not shared by Martin. Overtaking, undertaking, he negotiated the bag people with impatience. Before him small groups of bodies seemed to coalesce into one impassable mass only to disperse again; but he had to keep moving. A side step to the right and he brushed past a plastic bag from Athena, a jink to the left and he set swinging another from C&A. "Oi! Watch where you're going!" But his ears were deaf to the protestations, his eyes focused on the gaps between the obstacles, gaps that he cut through with locomotive directness.

The short side street that led to the rear of the Opera House was filled by a white delivery van, which had reversed up to the stage door. Martin slowed and rounded the vehicle. He looked in the back and saw cardboard boxes and crates of bottles. He turned his head to see that the fire extinguisher, which last night he had thrown in anger, was now holding the stage door open. Not a soul was around so he slipped in. Dennis' booth was empty of both Dennis and the smashed closed circuit television, and other than the void where the monitor should have been there was no sign of last night's destruction.

He walked a little way down the narrow corridor to Matcham's. A man appeared from the artistes' bar carrying a crate of empty mixers. "Alright, mate," he said as he squeezed past, to which Martin, dressed appropriately, anonymously in black, replied with a grunt. He searched the wall of photographs, sucking the jet ring in concentration. Each frame was screwed to the wall through two brass plates. Russ Abbott still smiled, his face smashed into a dozen radiating triangles. "Sorry 'bout that, Russ," he whispered, raising his bloodied hand and tapping gently the glass, which gave with a scrape. In no time he located the photo he had spied last night, the one he still saw whenever he closed his eyes. Once more Gerry Neon, not much older than Martin himself, regarded the lad with arrogant indifference, the cold goat's eyes making him shudder. He drew a flat blade screwdriver from his seat pocket, swapped it for a Phillips and removed the photo from the wall. Casually, but feeling more than ever that sick excitement, he walked out of the building, once more grunting to the Schweppes man.

***

Away from the Opera House and the shoppers, Martin sat alone in a sunken rose garden. One of several along the seafront, this walled hollow offered shelter to the pink and yellow roses that grew there and privacy to anyone occupying its single bench. Like a thief in a safe house, Martin prepared to examine and to reckon his swag: the framed photograph on his lap and its possible companion piece, the jet ring hanging around his neck.

But what value or significance could these items hold for him? And what did he want to find? A positive verification – a match between ring and image – would point to his mother's finger, her hand, her arm… It would signify an acquaintance, a coupling perhaps, between her and Gerry Neon. And if that wasn't sickening enough, there was the possible dreadful consequence of such a coupling. Him; himself. An obvious difference between the two rings, however, would leave him none the wiser and fatherless still. It was the devil or the deep blue sea, as his mother herself might say. Therefore, for all his earlier single-mindedness and the tachycardic thrill of the theft, it was now with a timid heart that Martin confronted what he was born to confront.

He lifted the string over his head, taking into his fist the ring as it swung, laying it down on the photograph with a tap and a scrape of the glass. Like a lid, however, he pressed his hand down on top of the ring, covering it securely, hiding it invisibly from his own eyes until he was brave enough to look. He examined instead a bee as it buzzed and bumped into rose heads, drunk on nectar, indifferent to the pollen it deposited on carpel after carpel.

The lightweight picture frame began to press into his thighs with urgent force. But still he couldn't bring himself to look at the photo, at Gerry Neon, his tight-trousered thigh and the ringed finger of the woman's hand resting on it, her face out of shot. Nor could he yet look at the other ring, the same ring, the ring under his palm, threaded with the sweat damp string that coiled and looped in figures of eight on the glass. The one question that plagued him, the only question in the world right now, was whether or not the two rings were one and the same. Without looking he convinced himself that they were and, as a second bee joined the first in the flower, he began to believe even more firmly the corollary that Gerry Neon was his father.

With almost physical effort he summoned enough courage to begin his dreadful scrutiny. Moving the string aside he looked first at the monochrome image: the slender finger and the item of jewellery, minute at this scale. It was difficult to tell if the black and white ring was silver or gold even. A memory of Antiques Roadshow came to him, an expert saying something about bezels and shoulders, but he hadn't the eye or the knowledge to make his own analysis; and besides, the size! Too small. It was hopeless: the ring in the photo was ring-like; it looked like a ring. Perhaps it was silver. Maybe it bore a dark stone of some kind, probably black, yes okay jet black, about the size of a pea, but little more than a crumb at this magnification. He looked, and he looked.

Then, steeling himself further, he took the real, three-dimensional ring between his thumb and forefinger and held it beside the possible miniature image of its younger self. He strained his eyes with obtuse obsession, trying to force an answer.

Breath-less, as in not breathing, his only movements were cardiac and ocular: his heart thumped; his eyes flicked. The rings, they looked… Similar, were they? Or slightly different…? No, similar, surely. Breath-less with tension, he didn't breathe out. Where was Hugh Scully when you needed him, he joked to himself, exhaling finally with a cheap laugh, but he felt no relief. The thing was… The problem was that for all his suspicion, for all his hope, even, for an answer in the affirmative, he could not with certainty confirm a match. It was possible – he had to admit – they might not be the same ring and it might not be his mother after all, and he couldn't deny his paradoxical disappointment. But then again…

Tilting is head back he screwed his eyes shut, thinking, straining for an answer. A tram bell rang out. A seagull cried. Minutes passed and still he searched his thoughts. The sun began to burn his face. He wondered if he didn't have an answer because he'd been asking the wrong question. Since forever he'd fixated on knowing an identity, a name, but perhaps this, like the ring, didn't matter. He understood now – or perhaps he told himself, it was hard to know the difference – that what mattered was the bigger picture. He continued, telling himself that no paternal identification could ever bring him a childhood of tuckings-in at bedtime or of kick-abouts on the field. No official naming could ever give him the feeling of sitting on daddy's knee. He needed to reframe his question. His *mother's* story was the thing. Understanding Lorraine Collier's past, through selfless empathizing, would reveal a more tangible truth. A truer truth. A liberating truth. That's what he told himself now.

He pictured her blooming as nature intended, but deserted and alone and unable to be happy; and then later as a young mum, all her dreams dashed, hitting the bottle. He realized that, same ring or not, it really didn't matter who his father was. He knew *his mother's* backstory, *her* truth, inseparable from his own truth, regardless of any heirloom worn on a finger. One of those acts, he told himself... One of those acts framed on that wall – a comic, a singer; he could take his pick... One of those *bastards*, and he didn't care which, had chatted up his vulnerable teenage mother, had impregnated her, and had left her holding his infant self. That was the as-good-as-factual, liberating narrative he could tell himself. That was the undeniable, all-applicable truth of fiction. Any one of 'em could be his father... and it didn't matter who... so it might as well be Gerry Neon.

So, with circular inevitability, he had his answer. He brought his palms up to meet his face. With his fingertips he pressed hard, pulling downwards with them, from oily forehead to cheeks to chin. His face massaged, he sighed and opened his eyes, thinking... But he'd done too much thinking. He needed to be practical. He knew he couldn't walk around all day with a six-by-eight photo frame, but he wanted the black and white inside. So, he flipped the frame over, looking. The back was sealed with tape, which he picked at for a moment before considering if using the flat-blade he might... But he didn't use the screwdriver. Instead he seized the frame and, with only practical violence, slammed it down glass side first on the corner of the bench's armrest. The eggshell glass cracked into triangles. Carefully he prised and pulled at the shards until without injury he could touch the thin, glossy card of the photograph. Scraping and pinching he worked it free, folded it without further scrutiny and slid it, and the ring, into his breast pocket for later.

***

That night, Martin dragged himself through two shows with all the vim and zest of a double-shift shelf-stacker. Almost wordlessly and with little eye contact he struck the stage and raised and lowered flies on cue, but wearily; and this he did wearing a face at times resigned, at times hangdog. Even when Helen approached him – lovely, breezy Helen – asking if he was going to the bowling after the show, all he could manage was a half-hearted "Dunno. S'pose." The trouble was that although he had now pretty much confirmed that Gerry Neon was his father, or as good as, he felt there was still a piece of his truth jigsaw missing; he wasn't free yet.

Meanwhile Gerry – the paternal possible; the chief suspect and symbol – was half way through his second house spot, not yet The King, but doing some similarly nostalgic patter about Andy Pandy and Looby Loo and a wholly inappropriate act between Bill and Ben the Flower Pot Men when his radio mic started playing up. His words through the PA began to fade and the audience held its collective breath. There was even a flicker of concern across the star's face until he raised the microphone closer to his mouth and the volume returned. Then as he moved to a different part of the stage the full signal came back with a surprisingly loud "flobadob". There was a burst of laughter and Gerry, the old pro, seized on the moment, milking the technical fault for comedy. He made his own voice come and go in a staccato manner, as his exaggerated lips continued to move. He paused, looked quizzically at the mic, slapped it with his free hand, tapped it against his head and then once more mouthed silently into it before balling at the top of his Leeds voice: "Work! You ffff…flipping thing!" To continuing, roaring laughter he strolled into the wings, stage left.

He threw the dead microphone at Martin. It hit his chest, not far from the ring and the photograph in his shirt pocket, and fell onto the floor with an unamplified thud. "You charge these don't ya? I'll fucking talk to you later, sunshine!"

An uncomprehending "Whugh?" hung dumbly on Martin's lips, as Kevin handed Gerry a replacement microphone.

Through the PA, but standing unseen in the wings, a charged Gerry addressed the audience calmly and suavely with the received pronunciation of a BBC announcer. "Ladies and gentleman, please accept our most sincere apologies… We seem to have experienced a minor technical fault, now rectified, and we trust your enjoyment of this evening's performance has not been diminished…We have conducted a thorough investigation of our operations and have ascertained the *cretin* responsible for this unfortunate episode." Pause for laughter. "After the finale, they will be shot." He turned to Martin. He made a pistol of his hand, fixed the lad's forehead in his sights and fired a single bullet, his forefinger snapping upwards in recoil.

Still slack jawed, eyes circles of incomprehension, Martin almost felt the imaginary bullet hit him right between those eyes. He even blinked.

Once the headliner had returned to centre-stage, to huge appreciation, the ASM turned to the stagehand and spoke firmly. Anger made him sound more Scottish than ever. "You got te start using yer heed. Discharge first, or the batteries will ne charge up. Dae ye ken?"

"I know, sorry."

"Don't apologise te me. It's him you got te worry about," said Kevin shaking his head, turning away. He thought of Gerry's reputation for bullying theatre employees with disproportionate, even physical chastisements, and he feared for the lad. He spoke into his headset, scribbled something in the book and then, before his next cue, turned around and looked directly at the teenager. He saw a six foot man-child. He looked scared but, and this gave Kevin hope, he also looked angry. He then said: "Sorry son, but yer on yer own this time."

Inside Martin something profound was happening. It was as if a gene that for nineteen years had been switched off had finally begun to function. Legs that had just now teetered like card towers in a draft became two solid piles of muscle and bone, vital with blood. His quivering, hollow gut became the iron core of a man who trained like a contender.

In a sense Martin had trained for this moment, this commencement at last with adulthood. Those hours alone belting the hell out of the heavy bag until it split and had to be taped, or doing sit ups until he thought his own insides would burst out, those formative hours were not an expression of who Martin was then but more the construction of the man he would need to be when the time arrived.

Now, the hour, fully formed, genetically switched on, it seemed Martin's maiden engagement with adulthood would be a fistfight. With teeth clenched, blood in his legs and iron in his core, Martin knew he was ready for it.

Emerging from his adolescent self, but still a prisoner of physiology, he began to pace. He felt as if he could punch through a wall. Flies went un-raised; other cues went ignored; colleagues covered for the absent, present stagehand. If Kevin hadn't been too busy working the corner to notice Martin's pugilistic bearing he would have phoned someone. He would have phoned several people. Martin was ready to meet his maker.

15

Earlier, Pete Wheeler entered Bloomfield's florists' feeling put upon. It was not yet a week since he'd reacquainted himself with Gerry, after months and years away from the man's malign influence, but already he was running errands as if he still drove for him. Admittedly *he* had sought out his former bandmate and boss – his sometime pal – with an ulterior motive in mind, and he accepted he may need to provide the occasional bag of speed to grease the wheels; but to be sent out of his way to buy flowers for a dancer, just so that this other man could get his end away, seemed an imposition belonging to a previous time. He grit his teeth and thought of all the club owners Gerry would phone – had *better* phone – and of all the bookings he would surely secure, for Pete Noble, Comedian, and without a glance at the flowers on display he approached the counter. "A bouquet, please. The biggest you got," he said, pulling a crumpled note from his crotch pocket, like the last tissue from a box.

That evening, with the bouquet wilting in the boot of his second-hand Mercedes, he drove two full lengths of the seafront before finding a space, far off, beside a grey toilet block. In light rain he marched to the pier feeling somehow disrespected by the distance and insulted by the weather. Resentfully he remembered other occasions, when working for Gerry, that he'd been used as a lackey: like when he had to buy a last minute birthday handbag for Mrs Noble; or when he was sent to Liverpool passport office to queue for three hours for an express application because again his wife – always his wife – had failed to post the form in time for the Noble's Caribbean January. Such domestic peripherals too often took centre stage. But even the most orthodox of tasks, reasonably required of him, such as driving Gerry to and from gigs, had quickly become a bugbear for Pete. Too often "driving" involved waiting interminable tick-tick-tick minutes in the early hours with the engine running to keep warm while his employer was finishing off with a dancer backstage.

With drizzle spilling from his eyebrows, earlier memories came to him, of their school days together and the daily trouble he'd get into just to make Gerry laugh: the calling out, the answering back. And his punishments: the endless lines he'd write the endless lines he'd write the endless lines he'd write; the stinging canes across the palm that, when given by Bomber Briggs, always seemed to catch the bone of the thumb so that it throbbed for an hour afterwards. For the first time in thirty years he remembered some graffiti that had gone unpunished: "Bomber can stick his grease gun up his arse". He'd daubed it in big dripping letters in the toilets above the urinals using paint and a brush stolen from Art, as Gerry, his pal, looked on, the two boys wetting themselves.

Pete almost laughed now, all these years after the prank,

but he choked on that laugh, censoring himself with a cough, hating himself for the memory of his inferiority even then. Yet again he realized what he was always so quick to forget: he wanted Gerry to like him, always had. He spat out the last traces of that laugh and told himself that once Pete Noble was established in the clubs, once *he'd used Gerry* to get those first few bookings, he would cut off all ties with the bastard, for good. Until then he'd walk a tightrope – he'd play the servile role that ashamedly felt so natural, but he'd also stand up to him, somehow.

The last quarter of a mile took him out to sea and once more into Gerry's dressing room and realm. The second house interval was almost at an end. In no time Pete's face ached from the tight rictus of a fake smile. Behind this charade he thought of the twenty quid the flowers cost him, and he itched to know if Gerry, his supposed manager, had even once picked up the phone in his name. He decided he owed it to himself to start a conversation, once the speed freak had stopped talking. Resentment gnawed at him like a dog with a bone and, despite outwardly going along with the star's brag and bluster, he felt more than ever that he detested him. "You're kidding!" he said, bellowing hollow laughter from his lungs.

"I'm not," said Gerry.

"A chess set?"

"Yep."

"What do *you* want with a chess set?"

"I know! I can't even play. It's the worst gift since Anne Frank got a drum kit!"

At this joke Pete couldn't help but laugh. "So who give you it, a fan?"

"Yeah, it was here when I arrived tonight. Came with a note... 'A king for *The King*'. I opened the box to have a look... It's one of those really ornate sets that you see in department stores, carved from kryptonite, or something. Must've cost a packet. The things these fans do to sleep with me, honestly... Save your money, love! Drop your knickers, that's all you need to do!"

And then, before Gerry could start again, Pete said: "Speaking of money... I got your flowers. A big bouquet. They're in my car. They were twenty quid..." It felt good, this subtle, deafening invoicing, and there was a moment of quiet in which the balance of power seemed to Pete to teeter and then shift before Gerry replied.

"You got a bargain then, didn't ya?" He turned towards the mirror with a smirk.

Pete stiffened instantly, his eyes flaring. In technicolour he imagined his left hand gripping Gerry around the back of the neck and smashing that smirking face into the mirror. And in that legitimate, penal imagination he pressed his mouth to Gerry's ear and snarled his fair ruling, saying *don't you smirk at me*, before slamming his right fist low and hard into his kidney.

But during the mental moment it took for this scenario to play out, Gerry merely straightened his collar, unaware of the justice being meted out upon his person. And before Pete had the chance to say anything never mind punch anyone, Kevin announced that the interval was nearly over: "Entr'acte and second half beginners, that's entr'acte and second half beginners. Thank you."

"Sod off you Scottish twat!" shouted Gerry at the speaker above his head, as was his wont whenever anyone was listening. "Right, then. I better go. You gonna wait here?"

"Yeah… I'll be down in a bit." When I've stopped wanting to kill you, he might have added.

***

As Gerry Neon started his last number, off-stage on the prompt side four dancers in body stockings and bikinis were perched on four-inch heels. A dresser was lifting an ostrich feather headdress onto the second of them, while the first preened herself. The remaining two, Helen and Vikki, were as yet unadorned with plumage and not yet dressed for their walk-on part in the finale. They were however as ready as they would ever be for tonight's after show bowling. With much flapping and chirping they demonstrated to each other their imagined techniques, as neither had rolled before.

"Alright Vikki, how about this…?" said Helen, skipping back a few paces to make room for a run up. She turned around with a sportsman's look of concentration on her face, very serious, and raised an imaginary ball in front of herself.

A giggle rose inside her and she had to purse her lips tightly to contain it. Vikki, however, made no attempt at containment and laughed her usual fruity laugh, prohibited noise that made Kevin look over and cough. "Shush!" said Helen "I'm concentrating." With balletic smoothness, she made a slow pendulum of her arm. Gliding forwards, she lifted the ball high behind herself and then swung it forwards again, releasing its zero mass down the imaginary lane behind the drum riser. A degree or two off balance, she exaggerated her instability, allowing herself to topple head-first, grabbing at Vikki for support. Both dancers fell about. "What did I get? I didn't see! It's got to be a ten, or a goal or something!" said Helen, once she'd stopped laughing.

"Yeah, for artistic interpretation…Okay, Hels, *that* was pretty good, but watch *this*…" Squinting, Vikki focused hard on the same distant pins at the end of the same long lane. She stood square on to the lane, with her feet wide apart, and held *her* bowling ball in *both* hands. Without taking a run up, she squatted slightly, thrust out her bum, which she wiggled three times, and began swinging the ball back and forth between her legs, a technique possibly borrowed from the Highland Games. Each swing arced wider and swung faster than the previous swing until finally she let go, hurling the ball like some massive stone down the alley. Still squinting, she watched the imaginary stone roll into the distance and then punched the air, claiming: "Strike!" Both dancers cheered, quietly, and then fell about some more.

"Wow! We are good," said Helen. "But, I think I've broken a nail."

"Girls!" hissed the dresser, holding a third headdress. "Which one of you children is next?"

"Sorry, mummeeeeeeeee…" said Vikki, lengthening the last syllable, shuffling over, presenting her bottom lip in playful contrition.

From the shadows Pete watched the mime act with amusement. The dog that had been gnawing at him, first from resentment and then out of sheer anger, was, for now at least, asleep. While in the band, he had always enjoyed being around dancers, for obvious male reasons, but also for the fun of it. With the exception of the stuck-up ex-West

Enders relegated to work the provinces, as they sneeringly referred to the North, or the oh-so-precious, la-di-darlings, suffering twice nightly for their art, most hoofers were bags of fun: scoffers, drinkers and shaggers, the lot of 'em.

He'd been watching the dark haired one, the pretty one. Just now she was inspecting her nails, frowning. She even frowned prettily. Privately she then began straightening her bikini, adjusting her breasts in their cups, retrieving the gusset from... *Dirty* old man, he thought, with a mixture of guilt and pleasure. Stop it! She couldn't be more than eighteen – younger than his daughter, for Christ's sake! But...so...what? An inner moral voice, which in recent years he'd at least *tried* to listen to, was once more drowned out by his resident mob of pirates and Vikings. Shag her, Pete, they told him. Suck her tits, squeeze her arse! It's not as if she's a nun, for chrissakes... she's a dancer! That's what they're for! He couldn't argue with logic like that. Excused, he continued his voyeurism, watching as she stretched the narrow hammock of her gusset, making it comfy and neat. An altogether different dog awoke within him. He puffed out his chest. Manually he inspected his square jaw and pinched clean his nose. Fine features, mostly. Not too many crinkles. Still handsome. Sod it, he thought, and began to approach her, to sniff her out.

Helen looked up from her costume adjustment to see a huge, dark presence standing only a stride in front of her. "Oh, hello," she said, a little surprised and a little embarrassed, "sorry, I was just, you know, smartening myself, anyway...erm... what can I do for you?" She didn't much like being crept up on, being made to feel embarrassed.

"I was very impressed by your demonstration of, what was it, fencing? Golf?"

"Ha ha, very funny, no it was tenpin bowling, obviously." In the dim light, Helen began to take in the face of this handsome creep

"Just pulling your leg. So, are you going tonight?"

"Well I wasn't practicing for nothing," she said, smiling blandly. He looked familiar. Had he tried to chat her up before, she wondered.

"Right. Fair enough. So, have you got a team, or something?"

"Yes. The Girls Only team."

Christ! Which West End musical did *she* come from? "You don't make things easy, do you?"

"What 'things'?"

"You know, talking…"

"No, I don't know. What do you *want* to talk about?" She had no interest in prolonging this awkward conversation other than for the fact he really did look strangely familiar. But the moustache…? She had to place him, or it would bug her. She moved towards the dresser's corner. There was more light over there, and in any case she was next up for a headdress.

Pete liked feisty, ballsy birds – the battle of the sexes, and all that – but this was different. *She*, was different, and not in a good way. A new *breed* of dancer, was she? He followed her, but before he could think of a charming, witty reply she caught him completely off guard…

Turning around to him, she said: "Do I know you?"

He was thrown, more by the tone in her voice than the actual question. In the past he had asked birds this himself to break the ice, to create a bit of intrigue. A chat up line, pure and simple. Clearly that was not the intention here.

She genuinely thought she knew him, this... What was her name? "I'm sorry, love, what was your name?" He tried to wrest some control over the conversation.

Still smiling, Helen said calmly: "My name *wasn't* anything, it *is* Helen. Do I *know* you?"

"I don't think so. Why?"

"Oh, its nothing. I'm obviously mistaken."

"I'm sure we haven't met... I'd remember a girl as pretty as..."

"Oh, pur-leeze!" She turned her back on him for good, and stooped an inch or two to receive her feathers, just in time for her cue. No, she didn't know him after all.

Suddenly an angry confrontation at the front of the wings could be heard above the band, and Pete, the dresser and all four dancers turned as one to see what was happening.

***

To a standing ovation Elvis bowed and blew kisses and applauded the musicians and bowed again and blew more kisses and left the stage a king amongst men. Entering the wings he searched for the lanky, gormless stagehand, the one that had cocked up the radio mic and made Gerry Neon look like an amateur. He wasn't hard to find. The ASM reached out a restraining arm, but The King strode through it like a turnstile, irresistible. He met the stagehand with the confidence of ten thousand performances and almost as many bollockings. From low down, he sprung upwards, pushing this teenage beanpole up against a brick wall, next to the safety curtain control panel. "You useless piece of shit!" he balled at him, stabbing him hard in the chest with his squat forefinger. "How the fuck did you get a job on *my* show! *My* show!" he repeated, stabbing his own chest in emphasis.

On the balls of his feet and with fists clenched, Martin saw early the star's charge and began inching forwards. Kevin flung out a restraining arm and briefly it looked as if the ASM might prevent their coming together, but thankfully the headliner's determination to reach him matched Martin's own. At first it was Gerry that had the momentum, shoving the stagehand backwards against the wall, shouting at him, hurting his ribs with finger stabs. But then the teenager, the man, quick with blood and muscle grabbed his attacker's wrist. Each felt the other's strength, but Martin was quicker. He spun out from against the wall, until he was behind the older man, still with his fat wrist in hand. With momentous satisfaction he thrust the star face-first into the brickwork, forcing his arm up his back for good measure. Gerry grunted and tried to wrestle free, but after months of bench presses and heavy squats Martin found he had the strength to hold him. The captive's furious spit spattered bricks, and sequins fell from the wings of the eagle on his Elvis jacket. Martin moved in close so that his words could be heard: "Listen, you bastard, would you bully me," he asked over the high collar of the ridiculous jacket, "…if you knew I was your son?"

Before Martin could repeat his seminal question, Pete was on him like a bear, hooking an arm around his throat and pulling him backwards, throwing him to the floor in the darkness. Disorientated, Martin grabbed at a leg curtain, a tall narrow drape flown to frame the stage, and he pulled at it to right himself. And Helen, a Head Girl in a headdress, without thinking leapt in to pacify, placing her slight, steel frame between the floundering Martin and the advancing Pete. By now Kevin too had begun to police the fracas, he having two arms locked around Gerry, Gerry whose face was red and whose mouth sputtered spit and laughter, and who was mocking Martin with his laughter, claiming victory with his laughter, shouting P45. And then Martin was on his feet again, eyes wide and wild with adrenalin, and he was being dragged away by two flymen, shouting as he disappeared into the light of the reception: "Lorraine Collier! Lorraine Collier is my mother!"

Front of house meanwhile, the observant in the audience may have noticed that leg curtain jerk and sway, and may even have thought it odd, but none could have guessed at the scene erupting backstage. Indeed few from amongst the plebian rows of check-out-girls and factory workers would ever have imagined the true, tawdry nature of this glamorous, family entertainment. And as the band repeated for the second time the final chorus of American Trilogy, with no sign on stage of Elvis or Gerry Neon or of any other member Seaside Spectacular, people became tired of their ovation and began to take their seats again. By the third repeat of the chorus and still no finale, couples and families began to stand once more and to shuffle and to follow the carpet up into the foyer, thinking it a dissatisfying end to the evening, but oh, wasn't he funny?

***

"I'll fucking kill him! Fuck... Fucking get off me!" demanded Martin, adrenalised to the point of swearing and pure biology.

Once in the reception area Alan and Gary struggled to

restrain never mind calm their colleague. All arms and legs, he thrust and grabbed and leapt desperate to re-enter the fight and fighting his fellow crew-members in the process. Under such an attack the substantial flymen resorted to lifting Martin and bundling him through the stage door and out of the building. With his proxy blows raining down on them and with bruises no doubt in the post, they deposited this swearing adrenal gland onto the boards of the pier, nonetheless a hero in their eyes.

"Let me in!" he demanded further, coming at them again. "*Let* me in!"

"Whoa, Martin. Come on… Take it easy," said Alan, blocking the entrance, palms raised pat-a-cake style.

"Fucking get out of my way!" Quiet Martin squared up to him.

"Oi, mate… Calm down. Just calm down," said Gary, trying to prevent a further confrontation. Better quit while you're ahead."

"What d'ya mean 'quit while I'm ahead'? What the fuck does that mean?"

"I mean you did great in there. Better leave it at that, before someone gets hurt. Actually…," he touched his mouth, "…too late. You must have caught me, I think you split my lip!"

Alan laughed, but Martin was deaf to all humour, still reptilian in his reasoning. "I'm gonna fucking kill him! Bastard!"

Whoa, Martin, whoa! Take it easy. Did you hear what Gary said? You were great in there! It's about time someone stood up to that arsehole, but perhaps you should leave it at that…"

"Great? How can anything be great?"

"Seriously, mate. You did brilliant in there. It's hilarious when I think about it, one of the crew pushing Gerry Neon's face into a brick wall. You're a hero!"

"I'm not a fucking hero. Nobody has a clue who I am."

"What? Look…Just leave. Go and calm down. Sleep on it."

The flymen watched as Martin turned and stormed off up the pier.

"Shame," said Gary, licking his wounded lip, "that's the last we'll see of him."

"Oh, I don't know. Perhaps Kevin can swing something? Y'know, self-defense…"

"Perhaps. I doubt it. That arsehole gets people fired for fun. Come on, let's go back in. I wanna finish 'ere and then get to bowling for a pint."

"Or six!"

"And why not," said Gary, before singing: "The Vicky Pier crew are on the piss again, on the piss again, on the piss again…"

Alan joined in the chant as the stage door rattled closed behind them.

16

Helen in flats and jeans and Vikki rather more glamorous beneath her Mac stepped out through the stage door. The boards were still damp from the day's drizzle but just now there was a gap in the weather and both dancers were relieved not to need their umbrellas.

"So," drum-rolled Vikki, "He's a bit of a dark horse, that Martin…"

"I know! Who'd have thought it?"

"He's only a boy, but I do like the strong silent type."

"You like every type!" said Helen.

"Oi, cheeky!"

"I hope he's okay."

"Oh, Gerry'll be fine. A bit of wounded pride, that's all."

"Gerry? Not Gerry! Martin! I couldn't care less about that big head."

"Oh really? I saw you two canoodling in the shadows."

"He's disgusting! He's started looking me up and down, touching me when he walks past. He came on to me the other night, trapped me against the wall, kissed my neck."

"Everyone saw that, Helen. You looked like you were enjoying it!"

"No way! He's vile! But he also has a reputation… I don't think he's the kind of man who would appreciate being turned down in public. You know, to, er, embarrass him in front of people might not be a good idea. That's why I'm worried about Martin. I hope he watches his back for a while."

"Aren't you leading Gerry on, then?"

"What else can I do? You know what some men are like. They won't take 'no' for an answer. It only encourages them. I'll just wait until he gets bored of trying or until he fancies someone else." Helen paused briefly before saying: "I went to see Mandy, you know, in her dressing room, to tell her he'd been coming on to me and that I *definitely* wasn't interested. I didn't want her to think I was trying to steal her man or anything. At first she acted like she didn't know what I was talking about. 'Oh come on, Mandy!' I said, 'everyone knows about you and Gerry. You're *always* in his room!' But then her face dropped. You know how bubbly she is, always chatting – I really like Mandy, she's nice – well she looked heartbroken, on the brink of tears. Anyway, it seems it's all finished between them. For good."

"Yeah, she's nice is Mandy, poor love. Still, I can't say *I'm* heartbroken."

"What d'ya mean?"

"Well, all's fair in love and war, and I am currently without a man…"

"No! Don't even think it!"

"…so, you wouldn't mind if, ahem, *I* made myself available to him?"

"To Gerry? Are you mad? He's disgusting!"

"Oh, I don't know... He's got charisma. He's rich. He's famous. And, speaking of reputations, there's something I've heard about him..." said Vikki, holding out both hands, her parallel palms describing some fantasized dimension.

"Vikki! You are unbelievable!" shrieked Helen. "No. Be my guest. But, you've heard the other rumours about him and Mandy, haven't you? How he knocked her around?"

"Don't you worry about me. I can handle myself."

"I'm sure you can! But take care, Vicks. Seriously. "

"Yeah, yeah. Anyway, rewind, it sounds to me like you fancy Martin..."

"Oh I wouldn't say 'fancy,' but he's a sweet guy, funny... a bit awkward, I know, but he talks to me like I'm a person. And I think there's more to him than meets the eye."

"He certainly showed that tonight!"

"Tell me about it! I just hope nothing happens to him."

***

"Nobody has a fucking clue who I am," Martin hissed to himself, saliva sputtering from his mouth, "not one fucking person. I might as well be the Invisible Man! Look at me! Who am I? What have I got? A crap job in a shithole theatre. Radio mics that don't work – I definitely docked them. A dry ice machine more Heath Robinson than high tech – I'm positive I plugged it in! All Kevin thinks I'm good for is pointing a spotlight at rubbish acts. That's right, *I* illuminate *them!* And who the hell are they? A creepy comedian who isn't funny... My best mate the juggler who drops more than he catches... Dancers who are all prick teasers or slags, that's right Helen, *you're* a slag! And as for my noble pater...

Well, so what, '*Dad*,' if *you* do 'the best Elvis'! Elvis is dead, haven't you heard? Bereft of life. Ha! An ex-King. Ha! He's shuffled off his Blue Suede Shoes. Ha! You see? *That's* funny! And you're an arsehole! In fact, you're *not* my Dad. Even if you are, you're not. I *have* no Dad. Oh I have a Mum alright, and she's crap, why would I want a crap Dad as well? That's right Mum," he said to himself, his voice croaking, his eyes welling, "*you're* crap, whatever Dennis says about you and your boo-hoo past! You're an alcoholic, dirty stop-out hairdresser! You say to me: 'If you're not in bed by twelve, come home...' like it's the funniest joke in the world. You've been cracking it since I was fifteen, as if you *want* me to sleep around. I'm your son, for fuck's sake! I'm not some sex protégé. *I* come home after work. Where do *you* spend the night? Slag. Lush. Dipsomaniac. I tell you what, Mum*my*, Dad*dy*... I'm not related to either of you two sexual perverts. Just fuck off, both of you! And you Helen as well, just fuck off!"

Martin spat this angry monologue, this hissed slurry of consciousness all the way down the pier, utterly uncaring that entire words and phrases were audible to the handful of people he overtook. Motoring, he wiped tears from his cheeks like Munch's Scream. He exited between the ticket kiosk, now boarded up for the night, and the video arcade, about to close. The doors to the arcade were still open, however, and through them roared a cacophony of electronic fanfares, whooshing missiles and explosions. Somewhere within this multi-coloured noise Martin could hear the menacing death march of Space Invaders. He'd played it ever since he was a kid, dropping into the slot one 10p coin after another, the crook of his forefinger blistering and then callousing where he gripped the joystick, and now these little green men were mocking him as an adult, goading him once more to fight them. He could see them in his head, with their crabwise procession, dropping down the screen, row by row by row, quickening in their descent, coming to get him.

He saw too an A-framed pavement sign. Wooden, heavy and hinged, he seized the object as if in the micro-gravity of space. Without a second thought he spun like a hammer thrower, came out from behind his pixelated barrier and fired at the aliens, hurling the sign at the nearest games console. More difficult to direct than a laser canon, however, the A-frame sailed into the glass front of a Grab-a-Teddy mechanical crane. There was a violent crash as shards rained down on the cuddly toys within, and the wooden sign remained wedged there, inside the cabinet. He felt something other than anger, something between hilarity and anaesthesia, but he felt it only briefly. With the chrome claw swinging like a chandelier in an earthquake and an employee approaching, Martin made off down the prom. His hands burned from the effort of his violence and he once again raged with anger. He aimed a kick at a pedestrian seagull, and to his surprise, made contact, sending the bird flightless into the water.

***

"Sod the Stage Manager, he's probably pissed anyway. I'm gonna ring Bernie!" Sitting in Gerry's dressing room, Pete watched as the star of the show balled demands into a telephone handset. He'd heard this kind of thing from Gerry a hundred times before and yawned and wiped a smudge of something from his trouser leg. "Bernie, if he's still here tomorrow night, I don't go on!" The star slammed the phone down on the impresario and stared at his pal. Breathing heavily, hot and perspiring in the stuffy room, he stood naked except for a quarter pound of gold chains and a pair of emerald green briefs. He clamped his hands onto his hips and stared harder, clearly expecting some expression of solidarity. Instead Pete yawned again, this time closing his mouth into a smirk. Exasperated, Gerry turned and marched into the en suite. Pete noticed a damp triangle of material just above his arse crack. He returned with a towel and began to dry the sweat from himself, rubbing both armpits angrily, burying his face hard into the white cotton. When he emerged from the towel it had become beige, stained with the foundation he wore on stage so as not to be bleached by the lights. Pete could see that the heat of these lights was still in him, his porcine flesh pulsing, melting through every shade of red, from the sausage pink of his belly to the gammon of his neck. And his face, now rubbed clean of the concealing powder, glowed like a red apple in the mouth of a roasted pig.

Gerry threw the soiled towel onto the carpet by the door and said: "Well, Pete, he won't be working here again, that streak of piss…"

"What happened anyway? I was chatting up one of your dancers when I heard something, turned around and saw you fighting in the wings! You shagging his girlfriend? Wouldn't be the first time…"

"No, his mother."

"I knew you were desperate!"

"No, his mother twenty years ago. He thinks I'm his dad!"

"Well, you could be, you pirate… I mean, the possibility must have played on your mind over the years? Let's face it, we've both put it about a bit, haven't we?"

Blank-faced and deaf to the man who knew him best, Gerry dipped into his thoughts briefly before bobbing up again. "Me? His dad? Hardly a family resemblance! Who does he think he is to say that! Probably after some pocket money."

"He had you licked," joked Pete, with some private satisfaction.

"Don't start!" Gerry's voice went up an octave and filled the room and most of the corridor, before normalizing again: "Pass me that paper bag, will you…"

"Oh come on, Geronimo. You've got to admire his balls. A stagehand having a go at the top of the bill? Here," he said, throwing Gerry the show sherbet.

"I'll have his balls *in a vice*! Whose side are you on, anyway?"

"You're just embarrassed at getting a pasting from a teenager!"

Wetting his finger tip and dabbing it into the amphetamine sulphate, Gerry now lowered his voice and spoke slowly, saying: "*Anyone* can start a fight, and *you* stopped me from finishing it." He opened his mouth and dosed himself.

"Oh, right, lulling him into a false sense of security, were you? What about your arm that was up your back? I suppose you were just about to take a swing with it, eh? And what about *your face*? I bet you were going to push off the wall with it, weren't you, you know, for leverage…Eh, Geronimo?"

"Don't fucking start, Pete. I'm furious," balled the star again, his words this time reaching the stairwell.

"What about 'Thank you, Pete, for saving my skin'?" the imagined hero said with a smile.

"What? Thanks for pulling that piss stain off me, just when I was about to give him what for? Are you kidding? Thank you? As if!"

Pete couldn't help but chuckle and only stopped when Gerry darted over to him, his fist clenched and his arm cocked. "Alright, Gee. You win. You're nails. Calm down you maniac!"

There was a tap on the open door and Gerry turned around to see Duncan, the Theatre Manager, standing in the threshold.

"Good evening Gerry. Can I come in?"

"Yes. Good. I'm glad you're here." Someone to bollock, he thought.

Pete watched as this old timer, spry and smart in a bowtie, stepped into the dressing room and closed the door with a smooth, exact action. He oozed composure, if appearing a little impatient at having been summoned, and began straight away, saying: "I understand from Bernard Giggs you have a grievance with one of our employees, a stagehand, Martin Collier... Normally the Stage Manager would be standing here now but he is, well... he has absented himself and so Bernie telephoned me and asked if *I* would come to see you, to see if we can work things out. So, er, what's the problem, Gerry?

"I'll tell you what the problem is, Duncan, that teenage pillock can't fucking charge the radio mics, can't fucking work the pea-souper, can't fucking do anything right!"

Pete then watched as this polite, dignified man found himself on the wrong end of a three-minute tirade, shouted at him by one of the biggest bastards in the business. He saw him try to interrupt, to clarify the grievance, to explain the mediation procedure, to pacify the star of the show... but clearly he was wasting his breath trying to reason with Gerry Neon when he was this incensed and this set on retribution. To the Theatre Manager's credit, thought Pete, he did keep *trying* to interrupt, even as he backed into the door he had just closed, and even as he pulled his handkerchief from his breast pocket and wiped Gerry's spittle from his cheeks. Pete could feel the poor man's frustration. "Actually it falls on the Stage Manager to select his staff," he heard him say, seeing him flush at the unfairness of one particular accusation.

Witnessing this reminded Pete of a line much used by Gerry during their school days together three decades ago, a line – a ploy – of which he never approved. *"Hit me, or I'll hit you!"* the School Bully would say, always with Pete by his side as back up, daring the intended victim to throw the first punch. *"Hit me, or I'll hit you!"* he could hear him say. If the poor chump did as commanded, Gerry could then justify beating them up on the grounds of self-defense, sir. If they refused to hit first, his position would be that he'd given his ultimatum fairly and squarely so the coward deserved what he got, in fact they had asked for it, sir. *"Hit me, or I'll hit you!"* in fact. Pete, however, never accepted this cruel logic. As a hard man he had his own eye-for-an-eye code, and God help any man who crossed him, but Pete Wheeler was no bully, and so this Hobson's choice of black eye versus bloody nose never sat well with him. And yet he would always go along with it, weak and corruptible every time, forever standing shoulder to shoulder with Gerry as he planted his dishonest dilemma, as he sowed the seeds of Pete's lifelong resentment.

He knew, now more than ever, the depth of his antipathy towards Gerry, with his fat finger fucking the air six inches from poor Duncan's face. He could see Gerry for what he was, a fat, spoilt bully in green underpants, stamping his feet, hurling his toys from his cot.

But, he had the contacts...

"Well, that was fun!" said Gerry, Duncan departed, diminished. "Poor sod, with his hankie. I thought he was gonna cry!"

"Yeah, you've still got it, Gee. Ferocious."

"You never lose it, pal. 'Ere, pass us those trousers, will you..." The top-of-the-bill then got dressed, and Pete listened to him variously congratulating himself on a job well done, and that that Martin kid was now out of work, and that he was "well in" with the youngest dancer on the show – fit as fuck – and that tonight he'd filled the theatre *to the gunnels*, again, twice more, so that's another two House Full signs that Darren Daniel can shove up his arse, 'cos its all about bums on seats, and when it came to bums on seats Gerry Neon was Box Office... "Right then," he declared with one last suck of his speed finger and a clap of the hands, "let's go bowling!"

17

Disembarking the pier, Helen and Vikki crossed tram tracks and tarmac before passing through a plate glass door between Slots of Fun and Corrigan's Amusements. The entrance to Grumby's Rock 'n' Bowl bowling alley lead initially into a bright, steep flight of stairs, topped with ceiling tiles and tailed with multi-coloured combat carpet, bullet-marked with blackened gum. Narrow, towering walls presented to the breathless viewer a series of photographs of soap actors and footballers, each smiling and raising two fingers to the camera, fingers that were enclosed in twelve or fourteen pounds of black, spherical polyurethane. At the top of the stairs a second glass door bore a taped flyer: "Tonight Rock 'N' Bowl With The Stars Open Late." Vikki's push on the hand plate lead the dancers into a dizzying expanse of the same combat carpet, dark and swirling with purple and orange and which made Helen *aware* of walking on it, as if on stepping stones within a river. Behind a tall counter a name-badged employee in short sleeves rested on his elbows. Seeing the pair, his eyes widened. They approached the counter.

"Good evening ladies," he said, straightening and broadening himself.

"Oh I'm no lady. Not tonight, love, any road!" said Vikki, Helen shrieking.

"You from a show?"

"Yes, er…," she clocked his badge, "…William. We're dancers, Willy darling. From the pier."

"Thought so. Had to ask." Vikki undid her raincoat and moved closer, but Helen turned around to take in the huge room, to see who was here. On the sound system Duran Duran's "A View to a Kill" played quietly, heckled frequently by the far-off woody clatter of bowling pins, which the low ceiling seemed to funnel into Helen's ears. Meerkat punters stood erect and alert, eyes wide and necks craning to see which of the promised stars had just arrived. The receptionist continued: "Right, so, you've got two free games. It's all automated, just key in your names. Up to six bowlers. The bar's over there on the left. You'll be on lane number… 17. They should be nearly finished. What size would you like?"

Helen immediately snorted and let out a giggle.

"Oh about this big," began Vikki, once more raising her hands in a demonstration of length, hands which Helen quickly swatted down.

"Size six, please. We're both size six," Helen interrupted, "and please ignore my friend!"

William pinked a little, smiling. He disappeared behind the counter and brought up the bowling shoes. Helen handed over one pair of comfy flats in exchange for another, while glamour puss Vikki, supporting herself with a hand on the counter, cocked her ankles and stretched and fingered her way out of two minutely buckled high heels. In stocking feet she stood four inches shorter and, taking the blue and red bowlers, failed to hide her fashion horror with a snort and a giggle of her own. "Oh these look perfect, thank you, Willy," she said.

"You're welcome. Any problems, just press the 'Call' button. And, er, can I just remind you that the bar is over there on the left…"

"You on drinks commission then?"

"Huh, something like that."

While Vikki practiced her flirting with Willy, Will, Willy-boy, Helen drifted over to a display cabinet containing bowling balls far more expensive and far more decorative in their design – glittering blue, iridescent grey – than she would ever have thought necessary. There were inscribed trophies topped with golden figurine bowlers in mid-bowl and bizarre black leather gloves with fingers missing and wrist straps, all very Frankie Goes to Hollywood. On the wall above the cabinet, a framed photo showed a fat man with huge glasses and a moustache smiling proudly beneath a TV monitor that displayed "300" in big red digits. Much was meaningless to her, and what little she did understand left her amused more than impressed. What *is* Vikki doing, she wondered. Turning around she scanned the room as far as Lanes 20, 21, 22. Was there anyone here amongst the meerkats that she recognized, anyone she wanted to talk to? A strike of laughter erupted from the other, lower-numbered end and she looked over, but they were just Joe Public. Martin wasn't among them. "Come on Vicks!" she called over. She wanted to explore. She wanted to find him.

"Right then, Hels. Let's get a drink."

"Oh, you've finished with William then, have you?"

"Yep. Gave him our backstage number."

"You are terrible!"

"I told him my name was Helen Patterson!"

"You minx!"

"Don't panic Miss Patterson, I'm pulling your leg. Come on, let's get a drink."

Helen paused a second before remarking: "What? You mean you'd like a 'stiff one'?"

"That's more like it! You're learning!"

Before long, people Helen recognized started to arrive. Sat in the bar area, sipping vodka orange, she smiled at Alan and Gary and waved girly hellos as other Jilly Conlan dancers appeared. Jilly herself came and sat with them. She asked how their digs were before becoming all gossipy and confidential with Vikki. Helen kept looking around but there was still no sign of Martin. She watched instead as one alpha male after another rolled in – impresarios and agents, tops-of-the-bills, and next-big-things – all of them with a spring in their step and a bird on the arm. There were trophies everywhere, it seemed. These were confident men; men with presence; men with status. It was all crushing handshakes and elbow power grabs and backs slapped into next week, and it was not in the least bit attractive. Except, that is, to the meerkats: staring, trusting people, nice people in new sweaters with autograph books and pens at the ready. They too were becoming confident, they were beginning to circle and they wanted ink on paper. And then, and this made Helen nervous, there were the shady, guarded men: the drivers, the enforcers; men on the edge of legit, or just straying over; thick set men with tattoos and sovereign rings; men who very possibly had done time. Perhaps it would be better, she thought, if Martin didn't come here tonight.

***

Carrying the wilted bouquet, Gerry entered the Rock 'n' Bowl with Pete just behind him. He began to talk loudly: "Stroll on, Pete! This is some place!" he balled, announcing his arrival. "Let's get a beer, I'm parched." Ignoring the reception desk, he made straight for the bar with a swagger. The place was crowded, however, and there was only a short cock-walk of carpet before the first punter pressed him for a photograph, a woman with the cameraman clinging to the star, her mouth a mollusc on his cheek. Next in line an autograph hunter held out a pen and a program for his attention. He bagpiped the bouquet under his arm and scribbled a version of his signature, answering that yes he remembered playing Wakefield Theatre Club in 1967. Immediately he sensed another fan hovering, another Hillman, another punter-azzo. He looked for Pete... He scribbled again, this time on a napkin, replying with lessening patience that yes he had played Fagin's, in fact he remembered, cue exit joke, how there used to be a hole in the wall between his and the dancers' dressing room and that, to hell with it, he always let 'em look! Cue laughter. Thank you and goodnight... At last he spied Pete ordering at the bar, but still they kept coming. He obliged a man and his Down's son with an autograph (well, he had to...) and granted another to a young couple, being good enough even to kiss and to squeeze the just-ripe girl (never let it be said that Gerry Neon neglected his fans!). With an appraising glance, he snubbed the forgettable remains of the queue that had formed for his ink, simply staring bar-wards and threading past them.

An even tighter scrum had formed around the bar and Gerry squeezed his way towards Pete and a much needed pint of Australian lager, too cold to taste. At every turn, however, it seemed someone in the business – an aspirant; a rival; a character from his past – wanted a minute with Gerry Noble or with Gee, or Gerard, or Nobby or whatever they knew him as. The already limp bouquet, which upon entering the room he had carried like the Olympic torch, was jostled in the scrum, and palm sweat even loosened his grip on the cellophane. One particularly vigorous re-acquaintance saw him drop the flowers in a gush of Nobby nostalgia. Once the first wave of glad-handing was over and Gerry was at the bar, the sorry bouquet was all bashed up and de-flowered.

"That's right, Pete, you just take it easy at the bar," he said loudly, with only half-joking indignation. "Didn't you see me getting mobbed? I'm lucky to get out with my clothes on!"

"What d'ya mean? I was buying you a drink."

"Yeah, well… Anyway, I can't believe you paid twenty quid for these weeds? You were ripped off. Look! That stem hasn't even got a flower on it! They're compost!" said Gerry, laughing, tossing the mangled flowers onto a drip tray. Pete did not reply. He couldn't even look at his soon-to-be-ex-again-mate. "Is that my pint? Cheers, pal."

***

Helen was on her second vodka orange, happily forking fries into her mouth. Vikki denied herself her own tray, but pecked at Helen's, sucking the salt from her beak-like fingers. They chatted about the older woman's previous work on cruise liners, and the three years she had spent hoofing in the Canaries, and about how *really* she wanted to choreograph her own routines, like Jilly did. They had both seen Gerry enter and could now observe him at the bar, with his back to them.

People began to make fours and fives and to decamp to their allotted lanes. "Come on, Viks. Let's try this bowling malarkey!" said Helen, aware of Gerry's proximity.

"Okay, Hels. But, er, you-know-who's at the bar…Shall we see if we can make a four with him and that big feller?"

"Um… do we have to?"

"Come on Patterson. I was gonna take Gerry off your hands, remember?"

"I'd rather not. Can't we just have a laugh with the girls?"

"S'pose so… I'll just have to play hard to get. For the first hour at least! Come on then, let's find the others."

Five dancers therefore entered their names into the console of Lane 17 – team name "Hel's Belles" – before commencing the alien, amusing, strangely embarrassing act of selecting their ball. "This one's too heavy, it'll break my wrist," said one, giggling; "which fingers do I use?" asked another, to no one in particular. The adjacent Lane 18, which shared the console and ball return rack with 17, was fast becoming the focus of the attention of many who weren't themselves bowling. Twos and threes began to gather until a small audience of punters and pros had formed. The reason was Darren Daniel, the handsome headliner from the Opera House, the Next Big Thing, the Man of the Moment… His team's name was "Double D" and, ever the showman, Daniel had even brought his own ball.

Helen felt the buzz of excitement, looking over at the tanned star with the sun-kissed hair and designer stubble. She knew as well as anyone in the business that he was gay, but allowed herself a moment of appreciation nonetheless.

As he removed his suit jacket and folded it neatly with T-shirted arms, she almost swooned.

"Come on, Hels," said Vikki, "it's your turn."

"Right then. Where's my blue one? Ah, here it is." She lifted the house eight-pounder – almost a child's ball – with both hands. Locating the holes and not wanting to break a single nail more than was necessary, she inserted only her thumb. She stood at the back of the approach area, gave a frown to Vikki who was seated watching, and then turned to face the triangle of pins, which might have been a stand of mighty oaks half a mile away. Still holding the ball with two hands, raised to chest height, she walked to the foul line and halted, as if waiting to cross a road. Standing still she lowered the ball, swinging it backwards now with only one hand, only one delicate wrist, before bowling it, or rather dropping it Barnes Wallace-style down the lane. To a well-intentioned chorus of laughter it sped geologically, rolling like a glacier over the slippery surface, in danger of not reaching its target. After what seemed a minute of surprisingly straight passage, the ball bumped into the front middle pin, at such an angle that a chain reaction of teetering and toppling ensued. Pin fell into pin until, as the ball dropped off the end of the track, a giant X appeared on the monitor. "Strike!" Helen jumped and shrieked with surprise and joy. Her lane mates screamed. Even Darren Daniel's crowd, until then enraptured by his every gesture, was distracted by the sight and sound of Helen's celebration. Daniel himself smiled charitably, as he buckled the straps of his hand guard.

When *he* came to bowl, a hush descended. Even bowlers on Lanes 19 and 20 paused to witness this exhibition. The anticipation was palpable. Only Tears for Fears, ethereal gatecrashers piped through invisible speakers, disrespected the occasion. Sockless in his own bowling shoes, his very own purple ball catching the light like a giant bauble, Daniel briefly stretched onto his tip toes as if about to swan dive, before sashaying extravagantly towards the lane. He cradled his iridescent ball with an arm that was curled into the handle of a teapot, short and stout. His palm faced upwards, the holes of the ball pointing down, so that when he released the ball with a whipping action, his cupped wrist would flip from palm up to palm down, imparting a rotation that would cause the ball to hook, like a hockey stick… Or so he visualized. But he had only purchased the equipment this very afternoon and hadn't bowled for years. Such was his delusional belief in his untested ability that when the ball naturally bounced straight into the gutter, with not a hint of the intended hook, he looked diagnostically at his bowling hand as if some minor adjustment to the guard or some fine tuning of his expert technique would ensure success next time. There were gasps of disbelief. There were sniggers.

"Get on with it!" shouted Gerry from behind the racks of balls. "Try a rubber glove instead! I'll see if they've a Marigold you can borrow!" A ripple of laughter spread throughout the audience.

"Gerry Neon! As I live and breathe! Good to see you, Gerry. Come and join us. Have a bowl," replied Daniel, as if they were the best of friends and all was well in the world.

"Nah, you're alright. I'll just stand here and watch you. You'll be enjoying this, having a crowd for a change…"

"You're a funny man, Gerry, very funny. Now watch this…"

Recognising his Leeds whine, Helen could hear that Gerry had encroached upon the action. Straight away his cruel humour put her on edge; she could *feel* his baleful presence. But, despite this, despite herself, she *had* to look to see him too, and what she saw was that he was holding some flowers. Instinctively she knew that they were for her. With a sinking feeling, she sought some time alone, to compose herself, to plan her diplomacy. Synchronising her departure with Darren Daniel's next unmissable bowl, she excused herself. "Just nipping to the loo," she chirped to Vikki, without a hint of the dread she felt for those flowers and for what they signaled. Walking to the toilets unnoticed she heard the crowd's reaction to Double D's latest exhibition of himself, and she heard yet more gleeful heckling from Gerry. "I'll just go and get my hard hat!" he was crying above the laughter.

Locked in a cubical she bent over and tried to vomit, to void herself of the knot in her stomach. Fingers that should have been inserted into a bowling ball she now thrust down her throat until her eyes watered, but to no emetic effect. Outside of the cubicle, staring into the mirror at those same wet eyes, she knew she had to do something, or else she'd be looking over her shoulder for the rest of the season. But Gerry was not a man to turn down or embarrass with people looking on so she would have to be tactful, cautious even; but she *would* talk to him.

***

When Helen returned to Lane 17 he was of course already there, sat amongst his dancers, holding court, waiting for her. The tall dark man was there too. She descended the single step to rejoin her girlfriends and Gerry stood up.

"These are for you," he said quietly, presenting her the flowers.

The simplicity of this statement and an apparent humility in his manner initially threw Helen, but she was not to be taken in. Looking at the wilted, petal-sparse, de-flowered bouquet, she resisted the urge to take it and thrash him across the face. Instead she accepted the non-flowers as if they were pristine, nosing them, breathing in their scent. "Thank you," she said, "they're lovely." After a few minutes of his toned-down, feminized banter and empty compliments, and of her bland, smiling replies, she accepted his offer of a drink. "I'll come with you," she added, boldly.

At the bar Helen sat on a stool, Gerry stood beside her and the flowers lay still dead on the same drip tray as before. Despite her protestations he insisted on buying her an alcoholic drink. She eventually submitted to a vodka orange, cursing herself for being weak, and barely touching it. He on the other hand swigged his way through two bottles of Pils, and it seemed that with each mouthful he moved closer to her, touching her knee or thigh. This unwanted tactility was intensely irritating to Helen, and it took great restraint on her part merely to stiffen with each caress and not to slap him. Itching to stand and walk, she reminded herself of why she'd accompanied him to the bar; but the right moment to speak her mind seemed elusive and with each passing minute she felt more and more nervous, fearing that she was in fact losing her nerve.

Gerry, despite the pilsner and his intoxicating desire for Helen, did sense her resistance to his touch. She wouldn't even look at him. But faced with such delineated, fawn-like beauty he buried his own irritation at what in the seventies he would have dismissed as frigidity, instead telling himself that she was only young, and that she probably needed more time. Betting she'd be worth it in the end, he conceded to take it slowly. "Listen, Helen," he began, "why don't we go out for bite to eat one night? I'm sure Tricolo's would stay open for me. We could go after the show on Friday. A bottle of wine? A couple of pizzas…? It'd be a giggle. What do you say?" To Gerry Neon this felt like begging.

"Gerry," she said abruptly, taking his hand, shaking but determined. "I'm glad we're talking, just the two of us, privately…" Dry mouthed she at last gulped her vodka orange, adding "because there's something I need to say to you. I don't know if …"

The taking of his hand, the momentous eye contact, the earnest demeanor; he could tell she was about to give him the brush off, and it seemed to him he'd been made to beg for the privilege. For the second time today a teenager – *a teenager* – had got the better of him. Before she could finish, he interrupted, saying: "You're worried about my reputation, aren't you?"

Misunderstanding him, Helen thought of Mandy Monroe, cast off and sorrowful, and of the reputedly countless other notches on his bejeweled Elvis belt. "Something like that. Yes. I don't want to be just another conquest. And besides, Mandy's devastated, you know? Poor woman. And I don't want…"

"She'll get over it," he said curtly. With meaty hands he grabbed her waist and moved in close. Then, alluding to an altogether different reputation, he said: "No. You misunderstand. You needn't worry about my size. I take my time and can be very gentle." Despite the meteorite of Women's Liberation, this seventies dinosaur was far from extinct.

"What?" she shrieked, prising his hands from her body, standing up to leave.

"It's okay, it's okay. I misjudged the situation. I'm sorry." He held up his hands, smirking.

"Look Gerry," she spoke politely, professionally, "I'm not interested in you. Please leave me alone."

Still smirking he said: "It's okay, it's okay to be a little scared. We can take it slowly. And there are other ways… You have a pretty mouth." He reached for her cheek, and pressed his thumb against her lips.

"What are you doing? You're being disgusting!" She threw off his hand.

"Oh, I'm sure you'll come around to me. Might be better for you if you did."

"What do you mean 'better for' me?"

"You like dancing on the show, don't you?"

"What? You're threatening to fire me if I don't go to bed with you?"

"I'm just saying… You want to dance on my show… I like to sleep with dancers. It's quite simple."

"There is no way I am ever going to sleep with you!"

"Well in that case you have a problem."

"No, I don't. I won't let you bully me. Martin stood up to you and so will I!"

"Martin? Why are you mentioning that streak… Oh I see! Now I get it."

"No, you don't. I…"

"You two are sweethearts, aren't you?"

"Regardless of whether I have a boyfriend or not, I'm not interested in you."

"I'll tell you what, I'll let lover boy Martin keep his job as well." Gerry smirked again.

"I've tried asking you nicely," there were tears in her voice and flames in her eyes, "just leave us alone!" She returned to Vikki and the other Hel's Belles.

***

After his act of glass-smashing violence at the arcade, Martin tore aimlessly around Grumby's seafront and centre. It took him a while to calm down, to get over his I-hate-everyone monologue. He reached the end of the main drag and marched back again; he climbed up steep steps and swung his arms down cobbled hairpins; he charged up this side street and down that… all until either by chance or subconscious design he found himself outside The Galleon. In a dry swallow he understood he had reached his destination. He forced a croaky "Alright, mate?" and tattoo-and-tendon-man waved him in.

He hopped and shifted at the bar, trying and failing to catch the barman's eye. Looking sideways he discovered that there was at least a football shirt and a cleavage ahead of him in the lateral queue. He filled his lungs with the damp air and prepared himself for the wait. Behind him the resident geriatric duo played nondescript jazz, and several times he glanced over his shoulder at their tradesmen's proficiency and their three good eyes, but each time his gaze would return immediately to the barman, the cleavage, the optics, the barman, the bar mat, anywhere, everywhere… With no mental focus and no striding and swinging to occupy his limbs, he began to shake. It was as if some cosmic percussionist had taken a hold of his muscles. Contract. Relax. Contract. Relax. Ten times a second he shook and could not stop shaking. It was absurd, funny even. Was he in shock? Had the fight with Gerry and the vandalism that followed resurfaced now as some delayed physiological response? He held onto the bar and laughed to himself.

Football shirt made a triangle of his hands and spun away with three pints. "I'll be with you in a minute, mate," said the barman reassuringly before turning to the woman, as if Martin's strange agitation was conspicuous and something to pacify. When eventually served, Martin flew the first pint of Export even before he'd received his change, which he then used to order a second pint, in a manner similar to that of a chain smoker who uses the remains of one cigarette to ignite the next. The slight, cadaverous, barman spoke to him:

"None of your lot in tonight, is it the Midnight Matinee?"

"What? Er, no. That's on Saturday. Tonight it's bowling."

"Didn't fancy it?"

"Not really."

"You alright, mate? You look… I don't know. How can I put it? I can't tell if you've just seen a ghost or just won the Pools." He thumbed the beer tap closed with a splash.

"Oh. I dunno. One or the other, I suppose. Yeah, I'm okay, thanks." Receiving his second pint Martin added: "I'll let you know once…," he raised a hand to catch a burp, "once I've figured it out."

Spilling a little, he walked over to a table and sat down. He held onto his low stool, tucking a thumb beneath each buttock as if to pinion his arms to stop them from flapping. He stared at his pint. Rising chains of bubbles reminded him of that school experiment in which oxygen would stream from an upturned sprig of pondweed, the outward signifier of some dark reaction. Count the bubbles, his teacher had instructed, as they sped to the surface, unquantifiable. He removed a burning thumb from under the seat of his jeans and drank his drink, still shaking, but less so.

Looking up he saw that The Galleon was about half full. A quick survey confirmed the absence of any of his "lot." This was a shame because he felt like talking. Instead he concentrated hard, on his beer and on his thoughts. His residual shaking didn't feel like the fright of a near miss or the fear of imminent doom. It was more like extreme eagerness or impatience. In Gerry he may have accused the wrong man but the whole ring-photograph-Son-of-Showbiz revelation had left him excited about what was to come next. The paternity secret was out! Perhaps the past could now be resolved, at least in his mind, and he wondered if he could even make peace with his mum: could she give confirmation to his truth; could he give her his forgiveness? He drained his glass and counted his coins.

"Back again, eh. Thirsty?" asked the barman.

"Yes. And drinking to something."

"Good, so you've figured it out then. Tell me more, drinking to what?"

"The truth!"

"The truth? Wow. I didn't expect that of a Tuesday evening. The truth will set you free…"

"I certainly hope so."

Amber pouring, he touched his breast pocket. He felt the folded photo he'd stowed there. Branded into his memory it burned once more, and he realized there was only one person in the world he wanted to talk to. "Listen," Martin said, "I've got to go. Just give us a half, just half fill it." He slapped the contents of his fist on the bar, said: "Keep the change," and necked the inexact half pint, before making for the exit like a man on a peace mission.

Another wet walk home in the small hours, but Martin had never before journeyed through drab urban Grumby with such hope. His route and the surroundings were unchanged, but there was, in his mind at least, the embryonic possibility that his destination from now on could be different. He hadn't moved to Number Six Glenside from Number Five, and he didn't yet live alone in a bedsit on Colville Road, as he aspired. No, his bricks and mortar destination remained the semi he grew up in, with the cracked concrete path and the stiff gate that scraped it. But, armed with *the truth*, his was now an address at which honesty and liberty could reside, where previously they could not. He believed he could now *live* with his mum, rather than just lodge under the same roof. This was the putative difference in his destination, a born again difference in his experience of living there, and the reason he walked with hope in his heart.

Seeing he was close to Lorraine's, his mum's hairdressers, he spontaneously crossed the road and stood on the pavement outside it. How uncharitable of him never to have been inside these premises, he thought. Perhaps he should visit her here...? Streetlights reflected off the glass frontage obscuring his view so he cupped his hands to his face and pressed them against the window. He scrutinized. The dim interior looked just like an authentic ladies' hairdressing salon, with two simple barber's chairs and a shampooing sink shaped for the necks of clients. There were shelves piled neatly with plump towels and a floor unit well stocked with a proud regiment of shampoos and conditioners with brand names of which Martin had heard. Even a stack of magazines had a neat, conscientious quality to it. This was Lorraine Collier's domain and it looked professional. He didn't know why this should surprise him, but it did. And then on the wall – the wall she must stand in front of for at least eight hours a day – he saw two framed photographs. Straining, he could just make out with his hand binoculars his brother's "Fame" tee shirt in one, and in the other he saw himself smart and respectable in his school uniform. It was silly but this prosaic detail confirmed what he now felt foolish to have doubted, that his mum loved him. He kissed the window. With both sadness and joy he continued his walk home, to his mum.

Inside Number Five, just beside the front door, there was a small windowsill on which there crowded a glass bowl of 1ps and 2ps, a telephone and two strongman-sized directories, never once thumbed. He hung his Yale on a key-shaped rack of hooks, just below the sill, and smiled to see his mum's bunch not hanging there but rather thrown in the bowl above with the coppers. He took *her* keys and hung them next to his. In the kitchen he filled the kettle with enough water for *two* cups and, hearing an echo of his mum's nagging, belatedly removed his shoes and placed them in the basket in the hallway.

A cup in each hand, he stooped to nose the hall light off and the landing light on, spilling a little of the hot beverage. He climbed the stairs, feeling hopeful and fearful, compassionate and cruel. Gently, and with courage, he toed his mum's bedroom door ajar, saying: "Mum, can we talk? I've got a brew for you." Nothing. Opening the door further a wedge of light illuminated her cocooned form. From her hair he could tell she was facing away from him. He entered and stood beside the bed. Her near corpse gave a questioning moan. "Mum, I've got a brew for you!" he said with greater urgency, placing the cup on a bedside chest. The room smelled of face cream and sour, volatile exhalations.

"Martin? What time is it?" Her words were quiet... slow...monotonous...

"Late, Mum. I need to talk to you. Here's a cup of tea."

"What? Can't we talk in the morning?" she slurred. "I need to sleep, sweetheart, I've got work tomorrow."

"But we always miss each other. Can't we talk now?"

"Shush, you'll wake Adam." There was a pause and a temporary stillness before she turned her head, looking over her shoulder in his direction. "Is it important?" she sighed, resignedly.

"Yes."

"Wait downstairs. I'll be down in a minute."

Lorraine Collier twisted and hauled herself until she was sat up. She pinched the bedside lamp on and saw that it was nearly half-one. "Bloody hell," she moaned to herself. She took a sip of too hot tea, feeling rather more annoyed and duty bound than concerned. Heavy-headed and dead-limbed, she slid her legs out of bed and sat a moment. Eventually, on her feet and tying her dressing gown, a maternal instinct awoke in her and she began to wonder what on Earth the matter could be.

In the lounge, Martin stood with his arms by his side and a photograph – *the* photograph – unfolded in his hand. His tea steamed behind him on the mantelpiece next to a carriage clock. Despite his chronological adulthood, somewhere inside he was still a ten-year-old boy and it felt as if he was acting above himself to summon his mum to a conversation that she would take as a telling off. Another thing was that despite his compassion for the earlier version, the pathetic sixteen-year-old Lorraine Collier, and despite his willingness to forgive the bitter, drunken woman she had become, she most probably would become very upset by what he had to say. After all, what mother would want to hear their bastard son name their deserting, untold of father, and to then hear them ask why for two decades they had kept the man's identity from them? Martin hated what he was bound to do. Even though it had been *her* secret, *her* dishonesty, and *his* lifelong deficiency, he didn't want to upset his mum. But, with the truth told they would both have so much to gain…

Lorraine entered and sat down on the sofa, almost hugging her cup of tea. "Well, Martin," she said yawning, looking at her son, "this had better be Earth-shattering. What is it darling?" Her face was an oval of kindness and concern.

Martin looked down on this open face with a profound feeling of unease. She appeared so credulous, so lacking in self-preservation. He would have preferred the worldly asymmetry of suspicion. Raising his hand to his mouth, a yawn bought him a few seconds more: he didn't know how to begin. Thankfully he didn't have to…

"What is it? You look awful. What's the matter? Are you in trouble?" she said.

"No. This is the matter." He held up the photograph.

"What is it? I can't see…" She sat forward.

"A picture of you and Gerry Neon. Here…" He held it closer for her to take.

"What?" The words took a drowsy moment to register. Gerry Neon, he said. The name sounded familiar to her, but wrong. Neon? A nickname, surely… Did he mean Noble? He meant Gerry Noble, that bastard Gerry Noble. "I've never heard of him?" It was her turn to buy time. She shuffled forwards and reached for the photo, clumsily dropping it on the carpet.

Martin's hair trigger pulled, indignation once more shot from him. "Yes you have. Ger-ry Ne-on! He tops the bill where I work. You know, the pier? There are posters of him all over town. His face is plastered on the side of buses!" Without satisfaction he added: "You'll remember him as Gerry Noble…"

"Yes, you're right, I know the one. Sorry, I'm tired. My mind's fuzzy. I don't remember ever posing with him for a photograph, though." Reluctantly she stretched her hand down to the floor and picked up the thing. Where the hell did he find it? She sat back and took it in. There in black and white was the image of the handsome, callous young man she had spent her entire adult life trying to forget; the man for whom love and hate still seemed indivisible. She stiffened and made a mask of her face. "Oh, is that him? Smug bugger, wasn't he? I don't see me, though…" She sipped her tea.

"That's *your* hand, mum, on his thigh."

"How can you tell? It could be anybody's."

"Look at the ring. Isn't that the one Grandma bought you in Whitby?"

"Oh, you could get rings like that anywhere. Still can. Anyway it's on the wrong finger. No, it's not my hand. Like I said, I don't remember ever being photographed with Gerry Neon, or Gerry Noble." She wasn't lying, she didn't remember. The photo was a profane revelation to her and she discarded it to the arm of the sofa, face down.

"But you used to work at the Opera House so it could be your hand, couldn't it?"

"What do you mean? I don't follow."

"I mean you were there, it *could* be your hand, and it might as well be!"

"That makes no sense, 'it might as well be'? I'm sorry, Martin, but…"

"Mum, I've been backstage at the Opera House. I've seen all the photographs, of the acts like this one, each of 'em grinning, all smug and smirking, each with their hangers-on, their girlfriends. You were a hanger-on, weren't you? A girlfriend? I mean, if that isn't your hand, if it's not you in *this* photograph, then aren't there others just like it where it *is* you? Seems reasonable to me."

"Martin, you're putting two and two together and coming up with five!"

"Am I? A pretty girl like you? Star-struck? Wanting to make the big time?"

"The big time?" Lorraine mocked her son with a laugh, and then looked straight at him, continuing: "I was only an usherette for goodness-sake!"

"And that's not all, is it?"

"What do you mean?" She began to panic a little; what did he know that she hadn't told him?

"Dennis said you *performed* there for a time as well, as a singer. The last week of the season you depped for the previous girl, who left without warning. You never told me that. But Dennis did. He said you sang there on stage, and you did really well, you went down a bomb in fact, until the last night…"

Martin's words exhumed long buried memories. The last performance… Dying a death in front of the world and his wife… The unspeakable, unspoken of episode in the dressing room that preceded it… These two events taken together constituted the defining night of her blighted life. "Oh, Dennis can exaggerate. I just used to sneak a go on the mic at sound checks, that's all. I think the organist had a thing for me."

"Well, somebody did because I popped out nine months later!" Despite himself, Martin sniggered at this cruel humour.

"Yes," she said, her eyes falling to the floor, "you did."

"I don't know why you've never told me you were a singer, a proper singer, unless there was something you were trying to hide…So, are you going to tell me now?" Martin took a step forwards.

"What?" She looked up.

"The great unspoken secret of this dysfunctional family? Or do I have to keep on guessing?"

"Don't talk so loudly. What are you talking about? I don't understand…"

"Are you going to tell me who my father was, is?"

Lorraine foolishly thought that she had dealt with this

absence, this congenital want long ago. "Oh. It's not…"

"What? It's not what? Look Mum, I'm *not* going to lay in bed another night, another day gone, just to stare through the velux at the clouds and the blackness, *still* not knowing what *every son needs to know*." He choked on the words. Neither party heard the light footsteps coming down the stairs.

"But… you wouldn't understand."

"You're right, I *don't* understand. 'Oh, he was just some fly-by-night character, who took advantage of me,' that's what you said the last time I asked. 'Just a ladies' man that I fell for when I didn't know any better.' 'You're better off without him.' 'He didn't deserve a son.' These are the things you've said to me over the years without telling me the one thing I wanted to know." He made a numeral of his hand. "His name! Well, I know now. *Gerry Neon*. Isn't it? Or someone like him."

"But, I didn't hide it from you – I *couldn't* tell you!" Lorraine pressed a knuckle to her tearful eye.

"Well, you're not denying it! It *is* Gerry Neon, isn't it? It's him!" Martin pointed at and then rushed over to the photograph, flipping it back to visibility, stabbing the image twice with his finger. "Him! He's my father!" He retreated back to the mantelpiece.

With naked eyes Lorraine looked at her son and said quietly: "Perhaps, yes, it could be."

"What d'ya mean 'could'? You don't *know*?" Martin shifted from foot to foot. Spittle flew on racing breath.

"No. You see… I was young and *stupid*," she hissed this word, before continuing more thoughtfully, with piecemeal phrasing. "I didn't understand. It was the sixties and I thought everyone was doing it, especially those in shows, on stage. Gerry said it was normal to share girlfriends, and I didn't know any better. I was too overwhelmed by it all to think about falling pregnant. I thought he'd..." she coughed with embarrassment, "...I thought he'd pull out. Perhaps I could have refused more than I did, fought more... But then I wouldn't have you. I wanted to be a singer, to go to Manchester, to Liverpool, to be famous. I thought it would make me a woman, a star. I thought Gerry would help me. He didn't, of course."

"I don't understand..."

Calmly Lorraine said: "I only had sex with Gerry a handful of times, always being careful. Except the last time. That time, in the dressing room between houses while the others were in the bar, there was another Noble there as well, the guitarist. He, well, he joined in. I struggled, a bit, but... I thought that was what people like that did. By the time I knew I was pregnant with you, the season had long ended and I didn't know where they were. So, I *don't* know who your father is. It could have been either of them. That's why I never told you. I'm so sorry, Martin. It breaks my heart." She sobbed.

"So...Right, but..."

She placed her cup on the carpet, stood up and walked over to her son, taking his unwilling hand. "Martin. I'm sorry I never told you the truth. I was embarrassed. Ashamed." He pulled it away, but she grabbed again. "I felt stupid. I didn't know how to tell you. I thought it would be easier when you were older, but it got harder. I hoped the past would go away but it didn't, it doesn't." Now with two hands she squeezed his one, pleading with aqueous eyes and a tight voice: "Martin, you're *my* son and I love you."

He didn't expect *this* truth, this uncertainty, this dual reality. It threw him. He didn't *know* anything anymore. He only *felt*, and he felt he needed to be alone. With his free hand he took a fistful of toweling from where the dressing gown crossed Lorraine's heart and he pushed hard, pulling his captured hand away. "How could it be 'normal'," he shouted, his younger brother appearing in the doorway, "to screw two men at once!"

"It isn't. It wasn't. Please don't hate me, Martin. What I did was wrong, but I was the victim. You must see that, please!" She could feel the situation unraveling, and in her son's eyes she saw contempt.

Martin at once understood why his mum was so against his work on the shows, his drumming, *his life*, but the compassion he felt earlier had evaporated and he was no longer minded to kiss and make up. "Maybe you *were* the victim, but so am I!" he said. He stormed out, pushing Adam aside, and ran upstairs.

"Oh, Adam… I'm so sorry you saw that. Your brother's upset about something. Don't worry, darling, it'll all be forgotten in the morning. Come here sweetheart." Kneeling, cuddling her youngest she heard metallic rattles and soft chimes coming from upstairs. And then unbelievably, with twenty-to-two showing on the carriage clock, she heard – the whole street heard – Martin knock seven bells out of his drum kit. The ceiling seemed to flex, the lounge door shook on its hinges and swung several degrees in the wind of sound, and the noise was thunderous.

Lorraine quickly became angry. She kissed Adam's head, got off her knees and ran upstairs. "What the hell do you think you're doing? It's two in the morning! Martin!"

Barricaded behind his kit, her son heard only Simple Minds: sixteenth notes on the hi-hat, the off-beat on the bass drum, d'ga, and the hammering snare – Mel Gaynor himself could not have hit it harder, and Big Mel was famed for hitting hard.

"Martin!" With no switch to flick, no plug to pull, Lorraine stood by the drum set and squeezed a cymbal in a futile attempt to silence her son. "Martin!"

Looking down, his head nodding with the beat, he perceived her in the top of his vision. He watched her pinch his eighteen-inch crash and he hit it. Take that, he thought. Triumphantly he looked up at her face and saw her lips forming his name, her face screwed into a scowl. He played with such aggression that he caught a knuckle on the rim of the snare, removing a divot of flesh. He did a grandstanding fill around the toms, blood spattering the skins as the wound bled freely. To hell with the time. To hell with the neighbours. A second rolling fill reverberated through the house, ending with another ear piercing crash smash. He stopped momentarily and snuffed the ringing metal with his bloody hand. "Yes, Mum? What did you say?" he asked, before commencing again, drowning her protests. He stopped again. "Sorry, I can't hear you," he said before yet again tearing into his rhythm, this time quicker, his hands a blur, globules of blood being flung this way and that.

Incensed, Lorraine forced her way around the kit to where he was sitting. She made desperate, flailing grabs for Martin's bloody sticks, lunging and falling over him. "Stop it, Martin! For God's sake, stop!"

He elbowed her away and kept playing. Duh – ga – duh, duh – ga – duh – d'ga – duh, duh – ga. The bass drum thudded, the snare cracked like a handgun. His mum screamed in his ear, just audibly, and grabbed at his hands and swatted his face, smearing blood that had landed there. Carelessly son caught mother with a stick, 5A hickory on wrist bone.

Lorraine pulled her hand away and wedged it in her armpit, wincing. Her son ended the barrage.

In ringing silence Martin threw down his weapons and stood up. "That was 'Don't You Forget About Me' by Simple Minds. I've been playing it for months, not that you'd know," he said. He took hold of his mum by her upper arms, moved her out of his way and squeezed past. "I'm off," he said indifferently.

"You bloody idiot! Why d'you do that?"

To a neighbour's wall-thumped reprise of the drumming, Martin walked down the stairs and pulled the door to. Lorraine, stroking her throbbing wrist, slumped onto the drum stool and sobbed, feeling sixteen again.

19

For the second time in less than an hour Martin again walked the dark streets of Grumby. His earlier aimless wandering had lead him by chance to The Galleon, but this time, even as he was pulling closed the door of his childhood home with battle drums still ringing in his ears, an instinctive notion of where he needed to be was already forming in his mind.

As a first staging post *en route* to this ultimate, abstract destination he went to the glen. This narrow, wooded valley that led unlit down into Pagoda Park was even on a bright summer's day as dim as dusk, but at 2:30am on a Wednesday morning it was as dark, and quiet, as a cave. He used to play here as a kid, chasing his toy boat as it rocked and bumped down the stream, or else he would sit high up under the bridge surrounded by graffiti, looking down on the dog walkers.

The path followed the silent, black water as it slid like crude oil through the glen. It occurred to him that he had not *slammed* the door. Or punched a wall. Or kicked anything. Even mentally he felt no anguish. His mum and he had just fought World War Three, and his chances of ever knowing the identity of his father had been exactly halved, dashing his previous, hypothetical certainty, and yet he felt nothing. Normally after a row he'd be raw like a blister and his thoughts would chafe him with all the things he hadn't said. But, by confronting his mum precisely with the worst thing, the only thing on his mind, all other words and phrases had been rendered subordinate. He had cross-examined her, he had presented her with photographic evidence of her past and his origin and yet still he was none the wiser. Only a blood test could confirm Gerry's paternity now – as if that would ever happen! And who was the "guitarist" anyway, the second perpetrator, Gerry's partner in crime? As if *he'd* still be around! There was nothing more he could say or do: the past had no answer for him. Walking in the dark, damp stillness of the glen, he realised the best he could do was to leave the past alone, allow the wound to heal and to live with the scar.

Nonetheless he felt he couldn't return home yet, not until his mum had left for work, which would be some time after eight. It wasn't that he didn't believe her explanation. Already he was beginning to accept that she had been the victim, and even now foresaw that one day he'd pity her, forgive her and put his arm around her. It was just that in the weeping aftermath, however numb he felt, he couldn't help but blame her in some way. Perhaps he'd go and visit her at work, in a day or two, when the scab of sympathy had formed.

As a matter of fact he wondered if he himself still had a job, but he didn't much fancy going in to find out. There was one thing, however, that made his doing so inevitable. In his joy-starved heart he hadn't yet given up on Helen, and he wanted to see her one more time, even if doing so would only feed his hopeless fantasy. With perverse humour he calculated she had always been unattainable and so his probable sacking and banishment from the theatre could hardly make her any more so. But he had to try…

With time stretching before him like a blank audio cassette he almost welcomed the prospect of being alone with his thoughts, of making *new* mental recordings. He watched the stream pour dark and glossily into the boating lake that ringed the pagoda. He crossed a small bridge and followed the now treeless perimeter path in the faint light.

He thought of the time he'd wasted racking his brain for a follow up to the Galapagos line: "Is there anyone in from… Tierra del Fuego?" or whichever location he'd decided on. It struck him that his real motive, for all his scriptwriting pretensions, had been to impress or even befriend Alan the spesh act. He understood now that this was a naïve, pointless ambition, but… He gave a mental shrug. And then there were the *years* he'd wasted on his unknown, and as it happens unknowable, father. Again, too bad. It seemed he spent far too much time worrying about the past and about other people. Well, not any more. He now knew his destination, but it wasn't a place, it was a time: he was heading for his future, and it began now. The past was history, and he was free of it.

He exited the park and angled across the road. A few stars shone in the indigo sky and an unearthly blue light glowed in the east. Striding out, he accelerated up Burnistead Road, past the municipal swimming baths. By the time he'd crested the hill, he felt his neck and forehead bedewing in the cool. He vaulted a low wall and landed on the front lawn of his old secondary school – a single story, flat-roofed, prefabricated, unambitious building set in plain grounds. The last time he'd visited Field Grove Comprehensive was to receive his A-level results, almost exactly a year ago.

On the un-mown grass, he felt oddly conspicuous and so aimed for the cover of the buildings. By the time he reached the path, his trainers were damp through to his socks. He cut between the kitchen bins and the still-used temporary huts where he'd flattened Philip Plumber in his only ever schoolboy fight. At Rural Studies he bent to drink from a tap by the greenhouse and then urinated with carefree zigzags. He finished his tour of the grounds at the severely double-faulted tennis court, taking a seat on a brick retaining wall and resting his back on the chain-link fence, which bowed out at the top from being scaled. He looked out over the playing fields towards the quickening east.

He remembered in the end liking Plummy, who had been a bit of a swot like himself. Their spotty, pubertal fight had started in Art, with a ludicrous argument over the hair drier that was used to speed the drying of watercolours. One of them had queue jumped and there had been some pushing and shoving. After the lesson Plummy had followed him, threatening to "eradicate" his face and pushing him in the back. On the second push, and with a gathering crowd, Martin recalled spinning around and landing a punch smack in the middle of his aggressor's cheek, knocking him flat. Like a champion pug he had literally been lifted onto shoulders and paraded to French. The last time Martin spoke to Plummy was results day, when they compared their similarly good grades with piss-taking good humour. Thereafter, one teenage intellectual with the world at his feet had gone to University, while the other had remained in Grumby, sweeping a stage for other people, illuminating other people's ambitions.

University, thought Martin: *he* could have gone to university. Still could, in fact. He'd have to contact his teachers again to ask for help with the forms and the whole application process, but nonetheless... And with *his* home circumstances he'd definitely get a grant to live off. And wasn't there even some financial help with accommodation? He *could* go to university, and in the silvery blue light he imagined that he might. He could go to *Sheffield* University to study something biological, say Cell Biology or Microbiology, or else Chemistry. He could grow his hair. Join a band. Listen to John Peel. In fact forget the sciences, he could study Philosophy or Politics. In Sheffield. Wasn't the so-called Socialist Republic of South Yorkshire a "hotbed" of politics, especially since the Miner's Strike? It sounded so dramatic, but was he interested? Nah, scrap Politics. But Sheffield... He remembered at school reading about its vibrant music scene. He'd found a copy of The Enemy lying around in the sixth form common room during a free. He remembered feeling self-conscious poring over its esoteric, cliquey content, as if it wasn't meant for the likes of him. It seemed more about novelty and fashion than crotchets and quavers; it seemed beneath him but also somehow beyond him. He read about this "*industrial*" music coming from Sheffield, "*industrial funk*" even, made by bands with strange names like "Chakk" and "Cabaret Voltage", or something. It sounded weird and exciting, and just reading the words had made him feel, well, cool. *So*, he could join a band in Sheffield and play industrial music. And his name, Martin Collier... *there* was a name destined for industrial music! Jeff

Porcaro could never play industrial music! He could meet people from London. He could get a girlfriend with dyed black hair called Candida. He could get a girlfriend full stop. And he thought that Adam, his little brother, could come and stay with him, in Sheffield, in his better future. And Helen too.

***

Hours later, in yolk yellow breakfast daylight, Martin stood hiding in the bushes and small trees opposite Number Five Glenside. Hungry was not the word, but cereal and eggs on toast would have to wait. Neither were cold or tired adequate adjectives to describe his tramp-like state, but a hot shower and duvet would have to wait too. His mum was still at home. He would eventually inform her of his plan for tertiary education, but not now, not while he was light-headed with hunger and drunk with fatigue. Hidden by vegetation, like a somnambulist woodsman, he swayed with a dreamy stare.

In the undergrowth he became aware of something moving near him. He heard quick fidgety movements through the leaves and branches; he heard rapid panting, whispered like a miniature steam train. But his conscious mind was something viscous behind the eyes and it was an effort to think, to deduce backwards from an effect to a cause. The fidgeting, whispering something touched his feet and he looked down to see a busy little terrier, a Scottie dog sniffing his trainers. And then he heard: "Freddie. Freddie. Come here!" There was a pause before the voice added: "Martin, is that you?" Like an oil tanker he turned to see

Dennis. For what could have been three seconds or a minute he stood dumbly, dazed and swaying.

"Martin," repeated Dennis, "what are you doing?" The dog scurried breathlessly back to his owner.

"Nothing. Just waiting. I'm so tired."

"Waiting? Have you been drinking?"

"Yeah. Until about eight hours ago."

"You're acting very strangely, Martin. Have you been home yet?"

"Yeah. About seven hours ago."

"What? Oh, and then you had a drunken argument with your mum and stormed out again, correct?"

"Actually no, I was quite calm. But we did fall out, and I did…"

"Come here lad. Let's talk about it."

"What's the point, Dennis? I'm going… I'm moving to Sheffield."

***

Mid-morning, Wednesday, Gerry Neon awoke alone, threw back the duvet and sat like a collapsed sand bag on the edge of his king-sized. Several ounces of eighteen carat swung beneath his sandpaper chin. He coughed and took a packet of cigarettes from the top of the bedside drawers and lit one. Inhaling deeply, he considered his words: hasty; we all make mistakes; one last chance. He hauled his congested mass to its full five and a half feet of height and crossed the deep shag of the bedroom to the expansive tiles of the en suite, where his piss echoed roundly. Downstairs in a dressing gown, he traversed further acres of ceramic and put the kettle on. He lifted his brief case onto the breakfast bar, thumbed the clasps and retrieved his little black phone book. He took a carton of milk from a desolate fridge and contemplated the remains of a pork pie on a plate streaked with brown sauce that lay next to the sink. The needlessly huge, Summer-rented, new build echoed like an empty bank vault to the sound of crockery for one.

With a dark brown brew in one hand, the plate of leftovers and the book of numbers in the other and with a second cigarette in his mouth, he shambled his way to the lounge. A large mirror hung on the wall, reflecting only the peach of a second, bare wall. On the arm of an apricot sofa rested the telephone. He sat, tapped his ash into the residue of brown sauce and phoned Bernie Giggs.

"Hi, Bernie. Not playing golf today?" The tarry tea, the nicotine, the pie – the breakfast of a king – quickly revived Gerry so that he was sparking and joking with the impresario in no time. He soon got to his point: "Listen, Bernie. About the young lad, the stagehand, Martin. Er, I think I was a bit hasty. Anyone can make a mistake and, er, well… Yes, that's right Bernie, yeah, keep him on."

The second phone call he made was to Dave Newhurst, his musical director. After further, appropriate banter he reached his second point of the day, a question: "Just had an idea for the show," he said. "Your keyboard, what's it called the DX… Yeah, DX7, does it have a church organ sound effect on it? Yeah, great. Could you play the Wedding March for me, you know "Here comes the bride…" You know the one? Great. Well, in the finale, either tonight or tomorrow, I might need you to play it for me…" If Helen preferred a teenage boy to a real man, he thought, couldn't he at least have a little fun at their expense? A little public embarrassment?

20

Alec Dennis Jeffreys had always looked out for Martin. Because he'd walked in on the act that had spawned him, because he'd been there at the moment of his creation, he'd always felt a pull of responsibility towards the boy. And over the years, watching Lorraine Collier prove herself with her chronic drinking and her reckless taste in men to be an unreliable mother, Dennis had come to view himself as a kind of guardian uncle. At times it had seemed he was raising the boy himself: *he'd* been the one to remove the five-year-old's stabilizers; *he'd* been the first to take him sledging during a particularly alcoholic, Glam Rock Christmas. And with each of these life events, with each benchmark moment, he'd found his affections for Martin grow and grow until he loved him as if he were his own.

With the surge of puberty he'd watched the adolescent's fuse shorten and the fatherless chip on his shoulder grow into a tree trunk. He knew therefore that the man's anger Martin had displayed at The Galleon over his drum kit, of all things, was only the most recent and most extreme expression of his character. However, the violence of the fire extinguisher thrown into the CCTV monitor, and the strange loitering in the bushes were new behaviours, and ones which played on Dennis' mind. And then there was the gap in the rogue's gallery outside Matcham's Bar: surely it had been Martin who had trespassed and stolen the Opera House's property, leaving a pale rectangle on the wall while trying to fill in his own blank? Who else would want a photograph of Gerry Neon taken, oh, *nineteen or twenty years ago?* Somehow the lad must have worked it out. And now that he'd crossed this Rubicon of criminality, Dennis was genuinely worried where the change in behaviour might lead him, especially with Gerry Neon in the frame. So, "Uncle" Dennis decided he should talk to Lorraine Collier before her son did something dangerous.

With Freddie full of rabbit-flavoured horsemeat and "the goodness of marrow bone", he left one sleeping dog lying in its basket in order to rouse another. He walked the short distance to "Lorraine's". Unsure of what to say and a little hesitant, he under-estimated the effort needed to open the weighty glass door and so entered the premises at the second push, feeling foolish and clearly pink about the gills. The inside of the salon, with its feminine smells and a back room for intimate waxings, was an uncomfortable place for a middle-aged bachelor, who cut his own hair with a trimmer from the chemist's, and Dennis' embarrassment burned through his cheeks.

The proprietor heard the door close over the roar of the hair dryer she was holding and turned around. Seeing Dennis, she silenced the Braun, excused herself and almost went for him. "Hello, my sweetheart! What a lovely surprise!" she said loudly, holding his reddening face between her two taloned hands and kissing his dumbstruck lips firmly. "What brings you here?" She didn't really listen to his vague reply and interrupted him, adding: "It's nice to see you, but as you can see I'm with a client and I've another wash, cut and blow dry at 11:20, and then... Actually, can you come back after two?"

At 2:05pm Dennis watched from across the road as a woman with huge and very lovely hair left the salon. He waited a few moments and then returned, this time pushing the door with adequate force and bracing himself, ready for Lorraine's torrent of affection. There was no repeat of her earlier outpouring, however. Instead she stayed at the far side of the room, topping up a "professional" shampoo bottle with Presto's own brand, and barely looking up to acknowledge her re-visitor. Dennis instantly sensed the change in her mood, now that there wasn't a customer to play the bubbly hostess in front of. He let the door close behind him.

"Oh, it's you, is it?" she said.

"Is this still not a good time?" he said.

"*Could* there be a good time for you to visit me?"

"What? Have I done something?"

"You tell me."

"Stop playing games, Lorraine, What d'you mean?"

"I mean, what have you been telling Martin about me?"

Dennis had guessed his words at The Galleon would come back to him, but Lorraine seemed ready for twelve bloody rounds, a reaction out of all proportion to the minor confidence he had betrayed. Martin must have put two and two together and worked it all out. "Lorraine, whatever I told him, and I didn't tell him much, I'm sorry. But it's only what you should've told him years ago. Listen, I'm here to talk about the lad. It's serious."

"Oh, God! What's happened? Tell me he's okay…" As quick as a yanked waxing strip her manner changed again, from woman scorned to frantic mother.

"Yes, love, he's okay. He's fine. I saw him this morning, hanging around in the bushes opposite your house, which was a bit odd, but he's okay."

"Oh, thank God." She became tearful, noticeably relieved. "We argued late last night and he left, upset. I waited up all night for him, but he didn't come back. I've been worried sick. I didn't know whether to call the police or not."

"No, no, you can stop worrying now. He's okay, but he *has* been acting strangely and I'm concerned about him. I'm worried he might get himself into serious trouble."

"Oh, Dennis. So am I. We need to talk to him, he needs our help."

"When I spoke to him this morning he seemed drunk. He said he was moving to Sheffield."

"Sheffield?"

"That's what he said."

"Why's he going to Sheffield? He's not going to Sheffield, surely…?"

"Like I said, he's acting strange."

Lorraine folded her arms across her bust and gently bit her thumb. Her eyes bored holes in the linoleum. For a good half minute she said nothing, and then remembered she had a score to settle with Dennis. "Anyway, what *did* you tell him about me and the Opera House?"

"Only that you weren't just an usherette."

"He *knows* that Gerry Noble might be his dad."

"Well, I didn't tell him that!"

"So how does he know?"

"Look, I bumped into him at The Galleon and he got all emotional, really angry about his drums and how you never take any interest in his life."

"Oh, those stupid things!"

"You see!"

"He's wasting his life."

"Well he doesn't think so. Anyway, I defended you. I stuck up for you. I said you were only protecting him, that you didn't want him to suffer the same disappointment that *you* did on your last night at the Opera House. But he didn't understand because he only thought that you were an usherette, so that's when I had to tell him about you singing. I didn't tell him about what I saw…"

"Well he knows about Gerry. He showed me an old photograph of him with my hand on his lap, or possibly my hand. He's convinced himself that it is because he thinks he recognizes the ring, even though it's far too small and grainy to be sure. He said to me 'It might as well be', and he's got a point. It *could* be my hand in the photo, and he knows it. I *was* star-struck in those days, after all…"

"That explains. He's worked it out…"

"But, Dennis…" Lorraine interrupted. "*I* told him the truth, the whole truth. I told him what I did, what you walked in on. I told him I didn't know who his father was because, well, because it could be either of them. It broke my heart to tell him, I didn't want to, but I told him. And now I feel terrible." She cried.

Dennis took her into his arms. "Well, you did the right thing. It must've been hard for you, love, but you did the right thing. It's a start, Lorraine. You can build a relationship on the truth."

"I hope so, I don't know him anymore." Her tears darkened Dennis' anorak.

He gently pushed her away from him and held her by the upper arms. He fixed her with intense eyes. "The trouble is, love, he's developed a violent streak. He came to see me after the show one night. He was fishing for information, about his dad of course. I left him for a few minutes while I finished off, and that's when he must have seen the photograph of Gerry. He went berserk and threw a fire extinguisher at my TV monitor, destroying it. If he's still upset, still angry, I'm worried what he'll do next. And Gerry Neon? Well, you don't want to mess with him."

"No. The bastard."

"*Or… Perhaps…Maybe* he's at peace now? Maybe telling him the truth was the best thing you could have done?"

"I'm not sure. You didn't see him, Dennis. Last night when he left the house he looked like he hated the whole world. Oh, Dennis, I'm worried. We need to speak to him."

"No, Lorraine. *You* do."

"But, what can I say to him? He hates me."

"No son hates their mother. You've got to find a way to reach him. You've got to show him you love him."

***

That evening, fed, washed and rested, Martin walked to work as usual. The more he imagined going to university the more excited he became. And, although spontaneous and born of sorrow, his plan did ring true; it really *was* a good idea, a brave and personal ambition worthy of the smug look that decorated his face. Martin Collier, Student, he envisaged; Martin Gregory Collier, Bachelor of Science (with Honours); M. G. Collier, BSc (Hons). Impatiently he wondered if it was possible for him to get to University *this year* (through "clearing", was that it?) even though he had never even applied to UCCA... He promised himself he would find out.

Regardless of the next three years, he had no idea what to expect from tonight. He didn't know if he had a job for a start. Kevin hadn't telephoned him with a verbal P45, or to reassure him, although he had been sleeping like a corpse, deaf to the world. He also didn't know if Gerry would continue their hostilities, jumping him in the stairwell. Mostly he approached the evening like an interested spectator: now that he was going to university he could take or leave his job, and as for Gerry, well, he wasn't afraid of *him*. His biggest uncertainty, and the one thing that drove him to the pier, was his status in the eyes of Helen. Would she see him as a brave hero or an unthinking thug? Realistically he doubted she had any opinion of him at all.

Approaching Victoria Pier he was reminded of his act of thuggery: the Grab-a-Teddy arcade machine he had vandalized was swathed in red and white tape and empty of its cuddly, eponymous prizes. He felt a shard of guilt prick his conscience and, scratching an imaginary itch on his eyebrow to conceal his face, entered the pier.

It was almost high tide and only a narrow hem of crowded beach remained. The sea swelled periodically with the shallowest of undulations, like the chest of a sleeping giant. There was hardly a breath of wind to ruffle the calm. Aesthetically Martin delayed his entry to backstage and instead walked twenty yards or so up the south side of the theatre, stopping and leaning on the railings. The sun was still quite high in the sky and he felt its warmth on his cheek. He took a moment to bask in the blue and the gold of the end of the pier.

Not far to his left was an old man. Slight and bent he rested his arms on the top rail. He wore a faded, once-smart striped shirt, with sleeves rolled beyond bony elbows, and the skin of his forearms and balding head was tanned the colour of the tobacco he smoked. Around him on the boards lay the paraphernalia of his day: a flask, a dog-eared newspaper, at least two plastic containers and a fishing rod, propped at forty-five degrees against a stanchion. The taut line led steeply down and he seemed to be staring at where it met the flat, navy water.

"Nice day for it!" said Martin, loudly in the quiet.

"Aye."

"Caught much?"

"Nah."

"Nothing at all?"

"Nothing big enough to take home."

"What you fishing for? Mackerel?"

"Not with this rig!"

"Rig?"

"Tackle."

"Oh."

There was then an uncomfortable pause before the fisherman said: "I'm fishing for bass."

Martin took a few steps towards the man and peered into one of his containers, the contents of which were wriggling. "What are they?" he asked.

"Maddies."

"Maddies?"

"You're a nosey parker, aren't you?"

"Sorry, I'm just interested."

"It's okay. They're ragworms. The little, lively ones are called maddies, by the likes of me."

"And bass like maddies?"

"Well, not today! The tide's right…" He looked at his watch. "…er, not far off high water, so it's nice and still. But it's too bright for bass, really. It's better at dusk, when it's dim, they're less cautious then. But that won't be for a few hours, and by then the tide'll be wrong, too much movement. Still, it's a glorious day."

"That's really interesting. Can you tell me, I've always wondered, how can you choose the kind of fish to catch? What's to stop you hooking a mackerel?"

"It's totally different. You spin for mackerel…"

"Spin?"

"I was just getting to that…" There was a hint of irritation in the man's voice. "A spinner is a metal lure. It's silvery and it looks like a bait fish when you reel it through the water. But you have to keep casting off and reeling in and casting off again, and it's tiring, even with a light rod. It's easy to do mind you, and you don't need to worry about digging for bait or anything like that. I prefer to fish the bottom, in the gully, where the bass go. I like to wait and let the fish come to me."

"What's the gully?"

"Well, it's a sandy beach, isn't it? The tide gouges out a big hole in the sand around each pile, and over time these join up to form a gully that runs the length of the pier. There are two, one on each side. This is a good spot, this side of the pier, because the tide is coming on to me and I can keep my bait in the gully."

"And bass swim in the gully…"

"Correct. That's where their food is, sand eels mostly, and these are prey for predatory fish like bass, which also like maddies, or not as the case may be."

"Why don't you move to another spot?"

"Nah, like I said…" the fisherman looked up from his line and fixed Martin with a wise, impassive half-scowl, saying, "I like to wait and let the fish come to me."

**

Once backstage Martin was intercepted almost immediately by Kevin, who led him to a quiet corner. "Well, after your assault on the top of the bill, it seems, unbelievably, you've had a stay of execution," he said. "For some reason Gerry *doesn't* want your head on a spike, so you've still got a job… Oh, and, huh," the Scotsman laughed and smiled warmly, "well done, lad! I've been chuckling all day thinking about it. Just keep out of his way for a day or two…"

Martin swept the boards. The sequins and the hypnotist's onion he collected may well have been diamonds and truffles. Unannounced a crisp, rich sound filled the stage as drummer Andy, enthroned behind his ten-piece, began his warm up. Instantly Martin's pulse quickened. With a glass to the wall of sound he focused his hearing on the discrete yet fluid playing. God, if he could ever be *that* good a drummer! And the maple kit! There were no rattles and no buzzing, straining overtones like his own newsagent's special; just pure, clean sound.

Inspired, he approach the drum riser, broom in hand, and marveled at the sticks man: his lightning speed around the kit; his interplay between bass and snare that was too complex to follow, never mind hold in your mind; his dancing, riffling thirty-second notes on the hi-hat. The muso paused and took a tuning key to a tension rod. "That was ace!" said Martin, "You are so good!"

"We're getting there."

"How long you been playing?"

"Couple of minutes."

"No, huh, I mean how old were you when you started?"

"Ten."

"Younger than me."

"Oh, do you play?"

"Well, not like you, obviously!"

"You got to start somewhere."

"I got to ask you, can you play the beat to Rosanna by Toto?"

"Oh, yeah, I've heard that track. Jeff Porcaro."

"Yeah, he's amazing. I've been trying for months. I can play it without the ghost notes, but as soon as I try to put those in…" He puffed his cheeks and exhaled in awe-filled speechlessness. He expected Andy to demo the beat, to give an *ad hoc* master class, but he didn't. To his surprise he said:

"Come on then, Rambo. Show me…" The resident drummer downed his sticks and stood up.

Rambo? Gob-smacked, Martin froze statue still. But as soon as he'd visualized himself behind the kit, he dropped the broom and was around the back of the riser and climbing up onto it before you could say "independence of limb". He took the stool, shuffled a moment to get comfortable and then, forgetting Rosanna like the high-maintenance beauty queen she was, tore into Led Zep's Rock and Roll, the beat every aspiring drummer first learns. The fine kit seemed amplified, its sound apparently coming from everywhere, such were its resonance and the acoustics of the stage space.

"Let's hear the Porcaro beat, then," said Andy, raising his voice to be heard.

"Well, erm, it's a shuffle, like this..." Martin played a few bars. "But he puts all these ghost beats in on the snare, like this... You see I can play the hand parts on their own, but as soon as I try to put in the bass drum, well, I just can't play it."

"Yeah, it's nice. It's a half-time shuffle. There's something like it on a Steely Dan track."

"Really? What's it called?"

"Oh, I can't remember. There's lots of great stuff, by 'em though. You should get yourself an album. Anyway, play... play something you *can* play..."

Martin, keen to impress, played his most difficult beat, a James Brown-style funk beat, and he smiled like a boy, whose Christmases had all come at once.

When he looked up, he saw that Helen was watching him, agape. He felt his arms turn to spaghetti and his hands to jelly, but he played on, *he kept his cool*. When he finished, she applauded and woo-hooed him like a cheerleader. "I didn't know you played the drums, Martin!" she enthused. "You're brilliant!"

Other musicians took the stage: Dave Newhurst messed around with jazz chords, while Perry tuned his bass. "Don't stop," encouraged Andy. "Play something else. Play a straight ahead rock beat. Perry'll join in, won't you Pez?"

"Always happy to nurture young talent," said the bassist, much to the amusement of the pianist MD.

"Ignore him, he's a piss-taker. Go on, give it some welly."

Not really sure what to expect, Martin kicked out a basic 4/4 beat, mid-tempo. Perry did indeed join in, with the riff to the theme from Peter Gunn. Was this a joke? Was it mockery? He didn't know. He didn't care: he'd never before played with another musician, and when he heard that walking bass line in synergy with his own playing, it felt magical, as if a kind of alchemy was at play, transmuting the bass and the drums into a golden rhythm section, into precious music. And then the lead guitarist followed the bass riff; and then one of the horns piped up with the melody. Before he knew it, Martin was jamming with the best musicians he was ever likely to meet – and Helen was watching him. Nineteen years was a long time to wait to feel cool, but it had been worth the wait.

21

Afterwards, beneath the stage, Martin was going about his business when someone spoke to him.

"Hello, drummer boy. I thought I might find you down here. You're not hiding from Gerry are you?"

For a split second he stiffened at the accusation of cowardice, but on seeing Helen walking his way, smiling, he laughed and relaxed. "Hi, Helen. No, it's, er, high tide and I'm just, y'know, checking for leaks." He cringed at his own poor comedy.

"Were you worried we were holed beneath the punch-line, or something?"

Oh, thank you, Helen! "Very good! You should write gags."

"Perhaps I should. Anyway, I'm glad I found you. I haven't had the chance to talk to you since you had your fight, with Gerry, and I was… worried about you. Are you okay?"

"Yeah, I'm, er, good, thanks. I thought I'd lost my job, though. It was pretty stupid of me to take on the top of the bill."

"Yes, but he started it. From what I could gather, you

were only defending yourself. And it looks like you could have finished it too, if it hadn't been stopped by that Pete creep."

"Oh, yeah, him."

"But you did really great. You're a bit of a dark horse, aren't you?" She prodded him in the abdomen, planting there a confetti of butterflies.

"I guess so. I just, I dunno…" Nervous, he pinched his chin, smoothing the cleft that resided there.

"Stop talking," said Helen, moving closer. "Listen, a few of us are going out after the show on Saturday. There's a burlesque act on at the Review Bar. Would you like to come?"

"What?" If nineteen years had been an age to wait to feel cool, as he just had while drumming on stage, this sensing of romance came with incomprehensible haste.

"You heard me, silly. Just say 'yes'."

"Well, yes." He laughed. He didn't know what else to do.

Helen did, though. "Good. And Martin?" She reached a hand around the back of his neck and pulled him down, raising her lips to his ear. "This is for standing up to Gerry," she whispered, and kissed him on the cheek. She let go, gave the sweetest of smiles and then turned and walked.

Martin had never known the rear view of a toweling dressing gown fill him with such assurance, and such desire.

***

"I can't believe he still has a job. '*If he's still here, I don't go on!*' that's what you said. Well, he *is* still here and, what's that?" Pete Wheeler cupped a hand to his ear, acting serious, stifling a smirk. "Yep, that's the echo of your applause from the first house. You've lost your bottle, Gee. He kicks your arse, and yet he's still working here. What are you gonna do? Give him fifty lines? '*I must not make a laughing stock of the top of the fucking bill.*' You've lost it, mate. Gone soft."

"Patience, Pete. Don't you worry, he'll get what's coming to him, and it'll be a lot easier if he's still working here."

"What you gonna do? Throw him off the pier?"

"D'ya remember Blackpool, 1972, South Pier? That Jimmy What's-his-face? Man overboard!"

"H'yeah. You're lucky he didn't break his legs, the tide was almost out!"

"Oh he jumped."

"Your honour."

"H'uh."

"Seriously though, what are you gonna do?"

"Dunno yet. Summat'll come to me."

Gerry strutted into the en suite, while Pete made two mugs of tea. "Got any biscuits?"

"Have a look in my briefcase. I bought some digestives on the way in."

"What about that young dancer you were on about? The one you were 'well in' with?"

Gerry emerged from the toilet, zipping up his fly. "That fucking prick teaser! Apparently fame, money and a big dick aren't enough for this new breed. She might have to be a Gerry Neon Last Night Special."

"You pirate!"

There was a knock at the door and comic Ashley Kidd came in. "Evening Gee, Pete."

"Alright, Ash. How's it looking out front?"

"Full."

"That's what we like to hear! So Kiddo, what can I do for you?"

"Just checking you're still okay for Saturday?"

"Saturday? What's happening Saturday?"

"Football! You remember. We're playing the Opera House…"

"A football match? I must've missed that one."

"But Gee! It's the local derby and you're our Midfield General…"

"Don't worry Our Kidd! Just pulling your leg. I've been doing shuttle runs on the prom, and practising my keepy-uppy, and everything!"

"You'd forgotten, hadn't you?"

"Er, yes."

"S'alright. Half the crew had forgotten 'n' all. It's on the playing fields, up by Field Grove School. Kick off eleven o'clock. There's a sign-up sheet on the notice board. Can I put your name down?"

"Is Darren Daniel playing?"

"He said so, when I arranged it with him. He might have a few ringers up his sleeve, 'n' all."

"Up 'is arse, more like. Go on then. I'm sure I can manage a run out for twenty minutes, or so. Just until I've messed up his hair do."

Pete laughed.

"It is a friendly, y'know! Good, I'll sign you up, then. And you, Big Man?"

"Suppose so," said Pete.

"Nice one! We've almost a team."

"Should I make a few calls?" said Gerry, "Get a ringer or two of our own? There's Barry Mann at The Sands. Scouser. He used to play a bit, had a trial for Liverpool or somewhere."

"Yeah, Toxteth Magistrate's Court!" said Pete.

"Ha! Yeah, why not? Might as well make it competitive. Nice one." said Ashley, turning to leave.

"But, Ash! Wait. I've got no boots."

"S'alright, Gee. It's just a kick about. You can wear trainers. You do own trainers?"

"Er, I'll sort something out. Ta, mate. Do a good spot." The door closed. "You'll get some boots for us both, won't you, Pete? Size eight should do for me." Pete didn't answer. Gerry too went quiet, thinking of Martin's long legs, a clumsy tackle and a pot and crutches. "Better get some shin guards as well."

***

Slowly the Earth rolled over into Thursday; a brilliant morning. Martin opened his eyes and spun out of bed, eager to begin the first day of the rest his life. The dual prospects of University and Helen, but mostly Helen, filled him with excitement. He bolted his cereal standing. His Walkman called to him from the breakfast bar. He grabbed it, pushed rewind and returned to his bedroom, running up the stairs while the mechanism whirred. He took his drum stool and let the foam lips of the headphones close over his ears. The spools halted with a click. Toto IV, Side A was now rewound to the beginning, and Track 1, "Rosanna", was cued up and ready to listen to.

He pressed "Play" and heard the drummed intro as he'd never in all his forensic listens heard it before. The snare, the hi-hat and the bass drum seemed to separate before his very ears. There were now three Jeff Porcaroes, each playing a different part, and yet each indivisible from the whole. At last Martin understood this trinity – the fiendish hand parts, with the unholy ghost notes at odds with the accented second and fourth; the independent foot, with the two off-beats on the bass drum. Moreover he *felt* the shuffle, the 1-2-3-1-2-3 feel, like the rhythm of a train on its tracks.

He removed the 'phones and picked up his sticks, confident that he would now master the beat. He played and played, at first erratically, for sure, but then mechanically and then fluidly. Within ten minutes he himself was three drummers in one and the beat was his. Giddy and proud, he was like a boy who *finally* could pedal and steer at the same time; and he felt a kind of fear too, like he might fall off the stool as he took the corner between bars three and four, or as if he might drop a stick as he steered between the bollards of bars seven and eight. After sixteen bars, twenty-four, thirty-two the fear had gone and he was tight and loose and playing the beat like Jeff Porcaro could play the beat.

For some reason today, rather than yesterday or the day before, it had all fallen into place. The reason, he knew, was Helen. At last night's sound check he had revealed to the world his drumming, and she had been there to see it, this secret skill of his. "You're brilliant!" she had said, looking like she meant it. She couldn't have known, but by saying these words of praise and acceptance it was as though she had given him permission to shine, and shine he just had. He couldn't wait to play her his new beat.

And so he busied himself. He jogged and lifted weights as he always did; ate eggs as he always did. But there seemed now to be a purpose to this regimen that was more than just the structuring of empty time, a purpose beyond the general preparation for some unknown, future calling. And this sense of purpose, just like the butterflies he still felt, he owed to Helen. He had to see her soon.

***

Later, at Victoria Pier Theatre there was still plenty of time before the first house Overture would set in motion the juggernaut that was Seaside Spectacular '85 – the Gerry Neon Show. In the wings Martin checked radio microphones, flash pots, the bomb tank and sundry props; later, in the interval, he would lower and then raise the crushingly heavy safety curtain, or "iron". The odd muso passed to or from the stage, and a very odd dresser came and went, but he was effectively alone, making his last minute preparations. Helen was sure to appear before long and so he tried to maintain an air of insouciance. He felt a pleasant ache in his triceps and pectorals, having earlier bench-pressed more reps with the heaviest weights he owned than ever before; he swelled to think he would soon need to buy an extra 10 or even 20kg of iron to pump. Squatting to double check that the dry ice machine contained sufficient water, he noticed the top of the bill was approaching him. He eyed the hammer used for breaking solid carbon dioxide, just in case…

"Martin, it is Martin, isn't it?"

"You know it is." the stagehand said, leaping to his feet like a geyser, ready…

"Come with me." Gerry turned and strode away again.

After a frozen moment, Martin followed – it was impossible for him not to – and he chided himself for his canine obedience. In the brightness of the reception area he found the star, star gazing in a mirror, apparently using a fingernail on something between his molars. The teenager stood close behind him, hands on hips.

Gerry turned to find Martin towering over him. He spoke quickly: "It's okay. At ease soldier. I come in peace, as they say. Look, I wanted to bury the hatchet, but, er…" He glanced over at the booth and confirmed to his reassurance that the doorman was there, working on his crossword. He liked to have an audience, especially when asserting himself. "But let's get one thing straight," he went on, loudly, "nobody tries it on with me, okay? D'you understand?" The doorman looked up.

"If you say so."

"Yes I do say so. But then," he lowered his voice again, "anyone can make a mistake. I've had problems with radio mics before, in other theatres, picking up taxi cabs and what have you, so I might have been a bit, y'know, hasty. So, er, let's forget it ever happened and let bygones be buried and we'll leave it at that. Okay?"

"You're the boss." Martin noticed some white powder in the corner of the star's mouth and thought of icing sugar.

"Yes I am the boss," and then almost at a whisper he added, "and you're mistaken about me being your father, without a doubt, hundred percent, so we'll forget about that 'n' all. Got it?"

"Yeah. I talked to my mum about that. Some things are better left alone."

"I'm not 'a thing' you can choose to leave or not to leave alone, alright sunshine? It isn't me. Never was, never will be. Still, wise words from your mum. Anyway, look at the size of you! You're a foot taller than me! I did have a six foot girlfriend once, you know? But I had to jack it in."

"What?"

"It's a joke. You know, jack?" he mimed a pumping action with his arms.

Martin laughed, despite himself.

"That's more like it. Anyway, listen, have you signed up for the big match yet?"

"What 'big match'?"

"This Saturday! A kick about between us and the Opera House. There's a sign-up sheet on the notice board, just there." He pointed; Martin looked. "I bet you're quick. You should play on the wing. Right or left-footed?"

"Right."

"Right wing it is then, like a tall Steve Coppell!"

"What?"

"Not a football fan, eh?"

"I never really…"

"Well, you can have a run out on Saturday, stretch your legs. And don't worry about boots. Trainers'll do. It's just a kick-about."

"I'll sign up, then."

"You do that!" Gerry patted the teenager on the back and made for the stairs up to his dressing room.

"Thanks, Gerry. Break a leg," called Martin, cringing at his own clichéd geniality.

"Yep, let's hope so…" came the reply.

22

"Adam! Come on bruv, get out of bed. Auntie Maureen'll be here soon. I've put an egg on for you…"

Sitting down to his own breakfast, Martin felt too excited to eat. A mixture of pre-match nerves and blithe terror over tonight's date with Helen had disturbed his usually voracious waking appetite. Nonetheless he persevered through his muesli, each laborious mouthful taking an age to chew and an effort to swallow; it was, of course, important to have some fuel on board to play football, he told himself, ever the responsible athlete. As he ruminated he read the nutritional information on the box. For all the reassuring quantities of thiamine and niacin, all he could think of were the whorls of wood that curled from a carpenter's plane. With relief he swallowed the last spoonful of the wet shavings and wondered if in the future he could get his RDA of riboflavin from a doughnut or a waffle instead.

"Adam! Do you want toast soldiers or bread and butter?" he called up the stairs. Privately he had countless, other questions about today's schedule, for which there were no answers easily available to him: for example, should he go to the playing fields already in his shorts? Or was there an arrangement with the school's Community Sports Centre to use their changing rooms? Would people be showering? Did he need a towel? Would there be a referee? Would Helen be there, watching? Should he talk to her if she was, or wait until tonight? On the way into work should he buy a packet of condoms, just in case? And who is this Burl Esk, anyway?

"Are there any Coco Pops left?" said Adam, entering the kitchen, rubbing his eyes.

"Ah, good morning! I think so. Look in the cupboard." Martin turned and smiled to see the sleepy ten-year old still in his Masters of the Universe pyjamas.

"Where's mum?"

"Er, still in bed, I suppose. So, anyway, for your chucky egg do you want toast soldiers or bread and butter?"

"*Mum* says that, chucky egg."

"Yep, she does, and eggy weggies – that's what she always used to call 'em to me."

"Not anymore?"

"Well, I usually cook for myself these days, don't I? I'm never in when you two eat."

"No," replied Adam, self-sufficient with his cereal, pouring milk. "Will you work at Victoria Pier forever?"

"Nooo! Don't be silly. So, what d'ya want, shoulders or bread and bupper?"

"Shoulders," said Adam, laughing, sleeve-wiping chocolaty milk from is his chin.

"Coming up." As the bread turned golden on setting three, neither boy nor man felt obliged to speak further. The toast jumped and Martin spread butter on it. He forked three soft-boiled from the pan and hot-fingered them into eggcups. He clicked a pinch of salt onto each of two plates.

He sat down and they ate together as brothers; eggy weggies for him, and a chucky egg for Adam.

"When's Aunty Maureen coming?"

"There's a note in front of you from Mum."

"Oh, yeah." He read. "Ten o'clock. When is it ten o'clock?"

"There's a clock on the wall, lazy!"

"Oh, yeah. Are we going swimming?"

"I think so."

"Ace! Will Cousin Matthew be coming too? I like him. He's funny."

"I expect so."

"He's *really* funny! He's naughty as well, and he tells rude jokes."

"Really? What like?"

"But it's rude."

"It's alright. I won't tell."

"Okay," he began, already giggling. "What's a wanker's favourite TV program?"

Martin gasped in mock shock, and then responded, whispering the term of abuse. "*I* don't know, *what's* a... wanker's... favourite TV program?"

"Wankety Wank!" ejaculated Adam, his giggling reaching a climax.

"Wankety Wank?"

"Yes!" he said, still climaxing.

"Matthew told you that?"

"Yes!"

"I'm gonna have to speak to Auntie Maureen about him! Corrupting my younger brother!"

"You promised!"

"It's okay, I won't, I'm only joking!" Martin stood up, relieved the fridge of a carton and glugged fresh orange into two glasses. "Here…"

"Thank you."

Martin loved it when they were like this, the two of them, all calm and sympathetic and humorous like brothers. Too often Adam was *too much* his age: selfish, impatient, a brat. And for his part, because of the near-decade age gap, he frequently felt cast in the role of embarrassing uncle or geek older cousin, compelled to impress his much younger relative with feats of dumbbell strength or drum kit talent. This morning, neither brat nor geek were present and Martin felt he didn't have to do or say anything, he could just *be*.

And then, things got better. He noticed that Adam was tapping his fingers on the table. More than that, he was tapping out a *rhythm*. He then picked up his tea spoon and began using it on the rim of his plate, so that his right hand was accented, as if the sharp ceramic ting was the bell of a ride cymbal. Martin didn't comment but he heard, and he saw that Adam was playing paradiddles, and in time as well.

Little drummer boy stopped, put down his metal drum stick and said: "Mar-tin?" The name was affectionately whined, from high pitch to low.

"Ye-es?"

"Will you teach me to play the drums?"

***

Martin stepped bare-legged into cool air and began running to Field Grove under milky skies. He'd never played a competitive football match before and he felt childishly, unashamedly excited. His previous non-participation wasn't because of any *dislike* of the game – on the contrary, with vicarious enjoyment he often watched the televised matches on Sunday afternoons, and today he *wanted* to play – it was just that years ago, in those first lunchtime kick-abouts at Big School, the popular football boys with their football dads had quickly, mysteriously coalesced into football friendships, and into cliques and onto team sheets. And once those September starting elevens had been posted, with Martin not even among the subs, it was easier for him thereafter to regard the playing of *team* football as something other boys did. He would still entertain himself with garden lawn keepy-uppy and would happily solo slam his Mitre against the garage wall at the end of the road – on the volley, on the sweet spot – but with sad pragmatism he henceforth knew that teammates and afterschool fixtures were not for him.

Until today, that is! *At last* he was to play a game of football, like other boys did, like other men did, and he was literally leaping at the chance to join in, to prove himself, but he had little clue where to stand or who to pass to. Still running, sweat seeped form his forehead. He wondered if Alan or Gary might help him along; they regarded him a hero for standing up to Gerry so perhaps they'd give a few pointers. And then there was Gerry himself; he'd pressed him into playing, so perhaps it behoved him as recruiting sergeant to offer guidance.

Or maybe he didn't *need* any help; maybe his superior speed and fitness would compensate for absent skills? Or maybe a previously dormant part of his brain – the *Corpus footballus* – might boot up and find him space and time?

Maybe he'd score the winner? With Helen behind him, anything was possible. Feeling like a champion he leapt the low perimeter wall that described the grounds of his old comp and eased himself into a stroll. He wiped the sweat from his brow and his cheeks, feeling that they were rough with stubble, glad that nature was making a man of him.

The Sports Centre's modest car park was already nearly full. Its two short rows held beaten up run-abouts interspersed with immaculate three litre saloons and sleek sports cars. Gerry's Jag was there, imperious, as was a gorgeous convertible Merc, in cherry red. Martin guessed it was Darren Daniel's and he speculated which other stars would be turning out this morning. Eyeing the reception, he moved to step off the pavement, to cut diagonally across the tarmac, when his progress was checked by a black XR3i, teenage fanny magnet and must-have for any boy racer. He halted abruptly and watched as Scott Mee cruised by, *footballer* Scott Mee, who at school had been in his form up until the fifth year when he had left to sign apprenticeship papers for Grumby Town. Would *he* be playing today, Martin asked himself, a current professional in a ragtag kick-about? And for which team?

On reaching Reception he learned that Vicky Pier were to change in the Boys', whilst the Opera House team had the use of the Girls' changing room, and everyone had to be showered and out by midday thirty, in time for the squash ladder matches at one. Martin entered the Boys' as he had done countless times before in P.E., but today did so only after bracing himself. The tiled room echoed loudly with the laughter, coughing and swearing of men. Chief among the swearers – and therefore the manliest of the men – was a stocky Liverpudlian, mid-forties, who was standing in only his underwear, folding his trousers and effing and blinding at imposing volume. He was totally bald with a red moon face and Martin recognised him from bills posted around town as Barry Mann, from The Sands theatre. His legs were thick with muscle, his calves in particular angled and jutting from years of use, if only in support of his barrel chest and taut beer belly. He was standing next to Gerry Neon, also in a state of undress, both fag in hand, and the two competing alpha male comedians, were feeding each other lines: "Bloody hell, Manny," said Gerry, prodding the scouser's belly, "if that was on a woman, she'd be pregnant!" "It *has* been," said Barry, "and she *fucking* is!"

Amongst the laughter and the masculinity, Martin chanced a buttock on the end of a bench near the door, telling himself that these would be his teammates, not opponents out to kick him. He looked around and was encouraged further to spot Alan and Gary at the back, both in shorts and socks to the knee but as yet shirtless. Next to them was emcee Dave Newhurst, appearing haunted by a hangover, as was one of his brass section, pinch-browed and pale.

Disconcertingly Gerry's mate Pete was here too, bent over and searching through his sports grip, and he hoped that his and Gerry's truce had reached those lofty ears. He watched as the giant retrieved a pair of shin guards – *shin guards!* –from his bag. Worse, Ashley Kidd sat tapping and scraping the tiled floor as he tied the laces of his boots, his *football boots*. Martin looked down at his own gossamer trainers, his socks visible through the mesh uppers, the rubber soles worn so thin as to communicate every particle of gravel, every blade of grass. So much for "not worrying about boots," he thought. And as Ashley's studs continued their assault on the tiled floor, he imagined the opposing team's studs, guessing that such violent footwear would be in their armoury too, and he kicked himself for agreeing to play. A few other combatants from the pier arrived and, although he didn't take a head count, it seemed they numbered a team.

Presently Darren Daniel came in dressed in his trademark copycat Miami Vice attire. "Morning, fellers," he said.

"Hi Darren," said Gerry brightly, "the Girls' changing room's next door."

"Yeah yeah, very funny." He said over a chorus of unsuppressed sniggers, accepting the dig like a sport, even running with it: "Actually, I've just come to size up your boys, Gerry."

"I bet you have!" The super star's genitals were delineated by the tightest of trunks, in bottle green, and he cupped them provocatively.

"I wanted to know if the rumours about you in particular were true. I can see now that they're not!" The sniggers turned to good humoured laughter.

"Oh I measure up, dear, don't you worry!" There was a petty, competitive edge to Gerry's retort. "So, are *you* playing today?"

"Yeah, I'll have a run out. But Gerry," Darren then pointedly scanned the room, peering through the cigarette smoke at the shapeless, pasty bodies, hearing the coughing, "you don't look much like a football team to me. How's the heart, Barry?"

"Still beating. Doctor say's I've got a cute angina..."

"And a nice pair of tits!" added Gerry.

"Brilliant! It's like it was scripted. You two should be a double act! Anyway, like I say, not much of a team, Gerry. You should have been on the phone, like I have. Should've got yourself a secret weapon!"

"Appearances can be deceptive, Darren. We'll give you a good game, you have my word."

"Let's hope so, Gerry. Good luck today! Byeee!" The young pretender skipped out of the room.

Gerry turned to Pete, saying under his breath: "Well, he can shove his secret weapon up his arse!"

"Huh, yeah. Where's the kit anyway?"

"We're playing skins, didn't you know?"

There was a minute or two of relative quiet, save for the coughing and the pained, manly groans that accompanied every bend and stretch, every pulling on of a sock, every tying of a lace. Martin felt he was in a crowded GP's surgery, a health nut amongst the bronchitic and the hypertensive, the jaundiced and the nauseous.

And then Scott Mee strolled in – a preening pretty boy with two others of his ilk following after; a triplicate of trendy. "Watcha, Gerry!" he said, standing there, surveying the room, all pout and nonchalance. He had a large kit bag slung over his shoulder.

"Hello Scottie Boy!" Replied Gerry. "Here he is fellers, my best mate. It is Scott, isn't it?"

"You've never met him before have you?"

"What do you mean, Barry? We go way back!"

"Oh yeah? How long have you known him?"

"Er, what time is it?" said Gerry, looking at his watch, to continuing laughter. "Nah, seriously, I know his old man.

You know Jonny Mee? Owns The Anchor? This is his lad, plays a bit apparently, and not just for the pub team...and I'm his Godfather."

"Godfather? You're joking?"

"Of course I fucking am! I'm a comedian!"

"Well, they look like Banarama to me!" said Barry

And then Scott, smiling, piped up: "My dad said I should get my usual win bonus, double if I score." His mates laughed nervously.

"Listen sunshine, I'll do the jokes, alright?" said Gerry.

"And he wants the shirts washing afterwards..."

"I said I'll do the fucking jokes."

"Yes, Guv," said the ringer, still smiling. "Anyway, here they are. Help yourself." He threw off the bag, slamming it down on the floor.

The teenager looked ridiculous to middle aged eyes, with his highlighted fringe and his long hair at the back, permed like a girl's, and his face smooth and pink like a girl's and with his earring and his black leather trousers, and Pete Wheeler, unbending himself to his full six feet plus, smiling straight back at him, said: "I used to fuck kids like you in prison."

For a moment, despite the roars of laughter, Martin believed him.

23

Out on the pitch, warming up. Despite the assorted shapes and girths of the players, the blue and white hooped Anchor team shirts were all the same size, and they hung like polyester ponchos on some and clung like Lycra on others. Martin, who had been last to the kit bag, did not get a shirt and stood forlorn in his own cotton strip. There hadn't even been a goalkeeper's jersey for him to wear since Gary, fancying himself a cat between the sticks, had taken the green number one and was now palming away practice strikes from Barry Mann and Scott Mee. Toes were touched and hamstrings stretched, and Dave Newhurst went to vomit behind the goal to much laughter. Martin too enjoyed this voiding and began to limber up, even showing himself to receive the ball. Eventually the ball did come to him from Alan and he in turn passed it to Gerry, and all was well in the world. Maybe he could come on as a sub, he hoped, or even play the whole of the second half; if Helen *did* come along to spectate, he didn't really want her to find him on the touchline, a spare part.

Gerry called everyone over to him for a team swear. "Right lads. We're gonna fucking beat these cunts. If Darren

Daniel gets the ball, fucking kick him. Kick him when he hasn't got the fucking ball. In fact, when you get the ball, run at him and do what, Pete?"

"Kick him."

"You got it. Listen lads, they do not win this pissing match! We get the bragging rights in this fucking town, not that bunch of cunts. And remember, keep your low balls high and you high balls low. I will now hand over to our team manager. How do we line up, Kiddo?"

"Well I've had a close look at you all in training, and I've been very impressed. But first of all can I just say how nice it is to have Barry back with us, after his stint in rehab…and also Pete Wheeler, after his six months in HMP Armley."

"Can I go to the toilet please, warder?" joked Pete.

"Go up against Darren Daniel's leg," replied Ashley.

"He likes that," added Gerry, to yet another chorus of sniggers.

"Focus boys! It's a big match. Right, so, Gary you're in nets, obviously. A back four of, er, Gerry right back, Pete and Alan centre backs…"

As Captain Kidd went through the line-up, Pete Wheeler found himself looking at the lad in the tee-shirt, Martin. There was something odd about him. He would either stare at his shabby trainers or else peer far off into the blue yonder, never making eye contact, as if shy, or perhaps superior. And then, like the class new boy, he would laugh eagerly at the banter, but only after first peeking around to confirm others found it funny too. And for a big lad he held himself like cooked spaghetti. He seemed boneless or bloodless, as if he lacked something basic, something universal, and Pete wanted to shake him… But he had stood up to Gerry, Pete remembered, and it says something that a teenage stagehand should stand up to a seasoned bastard like Gerry Neon. So, spaghetti boy had steel; he had fight. Pete was no anthropologist but he saw a humanity in his subject that he recognised. Furthermore, Martin's entire head was eerily, unknowably familiar to Pete, like when you visit the changing rooms of a department store with mirrors on three walls, and you catch your reflection as others see you – your profile, the back of your head – and you turn your head but the strange image moves the wrong way, and your features look the same as they always do but somehow different like a back to front copy, on parallel mirrors, reflected into infinity. Pete had to force himself to look away from this apparition.

Martin began to jog on the spot, displaying his readiness for selection, but mindful of his own untried abilities he half hoped he didn't get picked at all so that he could go home and forget this foolishness. He looked over at the opposition, who seemed a bit thin on the ground, and saw that Darren Daniel was walking towards them.

"Barry, will you play centre mid?" continued Ashley Kidd.

"Yeah, but I'm not running!"

"S'alright, the young'uns can do that. Scottie, where's your preferred position?"

"In the kitchen," said Barry.

"Huh. Don't mind. Anywhere really."

"Right, well, you're up front with your two mates… What's your names, boys?"

"Craig."

"Benny."

"So, Craig, wide left, and Benny wide right. Got it?"

There was a mumbling of "yes bosses" and "yes guvs" and "come on, lads" when Darren Daniel engaged Gerry and Ashley in quiet conversation, before returning to his teammates.

"Martin," called Gerry cheerfully, beckoning him. "Apparently Diego can't make it today and they're a man short."

"Right."

"So it's good news."

"Right?"

"You've made the starting eleven. *Their* starting eleven!"

"Right, but…"

"Look at him, poor lad, doesn't know whether to shit or piss," said Gerry to Ashley. "Go on, off you trot."

***

| GOAL: Victoria Pier | 1-0 | Opera House Mee | 3 |
| GOAL: Victoria Pier | 2-0 | Opera House Mee | 5 |

Right from the kick-off Mann and Mee played with a sympathy and skill that was a league above the fog and flap of their amateur opposition. Barry would command midfield, deploying Scott with incisive passes behind the Opera House's defence, and the youngster would hover and then dart like a dragonfly. The older man's quip about him not running wasn't far from the truth, however. He might lunge to make a tackle or to intercept a pass, or having won possession might skip half a dozen paces to find space, but thereafter he would occupy the centre circle, shielding the ball with his rampart back and barricade arms, loosing off passes to feet, short and long, square and through.

Martin's team of strangers had no reply to this exhibition and were reduced almost to spectating, not that the last-minute transfer cared. Instructed to play wide left, he held to the touchline with distracted obedience, growling to himself: "Shit or piss? I'll fucking shit all over him!" It annoyed him that just when he'd psyched himself up to play without boots, to join in with his workmates Alan and Gary, and to prove himself amongst men, the goalposts had been moved, literally, by a distance exactly equal to one football pitch. He could see the humour in this irony but knew only its discourtesy. He felt like a chattel in a transaction. He felt he was being toyed with.

As far as he was concerned there was once again bad blood between him and Gerry and he readied himself for an opportunity to even the score. He didn't have to wait long. Amusingly, and within only minutes of the kick-off, it became clear his nemesis did not belong on a football field. He gave away possession twice, stood on the ball and fell over, kicked fresh air and generally staggered around gasping. Barry Mann mocked and goaded the superstar: "Put your round head on, Gee!" he yelled after a wayward header; "Bloody hell, Gee! I've seen milk turn quicker!"; "Jesus, Gee, you've the touch of a rapist! You *control* the ball further than I can kick it!" Each gibe was met with audible appreciation from both teams, but Gerry was too breathless with coughing to come back with anything more elegant than four-letter expletives. Martin felt more than justified to join in with this gallows humour and so jeered loudly. More to the point, playing out on the left even he fancied his chances against such an ailing, inept right back; all he needed was the ball at his feet and Gerry in position.

**

Meanwhile a Ford Fiesta turned into the car park: "There's a space, Vicks!" said Helen, pointing. Once stationary, both women checked their make-up: Helen pulled down the sun visor and saw cheeks that glowed faintly and lips that may or may not have had cosmetic applied. Prettily pleased, she sat calmly in leggings and a baggy sweatshirt, just aware of her heart beating.

Vikki, however, reached across Helen into the passenger foot well, retrieving her large chaotic hand bag, which she lifted onto her lap. Its plastic leather felt cool on her thighs, bare in linen shorts. She searched for powder and lipstick, which she re-applied in the rear-view mirror, before fussing with her big, provocative hair. "Victoria" in silver hung and bounced in a cleavage displayed. She turned up the collar of her stone-washed denim jacket and, grasping the door handle said: "Right, then. Let's go and check out some muscly legs and nice bums!"

Helen, thinking of the time she'd seen Martin jogging in tight shorts, did not argue with this sentiment. "Ooh, cheeky!" she said, giggling.

**

Gerry was *sat* on *his* bum. He'd stretched out a leg in an attempt to control the ball, missed it and, stranded off-balance in an X shape with his arms waving, had dropped backwards onto the grass. He probably could have avoided falling over, but he knew it would look funny; if he couldn't catch the eye with wizard dribbling or slide-rule passes, he guessed he might as well clown around and hijack the attention that way; he *was* the star of the show, after all.

Helen and Vikki joined the tiny crowd of hangers-on from the two theatres that milled around on the touch line, half spectating, half larking about. There were jokey comments about the players and their actions, and uproarious laughter at the merest suggestion of comedy on the pitch. When Gerry collapsed on his fat arse there was a reason to laugh; when he took a throw in, his shorts dropped to his ankles, his cock lolling like an Alsatian's tongue, there were incontinent shrieks and howls. "Nice tackle!" shouted Vicky, predictably. Pete Wheeler had seen it all before, of course, thinking it was thirty years since they were at school together and *still* Gerry was getting his cock out!

With the score at three-nil, Darren Daniel was allowed a moment's possession. "Kick him!" shouted Gerry.

Darren paid no mind to such an inelegant game plan and instead made his own play. "Marty!" he shouted with urgency.

The stagehand was all eyes and watched as the midfielder passed the ball square. Almost in slow motion it rolled towards him; he received the ball; he controlled the ball. He turned and looked up to see Gerry in position, twenty yards away. He didn't need to think twice. To dribble was too grand and technical a word to describe Martin's next course of action; more literally he kicked the ball down the wing towards Gerry and chased after it. He heard but didn't register a female voice: "Go on Martin!" it cheered.

Fifteen yards from the right-back, he took a touch and eyed his target; Gerry was waiting for him, stationary, feet wide apart. Ten yards and he took another touch. Eight and he knew what he would do. Five, he shaped his body. With three yards to go, Martin toe-poked the ball, aiming for a spot half way between Gerry's rooted boots, intending to nutmeg him, to round him and to receive his own through-ball on the other side.

Gerry saw that Martin was in possession, the same Martin who had cocked up the dry ice and the radio mics, the same Martin who had made a fool of him in public. He watched as he set off towards him like an over-sized puppy, thinking: "That streak of piss is not getting past me." He adopted a stance not often seen in association football. He crouched slightly with a wide base, shifting his weight this way and that to anticipate the teenager's run. He raised his hands, holding them before him like a wrestler about to clinch. With the left-winger bearing down on him he imagined his hod-carrier's shoulder thrust into the youngster's ribs, and he could feel his labourer's arms tight around the lad's torso. He sensed that Pete had moved across from centre back to support him, hearing him call: "Stand up, Gee. Be strong. Show him into touch," which was all the approval he needed.

Martin's toe-poke found its target, barrelling between Gerry's legs. Sensing his chance, the lad swerved to side step around the right-back only to be clumsily body-checked and pulled to the ground with a crude British Bulldogs tackle. There were gasps and loud exhalations of laughter from the touchline. Pushing himself back onto his feet, he tried to continue his run, but Gerry was still clinging to his left leg, trying to bite his calf, or at least miming to do so, shouting:

"Come 'ere, you bastard! I'll bite yer! I'll bite yer!" The laughter increased at this demented comedy; Helen raised a hand to her open mouth. His mad up, Martin kicked out, catching Gerry in the face, and then dragged his cannibal assailant two strides before breaking free, but losing a trainer.

Still rolling, the ball was almost out for a goal kick, but Martin accelerated anyway, desperate to keep it in. Almost at once he saw from the corner of his right eye the dark, lumbering form of Pete Wheeler just before he slid under him. He almost managed to ride the impossibly early tackle, hurdling with his right leg the centre-back's lunge. His standing foot, however, the left one, the one with only a sock for protection, took the full force of Pete's careless studs. In several places around Martin's inside ankle, metal screw-ins with the force of fifteen stone rammed into skin and bone. "I was going for the ball!" shouted Pete, with comic untruth.

Ironically, Martin's bootlessness saved his fib and tib. Had he his own studs, his sole would not have slid with the impact but would have remained fixed in the turf, his lower leg bones snapping like two breadsticks. Luckily nylon socks and grass do not adhere to each other and so although marked with a dice pattern of bruises he might not necessarily need a trip to the fracture clinic. Lifted into the air he came down hard on top of Pete in a tangle of arms and legs, before rolling off him onto his back and grasping his ankle as if to contain the pain. "Fuck!" he hissed, craning his neck to look at Pete. "You could have broken my leg! You maniac!"

Incongruously many of the spectators, and even some of the players, continued to laugh. It was as if this foul play was phony and little more than the slapstick that would break out in one of those pro-celeb matches, in which the gate receipts went to a lifeboat charity and a hospital radio deejay did a live commentary.

Pete however saw real pain in the Martin's eyes and in a heartbeat regretted the foul. He hauled himself to his feet. "Yeah, bit late, that. Sorry Martin. Which ankle is it?"

"The two on the left. Fuck, it hurts."

"It's alright, you can run it off. Here, let me help you up."

Martin took the offered hand. Once again he avoided eye contact, instead looking through his physio and finding Helen in the small crowd. "Thank you," he mumbled distractedly. With his weight on one foot and his arm around Pete's shoulder, Helen appeared concerned and as if she might be about to come over.

Pete held Martin up, transfixed once more by this apparition made flesh, with the pained face, the faint chin cleft, the distant, familiar eyes...Thunderstruck, Pete knew why he recognised him. He recognised him because he'd seen his face before, or one very like it: not backstage at the theatre, because he hadn't properly seen him there, in the dark. No, he'd seen it elsewhere and previously and innumerate times. Pete had seen the spitting image of Martin in the back of a spoon, in the frame-by-frame windows of a passing bus, in the polished paintwork of a showroom sports car and in the black screen of a turned-off television set: it was as clear as the fine nose on both their faces. He saw too this image of Martin in the smoked-mirrors of hotel lifts and the dusty, optic-obscured mirrors of city centre boozers. He saw the lad brushing his teeth this morning and shaving yesterday morning.

He saw him in his thirties; he saw him in his twenties. Without knowing it, the man old enough to be his father saw Martin each and every time he peered ignorantly into any mirror. Looking at the teenager now he saw himself – not the moustachioed, time-worn, collapsed-faced version of today, but the handsome young Peter Wheeler, with the fine features, of Gerry Neon and the Nobles. He saw himself because heredity is observable – Mendel and Darwin understood this; pigeon-fanciers and dog-breeders still do. And to those who *know* what they see, heredity is also retrospective, the past being visible in the present. This is what Pete, palming stubble as if to hide the family chin, understood now. He had never known nor dreamt he had a son but, just from looking into the face of this eerily familiar, beautiful man-boy, he knew now.

Martin however, his foot throbbing and with eyes that watched only Helen as she marched over to them, had no conception of the mind-quake shaking Pete to his core. He tried to stand by himself, thinking that the dancer looked cross, as if she was about to rebuke someone, but also that she looked great.

Others in the crowd were still in high spirits and Gerry continued to court their appreciation. "Come 'ere! I'll bite yer!" he repeated ever more crazily, crawling after Martin, growling like a dog. He tasted metal and paused to touch the inside of his lip. It was nothing, a minor injury from Martin's kicking, but the red on his fingers incited the touchline to yet another paroxysm. From canine all fours he got to his feet and, still riffing on the theme of funny is funny is funny, he sprinted after the lad, now injured and barely standing.

In quick succession there had been Gerry's wrestler's body check and his attempted leglock, and then there had been Pete's sliding take down; now, like a tag team partner re-entering the bout, Gerry attempted a Big Gee Splashdown, with submission. Sprinting, with a yard to his target, he planted both feet together into the ground and sprung with a punk pogo as high up into the air he could before falling down hard onto Martin's back.

Meanwhile, with his own leap of faith, Martin relaxed his grip on Pete's shoulder and tentatively tested his weight on his bad foot. He felt an immediate sharpness and reflexively bent down to hold and protect his injury. From out of nowhere a heavy load descended onto his back like a bag of cement, forcing him rapidly forwards and down. He threw his hands up to guard against the impact.

Normally the radii and ulnae of even a streak-of-piss teenager have a tensile strength sufficient to withstand a fall from standing. However, under certain conditions the human forearm, like the lower leg, may also behave as if skeletoned with breadsticks. Indeed, under the weight of *two* men the deceleratory forces upon impact may be so great as to fracture either or both of these grissini.

And so for the second time in a minute Martin lay in a heap with a middle-aged man. On this occasion, however, his mugger was intent on keeping him on the ground.

Without resistance, Gerry quickly manoeuvred himself so that he was sitting on the small of Martin's back. Clowning, but with obvious roughness, the star pushed the stagehand's face into the grass. "Eat dirt!" he commanded, smiling like a lunatic. Then, knowing that physical violence was almost always funny, he pretended to punch Martin in the kidneys – right, left, right, left. His fists connected with the turf but perspective gave to those on the touchline the semblance of an assault, and there was a collective guffaw. Gerry ensured however that his final punch did in fact connect with Martin's body, in the area of his floating rib, and with that blow he lowered his mouth to speak softly into his subordinate's ear: "That's for messing with me, sunshine."

Martin barely flinched at this caress, for he knew a worse pain.

Immediately after being forced to the ground, Martin knew only shock and pressure. Disoriented, as if in an avalanche, it took two or three seconds for him to realise he was facing downwards and that a great weight was pressing him from above. And then from some undiagnosable part of his body – from everywhere and nowhere, from every ganglion and from off the grid – there radiated a visceral nauseating agony, a white pain he feared might overwhelm him. Gradually he triaged the anatomy of his injury: his upper body, somewhere; one of his limbs, the right one; his wrist or his elbow? Not sure; the bone *or the skin* of his right forearm? Both. A terrifying moment passed with him unable to move, and it was then that he had felt a minor blow to his side, merely an insult to his injury.

And as his paralysis continued, the passage of time became all the more terrifying because Martin, winded and pressed by the weight of a man, found he also couldn't breathe. Scared for his life he fought to squeeze his uninjured arm out from under his abdomen. With great effort he freed it and urgently pushed against the ground, raising himself just enough to inhale and to utter a desperate "Get off me!" His right arm however was trapped under his chest, immobile and in an unnatural orientation. He tried to pull it…

…when Martin came round, he was lying on his back, breathing freely and looking at milky skies sunned by an upside down face, Helen's face. Pain quickly returned, however, eclipsing this paradise and causing him to cry out. He raised his arm to see the injury, but Helen covered his eyes with her hand; "No sweetheart, don't look," she said. He could *feel* however that his sleeve was warm and somehow wet and that it clung tautly as if it had snagged on some unknown part of his forearm. There was an outburst of shouting nearby. He turned his head and what he saw surprised him.

For some reason, Pete was squaring up to Gerry. The stocky man got his retaliation in first, however, pushing Pete with both hands, hard. The taller man rocked backwards a step or two, but that was all, and then, smiling as if off the leash at last, he went for Gerry. For once there was no laughter; the altercation was visibly serious, the intent genuine. Though in agony, Martin found distraction in this "Fight! Fight! Fight!" on the school field, and even felt himself willing on Pete.

Never mind their run-in at the theatre, Gerry had just broken Martin's arm and so it was only natural for the lad to want to see the star hurt too, *whatever the reason* Pete had to hurt him. But there was something else. Martin backed Pete because he had shown him a moment's kindness. True he had earlier murdered his ankle, but then he had helped him to his feet apologising, and had looked at him with a face that showed at least a flicker of sympathy and concern. Though in agony, Martin backed Pete because he sensed in him the gentleness of a shared humanity.

***

With Helen holding his good hand, Martin watched from ring-side. Only ten feet away Pete had a hold of Gerry by the collar, a white-knuckled fistful of football shirt at the end of his left arm. His right hand too was held in a fist, held high and cocked ready for a haymaker. However Gerry, with his chest out and his jaw proud, seemed not to believe that the punch would be thrown. In fact with building site bravado he laughed in the bigger man's face daring him, in front of the crowd, to: "Just try it!"

Pete then said: "Hit me, or I'll hit you!"

"What?" Gerry seemed taken aback, his eyes narrowing in confusion.

"You heard. It's what *you* always used to say, when you wanted to give someone a kicking. And now *you're* getting one."

"What're you talking about?" Doubt crept onto Gerry's face. "Behave yourself, we're still mates, really."

"Not anymore. You're a soft-as-shit bully, always throwing your weight around, and you broke…"

"No, *you're* the bully." Gerry grabbed at Pete's iron hand and tried to prise it from his collar. "Get off!" he shouted, his voice containing a hint of fear.

"…you broke that poor lad's arm. And for what? For standing up to you. Well, good for him. And now it's my turn. *Hit me*, or I'll hit you."

Martin's pain sank slightly beneath a flood of endorphins, and he was moved to learn that Pete was actually defending him. And the drama was there for all to see: the blunt ultimatum; the suspense of a cocked fist; Gerry's facial semaphore, from arrogant smirk to wide-eyed fear. Martin, now rooting for Pete, his avenger, watched as the fearful prisoner tried to break free. He saw him struggle with two strong hands to cast off his gaoler's immovable left; he watched him thrash from side to side, as if to hide his face from that loaded, menacing right. The blue and white material tore and became loose in Pete's hand. Partially liberated Gerry ducked and pulled away until the shirt came over his head and down each arm. But the snug sleeve material rolled upon itself tightly and became bunched and ensnared around his wrists, as if he was wearing a pair of polyester handcuffs with Pete holding the connecting chain. Gerry, topless, remained bent over, pulling backwards, like the rear-end of a refusing pantomime horse.

Pete let go, catapulting Gerry onto the turf. He snorted his satisfaction and then said: "Get up, you sack of shit!"

Like speak-no-evil monkeys the onlookers responded with concealed gasps and sniggers. Gerry, clearly humiliated at dying on his arse, began to rave with anger. With Pete advancing he sprung to his feet and pushed and pulled and threw off the rest of the football shirt, as if it was on fire.

"Come on then! I'm gonna fuck…" shouted Gerry. But no one within earshot learned of Gerry's exact intention. Pete, later swaggering to his car with his knuckles stinging, comprehensively saw to that.

And Martin, avenged, victorious in his spectatorship and triumphant in his pain, couldn't help but sense something curious in Pete's actions.

24

A dry mouth and brightness. Smooth movement. A gentle breeze. Strip lights that came and went. The nauseating smell of breakfast. The rush of a curtain being pulled. From recovery room to hospital corridor to male surgical ward, Martin's perception of reality was fragmentary.

Bedded in his cubicle he saw, whenever he opened his eyes, only curtains; asleep, however, he saw whichever feature presentation his flirtatious reel-man chose to project for him, and presently he chose to show Helen: The Movie. Swept along by the film, Martin watched the leading actress, curvaceous in her dressing gown, naked beneath her dressing gown, as she walked away from him, but turning, always turning around and smiling. On this cerebral screen of infinite size he feasted his mind's eye on her face and body, as she led him to some unknown place, to some intimate act. Although dreaming, the hydrostatic reality of his own body entered his unconsciousness, as he felt himself becoming erect, his erection pressing against the sheets. And thus ready he followed her, and he caught up with her, and her dressing gown came undone as she took his hand.

"Martin. It's mum."

Waking, there then followed a frustrating intermission. He opened his eyes and saw a kind, familiar face. He felt fingers, firm and warm around his own… a thumb massaged his knuckles as if to squeeze toothpaste from a tube… they belonged to… not Helen, but someone else, also beautiful… someone he knew. He sensed with abashment the tent he was making of the bedclothes and so shifted his buttocks, twisting himself just enough to de-mast it. That someone spoke to him.

"Martin. Martin, it's Mum. How are you?"

He could almost see the woman's words as they rode slowly the still air between them, descending finally like birthday balloons into his understanding. But without greeting his mother, he again dipped into his alternate consciousness, his narcotic reality, this time willing it as he ached to find Helen again, to follow her and to arrive at wherever she was leading him. With relief he found that the film was still playing, the same reel as before even, only this time it was different. He was back in his dream no doubt, his sexual dream, in which Helen and he were about to be lovers, but it was not the same. He searched for her, racing along the corridor and up the stairwell – the projectionist allowed him this. With great joy he found her, only this time she wasn't always Helen; she could change or revert in an instant. This strange Helen / Not-Helen duality was dancing on the stage, in the same dressing gown as before. At times this hoofing Heisenberg had the distinctive chocolate pony, whipping in circles as Helen, definitely Helen, twisted and hand-jived. At other times, the obscene projectionist presented to him Lorraine Collier, his mum but not yet his mum. The Lorraine on screen was around his age, a teenager, and she was smiling and dancing in the same bright lights as

Helen, in the same gaping dressing gown, but with a mane of fine platinum hair, which bounced as she shimmied and hitch-hiked. And then he was with them, intimately, intimate with both of them, inside their one gown, and sensuously, their one naked body warm and soft to his touch. He felt a great rising of heat, the heat rushing up his own body towards his head, and he awoke, his face hot with embarrassment.

"Martin. Martin, it's Mum. How are you?"

His reply came slowly, his dry lips moving silently for a time before his word emerged. "Mum," he croaked.

"That's right, sweetheart. You've had an operation. Your arm, you hurt it playing football. Remember? They've put a plate in it."

There was a pause while he tongued his palate and half swallowed, but no saliva would come. Indistinctly he croaked again: "...thirsty."

"What? Let me get you some water." She filled a beaker from a lidded jug and held it to his lips. "Here, sweetheart. Drink."

He lifted his head and pursed lips that were dry. The hours-old liquid soaked into his mouth and throat like a thin oil. "I feel sick," he said, slurring freely.

"That'll be the anaesthetic. It'll wear off. Are you in pain?"

"Mum."

"Yes, darling?"

"Where's Helen? I saw her."

"Who's Helen? I don't know a..."

"I saw her in her dressing gown."

"Perhaps you saw a nurse. Try to rest, sweetheart. Go back to sleep."

"I love her."

"I'm sure she loves you too," said Lorraine, laughing. "Now get some rest. I've got to go soon, sorry. I waited for you to come out of surgery, to check you were okay, but I've got to go. I've a wedding to style for. Dennis will bring me back again after, though...Won't you, love?"

"Yes, love. Hello, Martin," said Dennis. "You've been in the wars, haven't you? How did it happen?"

"Dunno." He searched his memory and then said: "I think it was Gerry."

"He's a nasty piece of..."

"Well, let's not worry about that now," interrupted Lorraine. "We've got to concentrate on getting you well, getting that hand of yours working, and your foot." With door-knock knuckles she rapped twice on his left shin, the plaster of Paris visible in outline beneath the cotton. "And Martin? I bought you something. They're on the side..."

"Uh? Thanks. What are they?"

"Oh, nothing much. You'll see. Anyway, got to go, got to go. I'll see you later. Love you."

"Yes."

"Ta-ta, lad," said Dennis. "Get some rest."

Martin watched them disappear through the curtain. He turned his head towards the bedside table and saw a brown paper bag, rolled into an oblong parcel held by a piece of sellotape. Intrigued, he couldn't reach it. Neither could he reach the beaker of water his mum had poured for him; surely she could have placed it nearer, he began mentally to complain... But he stopped himself short and smiled a weak smile. In fact, despite his thirst, and his nausea, and the drip in the back of his good hand, and his other butchered, bionic arm, he sensed the beginnings of a happiness even the morphine in his system couldn't explain. He felt overwhelmed by narcosis, closed his eyes and eased into the superior seating of his cinema for one.

***

"Do you want some cream rubbing on your bottom?" During the course of the morning, in the transient gaps between daydreams and sleep-dreams, Martin inside his cubicle had heard numerous kind offers regarding the care and toileting of the other patients on the ward. Now more permanently awake, and with the curtains drawn back from around his bed, he could see as well as hear the owners of these high, melodious, nursery voices; he could now witness the skill and attention of the nurses. The commode was not merely pushed but rather chauffeured from one straining defecator to the next; the bloody piss bags of those relieved of their prostates were inspected with a vintner's eye; fat, immobile lifers were turned at intervals by four or six hands in a ballet of nursing; and, as a further measure taken to prevent the development of bedsores, emollient was now being applied by the prettiest of nurses to the infant buttocks of septuagenarians made grateful of their second babyhood. "Do you want some cream on your bottom?" she asked the terminal cougher with the oxygen in the next bed, almost winking as she did, or so Martin imagined in his incongruously sexualised state. Because never mind those sexy dreams, those morphine blue movies, there was something erotic in his vulnerability, his lying there in the care of young women, his body as naked as the day he was born beneath only light sheets, and yet with the blood flow of a man, his body defenceless and yet unrestrained by a flimsy surgical gown. Vulnerable, he feared this nurse, with her trim white uniform and a fob watch that swung from her breast when she leant forward, this pretty nurse with her tub of cream to rub privately; he feared and yet hoped that she would make the same personal offer to him too.

"Do *you* want some cream on your bottom, Martin?" asked Helen.

"Helen! What are you doing here?"

"Charming! It is Visiting Hours, you know! Aren't you pleased to see me?"

"Of course I am…" She kissed him on the lips, as if it were the most natural thing in the world. "Delighted, in fact. I just… I wasn't expecting you, that's all."

"Why wouldn't I visit you? I was worried. I care about you…"

"Wow. I should get injured more often."

Helen giggled and sat down, before shuffling the chair nearer. Straight away her pony tail made an appearance, whipping the air behind her as she jerked herself forward. She was wearing a stone-washed denim jacket over a top that was cut low. "So, how are you feeling?" She took his hand.

"Absolutely stoned, if I'm honest." He exaggerated what little slurring remained in his speech and rolled his eyes in their sockets, making a similar motion with his head. Helen again giggled. "I'm alright, actually, thanks. Er, I'm on morphine for the pain, so I don't have any, well, pain. And I'm doing a lot of sleeping, as you'd expect from the God of Dreams."

"What?"

"Morpheus, the God of Dreams? No? Don't worry, sorry. So, er, I'm doing a lot of sleeping, as I've said, and you wouldn't believe the dreams I've been having."

"Really?"

"Yeah, like cheese times a million. Amazing! They're not surreal, like a Salvador Dali painting or anything, they're more about everyday things and people but in really weird combinations. Like, in one I was playing my drum kit, but I was in amongst the bushes across from my house, and that was it… But it was really vivid and went on for ages and I could control what I played. I was really good! And *you've* been in a couple as well." As soon as the words left his mouth Martin regretted revealing this last detail.

"Me? Really?"

"Yes."

"What doing?"

"Oh, er, nothing much."

"Come on, you've got to tell me!"

"Nothing, really."

"Nothing? What, I'm just… *there*, but not doing anything?"

"You were on stage, dancing, but in your dressing gown, and then you were talking to my mum, but I can't remember what about. Like I said, weird combinations."

"Are you sure I wasn't naked?"

"What?"

"In *my* dreams I always forget my clothes, or lose them, or take them off when I shouldn't. So what about in yours? Did I take my clothes off?" She smiled at him, tilting her head to one side.

"No!"

"Oh, that's a shame."

"What! I wouldn't have known where to look if you had."

"You're too much of a gentleman, Martin. Too polite. I'm going to have to teach you some bad manners!"

Helen was definitely flirting with him. He couldn't believe his luck! She was as fit *as...*! What was it about hospitals to turn everyone – well him and Helen, at least – into sexpots? *He* had that *minx* morphine to blame, and pretty nurses rubbing cream into private places, but what was Helen's excuse? She couldn't fancy him, could she? Really fancy *him*? Martin felt ignited with desire, he wanted to leap onto her, to burrow his face into her. "Could you pass me my water, please?" he asked, coughing.

"Yes, of course, here..." He drank from the cup she put to his lips, but he took hold of her wrist and held her hand there, kissing her fingertips.

Helen flushed a little. "That's more like it," she said and then, for maybe half a minute, neither of them spoke. Helen looked around the ward. She saw first the immortal grandchildren with their toys and comics to keep them quiet, and then, as her eyes passed from one sickbed to the next, she saw worried grey wives in anoraks, not far from the grave themselves, and she thought of her own grandparents, her granddad's "dodgy ticker". She shook the thought from her head and asked: "So, where's your mum? I thought she'd be here. I wanted to meet her."

"She came earlier. She was here when I first came out of surgery, I think, I can't really remember, I was still woozy from the anaesthetic. No, she was definitely here, but she had to go. That's right, she had a wedding to do."

"What is she, a florist or something?"

"No, a hairdresser. 'Lorraine's'. Do you know it?"

"No, but I might go now. I hate my hair, can't be bothered with it. That's why I keep it in this stupid pony tail."

"I like your pony tail. You have a nice neck."

"What's got into you? First you kiss my finger and then you give me a compliment!"

"Two. I like your pony tail *and* your neck."

"Even better. No, I don't like all this big hair, so I was thinking of a bob."

"I call my hairstyle 'Peter'"

"Funny!" Helen giggled yet again before coming back with: "You have a hairstyle?"

"I brush it, does that count?"

"Hm. What's this?" Helen touched the brown paper parcel, which lay still unopened on the bedside table.

"Oh, yes, I'd forgotten about that. My mum brought it. A get well soon present, I suppose."

"What is it?"

"Well, it's not a football!"

Helen picked up the parcel and weight it in her hands. "It feels like a stick of rock. Here, open it."

Martin took the imagined candy from Helen and, holding one end between his teeth, tried to peel off the sellotape with his one good hand. Biting and picking, he struggled for a moment and then said: "I can't. You do it."

"Ookaaay." She took back the package and, ignoring the end slightly wet with saliva, began to open it for him. "They did a good job with the wrapping, didn't they?"

She looked fantastic, so absorbed in her task, her slack

mouth pouting. Martin only wished she was opening a gift from him.

"There we go!" she said triumphantly, tearing off the tape, unravelling what was in fact a paper bag. There was a scraping, xylophonous sound coming from the bag.

Wood, thought Martin.

She reached inside, grasped the contents and, looking at Martin to see his reaction, pulled out a pair of drum sticks.

"Drum sticks, she's bought me some drum sticks."

Helen immediately started laughing. "Sorry but, you break your arm and your mum buys you drum sticks... It's funny! I mean, I don't know her but she must have a... a quirky sense of humour. What are you going to do with them? Use them for splints? Here..."

"Huh, yeah." He went along with the joke, laughing unconvincingly, still not quite believing what his mum had given him. He took the sticks from Helen and read the markings: Vic Firth, 5A. They were a good brand, the best, the only one he used; and the correct size too – how could she have guessed he used 5A? And with wooden tips as well, *not* nylon. They were exactly right. She must have gone into his room, squeezed herself behind his kit and delved into his stick bag to find out, and all this from a woman who not once complimented his playing, who was dead against it in fact. He could feel his throat tightening. Maybe because of delayed shock from Gerry's assault, or because of the surgeons secondary assault on his body or the magical drugs now dripping into him, or because of his invalid's vulnerability, or because of lovely Helen, or maybe because of these sticks he was holding, his mum's selfless gift... Maybe because of all of these things he realised that for a long time now he hadn't given his poor mum a chance and, screwing his eyes tight, he began to cry violently. He cried tears of happiness; he cried tears of remembrance of a son's love for his mum.

Helen too felt a surge of emotion. She stood up and half-sat on the side of the bed, putting her arm around her Martin. She felt him lean into her, shuddering, and she squeezed him tightly. She placed her hand on his rough cheek, wet with tears, and kissed his head. She had come today to visit simply because she fancied him, like girls do, and believed there was a chance she might want to get to know him better, perhaps in new ways to her, but now, listening to the sobbing of this beautiful boy, holding the broad shoulders of this handsome man, she could see beyond her teenage desire, she sensed that here was a man she could be with.

FINALE

In the dark of the wings a manicured fingertip traced the mortar work of a brick wall. With a nail painted red it nonchalantly stroked the furrows between the bricks, caressing their roughness this way and that; left towards a vertical pipe of some kind and then right towards the safety curtain control panel, and its emergency release lever. An American Trilogy had only just begun and the scheduled second house finale – the very final finale of Seaside Spectacular '85, in fact – was still some minutes away, and so the owner of this elegant, idling finger knew she would just have to bide her time. She had already delayed two weeks longer than she first thought necessary, the hugely successful run having been extended almost into October (to a chorus of groans from the cast and crew), and so to wait these last few tantalising moments would be a piece of cake, she told herself, a period to savour even. She listened closely as Gerry Neon sang:

"Glory, glory hallelujah."

Under the cover of darkness and beneath her folded Mackintosh raincoat, a large new handbag sat heavily beside her smartly heeled feet. It strained at the zip, being filled to bursting with the possessions she would need in her new life, and the bag seemed to her to be calling for attention, for she ached to delve into that bag, to inventory yet again her getaway accessories: the cash for a taxi; the train ticket; the plane ticket; her passport. But she was certain she had left nothing she needed upstairs in her dressing room, and was sure she would be good to go, as soon as…

"Glory, glory hallelujah."

Still listening, she noted Kevin busy working the corner, his back six feet from her, and a telephone handset pressed to his ear. Inside herself she *was* a little apprehensive; not of the gig on the cruise liner she would board on arrival in Grand Cayman, but of what remained for her to do here – her bowing out; her final act – before she could finally bid goodbye to Victoria Pier Theatre. And, being conspicuously early for her finale entrance, she did feel a little uneasy her apparent loitering may invite attention. She breathed deeply, exhaling with a faint volatility of vodka, and affected the appearance of a seasoned pro, neither early nor impatient nor nosey nor anything untoward, but merely awaiting her cue, looking glamorous, looking like a star, because she *was* a star.

Miss Amanda Monroe had finally come to believe, really believe in her own star quality the week of Gerry's convalescence, when he couldn't work on account of that other bastard, Pete, breaking his cheek bone and giving him concussion. Throughout those four nights un-reminded of Gerry's hateful existence, and during those eight shows her every note un-listened to and un-judged by his cruel ear, she had shone; simply without him *being there*, she had shone. And in her temporarily longer spot, lengthened to help fill the headliner's absence, she had road-tested her new material: "Misty" and "Crazy"; classy numbers, destined, like her, to be heard on cruise ships; timeless standards, which she had sung faultlessly, in her new, sophisticated style – and they'd gone down a bomb too, because she was a star.

"Glory, glory hallelujah."

Pointless things, finales, she thought, as she removed her red-tipped hand from the brick wall and touched instead her new, better necklace; you did your spot, sometimes an hour and a half previously, and then you returned to the stage just so that the audience could once again give you a clap. It was hardly worth all the waiting around! And what was a singer to do between her performance and her curtain call? Sit alone in their dressing room, all dolled up with nowhere to go? It was demeaning to one's talent, she thought, toying proudly with her new, superior, eighteen carat crab.

"His truth is marching on!"

Unseen a sly smile illuminated her face, however, as Mandy Monroe reflected there would be *no* finale this evening, not in the conventional sense. No, not tonight, because she, like spesh act Al and comedian Ashley and like all the dancers, would make no reappearance on the stage. In fact the bow she took and the kisses she blew at the end of her second house set would be her last in this country. The new and improved Miss Amanda *Minnelli*, on the other hand, would in only a matter of days be sure to revel in prodigious applause the Caribbean over, but tonight she had other plans. With grace and swiftness she bent down to her raincoat, which she had folded in such a way that one of its outer pockets was exposed and accessible. She eased a hand into that pocket and retrieved a pair of white satin evening gloves. In no time she had pulled them on, snug up to her elbows, and was standing again, her smile yet more foxy and furtive.

"His truth is marching on!"

Also unseen – in the backstage dark; being as she was *behind* Kevin – was Mandy's tactile hand, cautiously gloved and preparatively caressing the release lever for the safety curtain, the steel framed, heavy and anything-but-safe safety curtain, a hazardous thing even with a drop time of twenty seconds. With a brief look over her shoulder, and seeing that the gossipy dancers were congregated far upstage from her, she even took the lever's hard iron into her grasp and imagined the effort needed to pull it, had someone cause to. With a kind of cliff-edge acrophobia, the cardiac kick of the fear of jumping, she let go, just in case...

Again she looked around, surveilling the scene, and saw only the mouth-to-ear dancers still engrossed, and she was satisfied that no one had seen her grasp the lever, and no one would.

Tracking Gerry's vocal performance – there were still eight, six, four beats remaining of his closing, operatic note – she knew it was almost time, but she wanted a visual on him. She stepped to her right and, peering around Kevin, found that she could see Gerry now as well as hear him. He was there, framed between two leg drapes, brilliant in his plot of stage, his head tilted to the heavens in feigned vocal ecstasy, his eyes screwed shut under the God spot. With abiding disgust she observed him – his short legs; his paunch; his fat, sweating face – and in observing him she remembered an earlier view of him, the worst view of him, the one through the guesthouse window with him outside on the pavement. Scowling, she no longer felt any apprehension or unease but only an iron certainty she would wreak her revenge.

No beats remaining, she watched him end his final note with an arm-waving flourish, before slumping into the most extravagant of bows. She gave a monitoring glance back at the lever, checking it was only an arm's reach away, before returning her glare to Gerry; judging if he was positioned exactly on her mark – now, this instant – or if he would be there soon. She visualised the lethal fire curtain descending towards his skull, slowly, but as quick as a girder under gravity if unseen. After all, continents move much, much slower than any curtain, imperceptibly so in fact, until an earthquake strikes.

But of course the safety curtain, the fire curtain, the "iron" as it is called, *would* be seen – by the audience – and Mandy only wished that tonight among the thousand souls here to witness Gerry Neon's final bow there could be all the women he had abused over the years: the half-willing dancers summoned to his dressing room, to keep the gig; the after-hours barmaids coerced further than they had bargained for; the vulnerable fans taken advantage of, the ink still drying on their autographs. And specifically the landlady, *there* in Row F, whose cat he was alleged to have hung; and the bride, *there* near the back, the bride he was rumoured to have groped at her wedding reception; and the tender-hearted singer, *here* in the box seat, who he had tricked into a prankish rape. And Mandy gave a thought too to the men Gerry had bullied and humiliated: the stagehands at each and every venue he'd berated routinely, because he could; the lesser artistes he'd grabbed by the lapels or even slapped, because he could; the guitarist into whose acoustic he'd reputedly shat, *just because he could*. Mandy wished all of them could be here tonight. But the theatre would not be big enough, she then joked to herself, without smiling.

Oblivious to his coming fate, just as she had been oblivious in the Belvedere, Mandy watched a moment more of Gerry's laughable melodrama. As if spent from the heroic effort of his performance, she saw him collapse further onto one knee. Exhausted, his eyes still closed in reverence, he then bowed his greying head to the floor in submission, genuflecting before the audience's higher power. But nevertheless he also held his right arm aloft in some kind of salute, an acknowledgement of their applause and adoration perhaps, and he raised his forefinger skywards, maybe triumphantly, for Gerry Neon was *numero uno*, and this ignorant digit pointed vertically upwards, directly at a ton of iron.

With Gerry bowed and blind and on her mark, Mandy sensed her moment had come. She slid back to her left and seized the lever. With the crowd's ovation audible over the band, she with blood-tipped fingers gloved in white satin pulled the lever, and the crushingly heavy curtain began its inexorable descent.

While that girder settled, while those continents crept, six unaware musicians sight-read their charts, eight dancers queueing for their finale entrance looked at each other's backs, the fly crew way up in the gallery focused on their hemp ropes, and in the prompt corner the Assistant Stage Manager eyed console buttons and pressed them. It was as if every one of the theatre's employees was unsighted by their duties; even the two follow spot operators, certain to see the steady fall of the iron, watched with detached curiosity as it moved unstoppably down towards the star of the show. It was as if the theatre itself had turned a blind eye to the act of violence and vengeance set in motion on the stage.

And without waiting for the impact that was sure to follow, Mandy gathered her bag and coat and walked calmly from the wings. Through the stage door she walked, and outside in a cool and cloudless night she heard muffled shouts behind her. With a reckless lack of urgency she slowed to a standstill, set down her bag and enrobed herself in her Mackintosh, leisurely doing the belt. Hearing sounds of mayhem coming from backstage, the sly smile returned to her face and she turned up the collar of her Mac like a parting insult. Walking again, cruising up the deck of the pier in fact, she knew she had acted alone and for herself, *but she felt* that she had acted for others too, a heroine. And as she stepped off the boards and onto the concrete of the promenade, with an ambulance's wail becoming louder – or was it a police siren? – and with a gibbous moon rising above Grumby's proud headland, waxing just for her, she felt that white-gloved she had struck a blow for all who had ever suffered at the hands of Gerry Neon, for all those victims of Variety.

ABOUT THE AUTHOR

James is a Biology Teacher and lives in Otley, West Yorkshire with his wife and two children. This is his first novel.